DIRECT HIT

Slightly under a minute later there was a thump and a shudder as the torpedo, after passing partway under the ship, turned up, slammed into her main engine room and detonated. The blast erupted up through the bilges under her house-sized diesel, its concussion instantly killing the assistant chief engineer and the one technician who'd stayed behind a few fatal seconds to secure some valves. The device had already broken the ship's back even before the cool blue waters of the Bay of Naples geysered in behind the explosion's scorching, white-hot gasses.

Tareq ibn-Ali stood beside a pine tree in a small park on the side of a hill about a mile inland from the villa at which Abdul and Magda were staying. He'd been there for some time, waiting, watching the *Rachael Spivak* through a pair of binoculars.

There, he thought. Had the ship shuddered slightly? She was so big it was hard to tell. He waited and watched another minute or two. Now the ship was turning to the left, out toward sea, and streamers of what looked like black smoke seemed to be leaking from the superstructure. The hint of a smile passed across his pudgy, baby face, a face totally at odds with his soul, which was as hard as the hardest rock.

He lowered the binoculars and looked around him. Not a soul in sight. He returned his attention to the ship again. Yes, she was continuing to turn slowly in the wrong direction and the smoke was continuing to ooze out. She was like a man—or woman—who'd been carefully and skillfully beaten. There was next to no external evidence yet that, after staggering a minute or two, the victim would fall and never recover.

SEA HAWK

MICHAEL HOWE

BERKLEY BOOKS, NEW YORK

THE BERKLEY PUBLISHING GROUP
Published by the Penguin Group
Penguin Group (USA) Inc.
375 Hudson Street, New York, New York 10014, USA
Penguin Group (Canada), 90 Eglinton Avenue East, Suite 700, Toronto, Ontario M4P 2Y3, Canada
(a division of Pearson Penguin Canada Inc.)
Penguin Books Ltd., 80 Strand, London WC2R 0RL, England
Penguin Group Ireland, 25 St. Stephen's Green, Dublin 2, Ireland (a division of Penguin Books Ltd.)
Penguin Group (Australia), 250 Camberwell Road, Camberwell, Victoria 3124, Australia
(a division of Pearson Australia Group Pty. Ltd.)
Penguin Books India Pvt. Ltd., 11 Community Centre, Panchsheel Park, New Delhi—110 017, India
Penguin Group (NZ), 67 Apollo Drive, Rosedale, North Shore 0632, New Zealand
(a division of Pearson New Zealand Ltd.)
Penguin Books (South Africa) (Pty.) Ltd., 24 Sturdee Avenue, Rosebank, Johannesburg 2196,
South Africa

Penguin Books Ltd., Registered Offices: 80 Strand, London WC2R 0RL, England

This is a work of fiction. Names, characters, places, and incidents either are the product of the author's imagination or are used fictitiously, and any resemblance to actual persons, living or dead, business establishments, events, or locales is entirely coincidental. The publisher does not have any control over and does not assume any responsibility for author or third-party websites or their content.

SEA HAWK

A Berkley Book / published by arrangement with the author

PRINTING HISTORY
Berkley edition / October 2009

Copyright © 2009 by Penguin Group (USA) Inc.
Cover illustration by Chris Cocozza.
Cover design by Judith Lagerman.
Interior text design by Laura K. Corless.

ISBN: 978-0-425-23065-7

BERKLEY®
Berkley Books are published by The Berkley Publishing Group,
a division of Penguin Group (USA) Inc.,
375 Hudson Street, New York, New York 10014.
BERKLEY® is a registered trademark of Penguin Group (USA) Inc.
The "B" design is a trademark of Penguin Group (USA) Inc.

PRINTED IN THE UNITED STATES OF AMERICA

10 9 8 7 6 5 4 3 2 1

1

Captain Solomon Weiss walked out of the air-conditioned pilothouse of his ship, the *Rachael Spivak*, onto the starboard bridge wing. The day was hot, as most August afternoons are in the Bay of Naples, and the bay itself was dead-flat calm. The water was a rich, deep blue, blemished only by an occasional clump of plastic bags and grapefruit rinds floating just below the surface.

Weiss looked forward. Thanks to the containers piled five high on his forward deck, he was unable to see his ship's gray bow as it cut through the crystalline blue. But he was well able to see an oil tanker about five miles ahead, along with a few fishing boats scattered here and there. And a very handsome, and very big, white yacht scooting southwest past Ischia. There was nothing, he reassured himself, that hadn't been on the radar when he had looked at it three minutes before.

His eyes felt gritty and ached slightly. He removed

his sunglasses and rubbed them gently. Was it just the summer sun or was it age? He neither knew nor cared. He then looked toward the distant, passing shore, which was also painted in various hues of deep blue by the afternoon sky. He raised his binoculars for a closer look and could see the off-white and red brown splashes of color that indicated the cities along the bay's southern shore. Some, such as Sorrento, were only a thousand or two years younger than the cities of Israel, but still alive and prospering. Others, such as Herculaneum and Pompeii, were ancient and long dead, victims of Vesuvius— the great volcano that brooded in the distance, casting a shadow totally unrelated to the sun's position, hazy blue and shaped like a pyramid designed by an architect plagued with cataracts.

"I can never get over the way those crazy Italians continue to live on the slopes of that monster."

Weiss turned to find David, his second mate, standing next to him.

"The soil produces excellent wines," replied the captain. "And they've always lived here. Are they any more insane to insist upon living here than we are to insist upon living in Israel?"

David, his shaved head only partially covered by his ball cap, didn't reply.

"Are the security groups all in place?"

"Yes, Captain. For over an hour now, ever since we started to approach Capri. The SONAR's operating, antimissile control is manned, and the three armed parties are on station—forward, amidships and on the fantail."

"Very well." David was Weiss's second mate, but he was also the ship's security officer. This meant, Weiss assumed, that he listened more to the Israeli Defense Forces Sea Corps—or to Aman, Israeli military intelligence—than he did to Weiss. It was to be expected, he thought. No modern captain is the true master of his ship.

Captain Weiss always felt a tiny twinge of unease whenever they approached close to land, which was one of the several reasons he'd passed to the west of Sicily rather than cutting through the Strait of Messina. The strait was where attacks tended to occur. That was also where the security people tended to get a little on edge. He wanted them sharp, but he didn't want them to over-react. They were young and tense, and he knew they worried less about the possibility of shooting up a pack of careless-but-innocent fishermen than he did. Years ago, when he was a young soldier, he'd been totally concerned with keeping himself alive and had cared little what he had to do to realize that goal. Now he found his range of preoccupations had expanded. He'd be damned if he'd let anything happen to his ship or his crew, but, at the same time . . .

He started to tell David to ensure that they were all alert and would be careful about their targets, but he refrained. He didn't want to expose his own minor insecurities to the younger man. It was just the sort of thing some might seize upon as evidence of advancing years and declining suitability for command. Instead, he turned his binoculars forward. He thought he could now make out the hazy, multicolored splotch that was Naples, although the two great jetties that formed its outer mole were still hidden by the horizon. "What did you say the registry of that yacht is?"

"The Commonwealth of the Northern Mariana Islands, Captain."

Weiss smiled. "Must be some American Internet or electronics tycoon." He then rubbed the top of his bald head and walked back into the shade of the pilothouse to await the arrival of the pilot.

* * *

He was short and on the wiry—or perhaps skinny—side.
At the age of thirty he was already losing his short, dark
hair. He maintained a small mustache and possessed the
sort of face that, when and if he lived past middle age,
would be described as unremarkable. He lay on a chaise
longue on the pine-shaded patio of a leased, shorefront
villa and looked through a pair of binoculars.

"Can you see it yet?" asked the maddeningly seduc-
tive but stony-eyed young woman lying on the longue
next to his.

"No, not yet," replied Abdul al-Jabbar. "But it won't
be long. There's only one way into Naples from the
south."

Al-Jabbar spoke English with an American accent
even though he was born in Jordan. To the world he was
the Middle Eastern technical rep of the Lindley-Roberts
Group, a midsized American IT consulting firm, and he
was in Italy on a well-earned vacation. Magda, his companion, was of about the same age. She also spoke English, but with a heavy accent that seemed to emphasize
her short, shiny black hair, high, exotic cheekbones and
eyes so brown they were black. A face, in sum, with an
almost Oriental cast to it.

Magda's homeland, Albania, may have thrown off the
yoke of Communism, but she herself had not. She remained a fanatically devoted party member, as had been
her father, a high party official who'd died impoverished
and disdained by those who had once been prepared to
do absolutely anything to please him.

Both Magda and Abdul had been born to nominally
Moslem families yet neither was a true *jihadist*. Magda,
having watched as her true faith was banished from
much of the world, had one driving ambition—to get
revenge on those who had destroyed her father and his

creed. Especially the Americans and their fawning little friends. For his part Abdul respected the Koran for its wisdom and moral standards, but his true religion was a totally secular one—a free, unified and prosperous Palestine.

When he thought about it, which he was doing more and more, Abdul kept coming to the uncomfortable conclusion that while he wasn't on the wrong side, he might not be on the right side, either. His cause was the right one, he reassured himself. But what about some of his teammates? Would blowing people up really succeed in intimidating the world's governments into doing what was right?

"It was most gracious of the Chinese to volunteer to help in the war for Palestinian freedom and dignity."

"Yes," replied al-Jabbar absently, continuing to stare through the binoculars. It was true the Chinese had provided the weapon he and Magda were about to use. It was one he could never have assembled himself, and it was one that would be totally unexpected. It was also true the Chinese weren't doing it because they were concerned about the misery of the Palestinians. Like everybody else in the world, they had a strong desire to stick their elbow in the Americans' collective eye. They also wanted to field test the weapon. Indeed, Abdul was coming to believe that the entire world—the Americans, the Europeans, the Chinese, the Indians and everybody else, even the other Arabs—was only interested in the Palestinians as a means of getting at somebody else. He felt at times that nobody, except him, wanted to release them from their four generations of impoverished captivity as aliens in their own land.

He smiled to himself, a little bitterly. He was becoming as paranoid in his own way as some of the Hamas fanatics.

Al-Jabbar turned his binoculars away from the deep

blue bay and scanned the lavish villas to either side. He and the Albanian girl had spent the past ten days living in the greatest of comfort in this magnificent villa. No crawling through the dusty rubble that much of the Middle East had become—or always had been. No midnight meetings in rancid little rooms in Rome or London or New York with wide-eyed madmen who could barely read. He wasn't, at the moment, living the sort of life terrorists were supposed to live.

Much to his surprise, the neighbors—thanks largely to Magda's stunning appearance, perfect Italian and skill as an actress—seemed to have taken them to their hearts rather than treating them with the disdain normally accorded summer renters. One neighbor had had them over for lunch the day before, and the Metellos on the other side had invited them for dinner that evening. In fact, Abdul thought, they may have taken them—Magda, anyway—too much to heart. Carlo Metello, the ancient goat, had developed a thing for the girl and was constantly peeking through his own binoculars at her.

Up to now it hadn't been a problem. The only incriminating work they'd done had been accomplished the night before they moved into the villa—when they programmed the weapon and dropped it from an old fishing boat. But in another few hours they'd be triggering the device. It was doubtful the old goat would have any idea what they were doing, even if he was watching. And the drama itself would occur miles out at sea. All the same, it would be best if Don Carlo Metello were taking his nap when Abdul and Magda completed the mission.

"Wake me when it's time," said Magda, closing her eyes.

"Yes," replied al-Jabbar, momentarily irritated. He'd wanted to take a nap. There'd be time later, he decided, as he sipped a tall glass of iced tea and examined his surroundings.

The villa was hundreds of years old, set into a stone cliff with a rocky beach below. Stone, plaster and tile, festooned with vines and nestled in pines and bougainvillea. Brilliant red geraniums in pots along the waist-high patio wall. A hundred other growing things shading the patio from the sun's fury and filling the air with delightful scents. Cool inside, bright outside. The building, the surroundings, the knowledge that it had all been designed and constructed based on thousands of years' experience creating comfort under the Mediterranean's blazing sun, made him feel at home. He was also of the Mediterranean, and even terrorists can have taste, he reassured himself. And given the chance, Palestine would blossom just as extravagantly. Not today but someday.

His eyes settled on the girl, who was lying on her side, her mouth very slightly opened. She looked asleep, although the tough casing of muscles that sheathed her near-perfect body looked far from relaxed. Without doubt, he thought, she was stunning. Old Metello might be a little fusty, but he had good taste. In another time and place, al-Jabbar might have made a fool of himself over her the same way Metello was, even though he was certain that short, prematurely balding Palestinians were not to her taste.

He caught himself. Such thoughts were dangerous at the moment. He was reasonably certain she didn't trust him. He wasn't sure exactly why she didn't, but he knew she didn't. Neither, however, had anything to worry about at the moment. Whatever his nagging doubts, he would execute the attack, because he was a soldier in a war and it is the business of soldiers in wars to attack the enemy, the oppressors. He would continue to do so unless and until some other, better method of achieving liberation became clear to him. And, he reassured himself, his determination wasn't based on the knowledge that Magda had a pistol somewhere within easy reach—she always did—and that she was a much better shot than he was.

* * *

Pat McGrath, the CIA station chief in Beirut, leaned back in his chair and eyed Beth, the middle-aged woman standing in front of him, as she reviewed the major events of the day. In fact, there'd been none. Nothing in the West Bank. Nothing in Gaza. Nothing in Beirut itself. No suicide bombings. No rocket attacks. Nothing of significance. There was a whisper of a new cholera outbreak in Gaza City, but that was of only limited concern at the moment. It was the UN's problem. Or Hamas's. Or maybe Israel's. Anyway, it was endemic there. Every week there was some sort of outbreak. Yet Beth continued to harp on it, and that was why he didn't really like her. She tended to bleed a little too much for the Arabs.

Pat McGrath was superbly equipped for his job. He spoke both Hebrew and several important dialects of Arabic fluently. He'd spent half his life exploring the history and customs of the various parties that continued to keep the Middle East at a constant boil. At times only a moderate boil, at other times an explosive one.

Despite his education, Pat felt little sympathy for any of the sides. Especially the Arabs. Ever since his earliest years he'd learned, from television and from those around him, to not trust them. Not the oil sheiks who abused women and were determined to impoverish America. Not the ragged, more-than-half-mad terrorists who would blow Americans out of the sky the second they let their guard down. Not the little guy who worked at the convenience store around the corner from his apartment in the Washington suburbs. The apartment he only got to see four or five times a year.

Pat's mission in life, and his sworn duty, was to defend The Homeland. To keep America great. That was all he cared about, and he viewed his cultural knowledge as nothing more than a weapon in a war to the death. It was the Cold War again. Only more so. And he was prepared to do whatever it took.

Thank God! he thought when he realized the woman had finally finished. "Okay, Beth, I understand what you're saying and I want you to monitor the situation. Let me know if it develops into anything."

"Roger, Pat."

After the pest had left, Pat applied himself to a pile of paperwork, rushing through it in his haste to get out of the office. He had an appointment at his apartment in two hours with the cutest little Canadian he'd run into in a long time.

* * *

Penny Arnold ran her hand through her short blond hair, shook it and pulled open the plywood shutter covering what once had been a window. She then looked out into the courtyard of the Universal Lifeline Foundation Medical Clinic in Gaza City. Her eyes settled first on the piebald grass, then on the small gathering of forlorn rosebushes and the one stunted oak that adorned it. Compared to much of the city that surrounded it, the courtyard was an oasis.

Most of the crowds were gone now, along with most of the tetracycline, leaving no more than fifty patients jammed into the clinic, still undergoing rehydration, still suffering from uncontrollable diarrhea. Fifty, far more than they were equipped to keep overnight. Cholera, she reflected, was a smelly disease, more so than many. It was also always present in Gaza City. Many of the residents had developed an immunity of sorts, but there were always others, especially the old and the young. It was also an easily prevented disease. All it took was the most basic sanitation—public and personal. But even such simple precautions seemed impossible when well over a million men, women and children—impoverished and in many cases hopeless after decades of imprisonment—found themselves trapped in a cage surrounded by sterile desert.

God how she hated Gaza! Her third one-year contract would be over in a few months, and she would not renew. She'd done her duty. She'd done her part to try to make the world a better place. She really had! Now she could go home, get a good job in a nice, civilized, clean, well-equipped hospital. A hospital where supplies were abundant, the lawn was green and the barking clatter of automatic weapons never once disrupted the orderly processes of modern medicine.

"Ms. Arnold."

Penny turned. "Yes, Dr. Fayez?"

"Every time I look at that tired old tree I feel a slight sense of hope. It's a miracle it still survives, that it hasn't been cut down at night and carted off for firewood."

The nurse smiled. Once upon a time, in another life, her face—especially her once-playful, round eyes and generous mouth—had borne an habitual smile. Now she had to force it.

"Once again we've somehow managed to deal with disaster," continued the doctor, thinking that Penny looked like a ghost. "Now we have to collect ourselves and prepare for more mangled bodies tonight. I have a bad feeling."

"We're very low on antibiotics . . ." said Penny, thinking of all the gunshot wounds, shrapnel and burns that the doctor was hinting at.

"More have been requested. Whether they'll arrive in time remains to be seen."

Penny sighed and swung the plywood shutter closed. She'd made her choice and now she had to live with it. She turned and looked across the room, her eyes stopping on a shriveled, elderly woman propped up on and strapped to a gurney because they'd run out of beds and cots long ago. An IV tube led into her arm. The woman's face showed discomfort and a great deal more fear.

"Don't worry, Mrs. Nasser," Penny said in Arabic, "everything will be just fine. There's an excellent chance you'll be able to go home tomorrow."

"Yes," said the woman. "Go home tomorrow." Judging by the tone of her voice, the prospect didn't thrill her.

* * *

"Magda!" said al-Jabbar about an hour after the girl had dozed off, or seemed to. "The target's in sight."

The Albanian was awake instantly. "How soon?"

"I think they're in range now, unless the Chinese are lying to us."

"I'll trigger it."

"As you wish."

The girl stood, stretched and touched her toes. Al-Jabbar struggled to keep his mind on the job. "Put a wrap on," he said to her. "Don Carlo the Goat is already far too interested in you. All we need is for him to start taking pictures to tack up in his bedroom."

She looked at him and smiled ever so slightly. It was a smile that didn't extend any deeper than her perfect white teeth. "His wife would never stand for that, and she's the one with the money. Anyway, they're not home. They're off at Carlo's club for the afternoon." Then she put on a terry robe and headed off toward the gravelly beach and the small stone jetty that ran between their beach and the Metellos'. Once behind the jetty, she removed the robe and glided out into the pellucid blue. In her hand was what looked like a small radio. When she was waist-deep in the Mediterranean, she pushed the radio underwater gently and held it there for about fifteen seconds. She then turned and placed the radio on a rock sticking out of the side of the jetty. "The water is heavenly," she shouted as she turned toward the villa. "You should really come in." She started to breaststroke back and forth in front of the villa, waiting almost breathlessly to feel a slight thump in her guts and groin that would signal the operation's success.

Abdul watched Magda a moment, then turned the binoculars back on the ship. How many would die this time? he wondered. He felt no hatred for the average Israeli. They were pawns, just as much as the Palestinians. The difference was the Israeli pawns were well fed and could come and go. His war was against the conspirators—the governments of Israel and the rest of the world. The true powers that kept the Palestinians in bondage, prisoners in their own land. He found the images of common citizens being blown to bits while buying groceries even more gut-wrenching and personal than he suspected many of the world's leaders did.

Despite his care, however, there were always some who had to die. It was a war. It was the way of the world.

* * *

Sol Weiss was standing on the bridge wing of his ship, watching as the Naples pilot boat, a large white bone in her teeth, sliced toward them across the flat blue water. Weiss had slowed half an hour before in preparation for the rendezvous, but the *Rachael Spivak* was still making several knots. The pilot boat slowed and turned when she was about amidships, preparing to come alongside to starboard.

"Captain!" It was the second officer's voice coming over the pilothouse transceiver. "SONAR detects what appears to be a torpedo approaching from the port side."

"What bearing and range?" demanded the captain as he tried desperately to convince himself he'd really heard what he thought he'd heard.

"Two nine seven degrees. Eight thousand meters."

The self-propelled mine the Chinese had provided was working brilliantly. The SONAR signal sent by Magda had launched the torpedo portion of the device and sent it on its way. Within seconds it had acquired its target. Its eight hundred pounds of high explosive were aimed precisely for a point fifty feet forward of the ship's huge propeller. Aimed precisely at the engine room.

Captain Weiss instinctively grabbed his binoculars and scanned the flat waters to seaward. He could see nothing. No periscope. No torpedo wake. "Eight thousand meters? Are you sure, David?" snapped Weiss into the transceiver.

"Yes, Captain."

"Where did it come from?"

"Some place out to seaward."

I already know that, thought Weiss as he continued to scan the empty bay. What in God's name was he to do? He couldn't dodge the thing; his ship was barely crawling, and it was next to impossible to maneuver a ship as large as *Spivak* even with way on. "Sound the General Alarm," he snapped over his shoulder to the mate of the watch, who was standing slightly openmouthed. "And get everybody out of the engine room."

"Have you detected a submarine?"

"No, Captain."

Then he remembered the pilot boat, which was approaching the starboard side.

"Naples Pilot, this is *Rachael Spivak*. Stand clear! I say again, stand clear! We believe we're about to be hit by a torpedo."

"A torpedo?" The disbelief was all too clear in the voice of the pilot boat skipper.

"Yes, a torpedo. Now, stand clear."

"Roger."

"Captain, the torpedo has turned slightly. It appears to be homing in on our screw."

Of course, thought Weiss glumly. Nobody uses unguided torpedoes anymore.

"How far is it now?"

"We anticipate it will strike in less than one minute."

"Hang on," he shouted into the pilothouse. Then he clutched the bridge rail and hung on himself.

Slightly under a minute later there was a thump and a shudder as the torpedo, after passing partway under the ship, turned up, slammed into her main engine room and detonated. The blast erupted up through the bilges under her house-sized diesel, its concussion instantly killing the assistant chief engineer and the one technician who'd stayed behind a few fatal seconds to secure some valves. The device had already broken the ship's back even before the cool blue waters of the Bay of Naples geysered in behind the explosion's scorching, white-hot gasses.

* * *

Tareq ibn-Ali stood beside a pine tree in a small park on the side of a hill about a mile inland from the villa at which Abdul and Magda were staying. He'd been there for some time, waiting, watching the *Rachael Spivak* through a pair of binoculars.

Ibn-Ali hadn't minded the wait. He was, when the

situation called for it, a patient man. He was also one of the most powerful and active disciplinarians in the Hamas movement, the infinitely more religious of the two movements that dominate Palestinian politics. It was his job to identify and remove those who threatened the movement, whether they were members of Hamas or of Fatah, the other major—and more secular—Palestinian party. Or outsiders, for that matter.

There, he thought. Had the ship shuddered slightly? She was so big it was hard to tell. He waited and watched another minute or two. Now the ship was turning to the left, out toward sea, and streamers of what looked like black smoke seemed to be leaking from the superstructure. The hint of a smile passed across his pudgy, baby face, a face totally at odds with his soul, which was as hard as the hardest rock.

He lowered the binoculars and looked around him. Not a soul in sight. He returned his attention to the ship again. Yes, she was continuing to turn slowly in the wrong direction and the smoke was continuing to ooze out. She was like a man—or woman—who'd been carefully and skillfully beaten. There was next to no external evidence yet that, after staggering a minute or two, the victim would fall and never recover.

He aimed the glasses at Abdul's villa but could only see the front. Al-Jabbar had carried out his instructions after all. Al-Jabbar would live another week or two. Long enough to complete the entire operation.

Tareq ibn-Ali didn't trust Abdul al-Jabbar. He was associated with Fatah, and Fatah was both weak and corrupt. Although he couldn't prove it, ibn-Ali believed at least ninety percent of the Fatah leadership had large bank accounts in Switzerland. Or Liechtenstein. Or someplace.

Al-Jabbar lacked discipline and he lacked God. He spoke of a future that was not the future Hamas saw.

He'd spent too much time in America. In Tareq's mind the very technological competence that had resulted in al-Jabbar's being assigned this operation represented a deadly danger. In time he'd have to be dealt with, and that time was coming soon.

2

Pat McGrath lay in the air-conditioned comfort of his bed and felt the breathing of the Canadian girl sleeping at his side. With a little training, he thought, she'd master doing things the way he liked them.

His phone rang. "McGrath."

"There's been an incident," reported Beth. "You'd better get down here."

"Will it require our immediate response?"

"No, I don't think so, but you'd still better get down here."

McGrath looked at the girl, whose eyes were now opened. He'd hoped to start her additional training today, but that would now have to wait. "I'll be there in an hour."

An hour and a half later, McGrath breezed into his office. "What's up?"

"Put simply," said Beth, "somebody called the 'Palestinian Naval Militia' torpedoed an Israeli container ship as she was entering Naples harbor."

"Naples? Naples, Italy?"

"Yes, sir."

McGrath had to think about it a moment. Somebody *torpedoed* the ship? "I've never heard of the 'Palestinian Naval Militia.' "

"Neither has anybody else until now. They e-mailed the *New York Times*."

As Beth spoke, she handed McGrath a piece of paper. On it, McGrath read, "Until today the fight for Palestinian freedom has been a wholly defensive action, conducted in occupied Palestine, and the victims have been Palestinians. Now the Palestinian Naval Militia has taken the war to the rest of the world. *Rachael Spivak* is the first. There will be others unless and until Israel and her friends get serious about peace."

"What does Rome make of this?"

"They say we're closer to the source and expect us to tell them what's going on."

"A torpedo? Do these people have a real submarine?"

"The ship was equipped with SONAR and claims to have been unable to locate a submarine."

"That doesn't prove there wasn't a submarine."

"No, it doesn't. But it might have also been some sort of mine/torpedo combination."

"Where the hell would the Palestinians get their hands on that sort of thing?"

"That's what both Rome and Langley want us to find out."

"Yeah? Okay. Get Greg and Samir into my office in twenty minutes. We'll go over what we might know and decide how to find out the rest."

Half an hour later Pat looked around the table, at the three top people in his organization. "So what do we have?" he demanded.

"Same as we had twenty minutes ago," replied Beth, who disliked Pat as much as he did her. "The Israeli container ship *Rachael Spivak* was hit by what they think was a torpedo two hours ago while preparing to enter Naples."

"Casualties?"

"Two, unfortunately, and the ship suffered very severe structural damage. Several tugs and a commercial salvage ship are on the scene. They think they can get her into port in one piece, but there's a chance the stern might break off."

"There's been no follow-up attack?"

"No."

"Do we have any warships there?"

"No, not yet. The Italians have two ASW ships on the scene, and we have one destroyer headed south from Gaeta. The Italians also have two aircraft there. So far they've been unable to find anything."

"One destroyer?"

"The rest are either staying at Gaeta to protect *Mount Whitney*, the Sixth Fleet flagship, or are at sea covering the rest of the fleet."

"The Palestinian Naval Militia . . . what do we know about them?"

"Nothing, absolutely nothing except that the announcement was made on a website we believe is run by the PLO. Or maybe by one of its splinter groups."

"What does COMSIXTHFLT think it was?"

"He hasn't the slightest idea, and he's busy collecting the rest of the fleet into ASW formations headed for either Gibraltar or Soudha Bay on Crete. They're sweeping the two anchorages for mines right now. Frankly, Pat, I think he assumes *you're* going to tell *him* what's happening."

McGrath didn't like the tone of Beth's voice, but he didn't say anything. Instead, he sat thinking for several minutes, until the phone on the conference table buzzed. "Sorry to interrupt, Pat, but its Greta Sabbagh at Langley. Can you talk to her now?"

"All right!" snapped McGrath. Greta was the coordinator, Mediterranean maritime analysis at Langley. He didn't like her any more than he liked Beth, and on top of that he was irritated that he didn't have anything significant to tell her.

"Pat," said the voice in his ear, "can you tell us anything significant about this attack on the container ship?"

Pat glowered at those facing him, then told Greta what little he knew.

"Our Director's going to want to know more before he briefs the director of national intelligence."

"We're doing what we can. Anyway, aren't you the maritime analyst? Why didn't you see any of this coming? Submarines don't just appear out of nowhere in this day and age."

"You said it might not be a submarine."

"If it's some sort of mine, then it must have been a damn sophisticated one, and *it* must have come from somewhere. I really don't think the Palestinians are ready yet to build that sort of thing themselves."

"Call me as soon as you come up with something." The line went dead.

"Shit," mumbled McGrath. "Okay, I want you to contact everybody and anybody who might be able to tell us anything about this. The Palestinian Naval Militia. A Palestinian submarine—or anybody else's. Sea mines. Torpedoes. Anything that fits in. Anybody who might have supplied it—the Russians, the Chinese, the North Koreans. Maybe the Iranians or the Pakistanis. Somebody who's got some real scientists.

"And anybody who's bright enough and technological enough to do whatever has been done. This wasn't some confused goatherd from Galilee. We must have a resource that knows something."

The three heads around the table nodded.

"Now go, god damn it. Hit the road and find something."

Angry, he returned to his office. The assholes at Langley—especially that freak Chaz Owens, the Agency's antiterrorist czar—were driving him nuts. The minute they arrived there and settled behind their desks they became masters of the universe and the guys in the field became fools and slaves. They never made mistakes. All the disasters were the result of the stupidity of guys like Pat McGrath.

McGrath had to get more information and he had to get it fast. He called Moshe Goren, his counterpart at one of the several Mossad operations in Beirut.

"We don't know much either, Pat," said Moshe, not certain he wanted to tell Pat even the little he did know.

"Was it a submarine or a mine? I've got to tell COM-SIXTHFLT something."

"We don't know."

"Then what the hell do you know?"

"We know that somebody code-named the Sea Hawk executed it," said Moshe, after deciding that no damage would be done by tossing this scrap to the Americans.

"Can you find him?"

"We can't do anything for another few days," he half lied. "We'll keep working on it, but I'm afraid we're all going to have to wait."

"Give me some info on him. We'll get him."

"We don't know who he is or what he looks like. It may not even be a him. All our source said was that the person who executed the operation is code-named the Sea Hawk. And I don't want any of your clumsy friends screwing up our operation, so just make do with what I've told you. In a week I'll be able to tell you more."

"A week, for Christ's sake!"

"Maybe sooner. Maybe not. Remember, it was our ship."

"Okay. Thanks. I owe you one."

"You owe me a lot more than one."

* * *

Admiral Reginald Tandy, the chief of naval operations, sat in his chair at the Pentagon and studied the large-screen display as he listened as Vice Admiral Robert Simmons, commander, United States Sixth Fleet, explained the deployment of his forces in the Mediterranean. Also in on the conversation was Vice Admiral Albert Hampton, commander in chief, U.S. Naval Forces, Europe, who was Simmons's immediate superior.

"As of this moment you've got six ships at Gibraltar and ten at Soudha Bay?" asked the CNO.

"Correct, Admiral," replied Simmons. "The Brits have assured me Gib is clean, and the Greeks will be finishing up at Soudha within a few hours. I intend to get the amphibs and the other ships that lack their own ASW capabilities—except the carrier—in port for the time being. *Bill of Rights* and the rest of her group will stay in the Eastern Med. Between Iraq, Iran, Afghanistan, Pakistan and who-knows-what's going to happen in Syria, we simply must have a carrier group there."

"And you?"

"*Mount Whitney* will remain at Gaeta. I've detached a destroyer to go south to Naples and work with the Italians. That leaves me four escorts."

"Does that mean you don't think we're dealing with a sub?"

"I don't dare rule it out, but two Italian ships have searched the approaches to Naples and have come up with nothing."

"It could well have been a small sub that's already

returned home, wherever that is. Some small inlet or harbor?"

"Or to some sort of mother ship," added CINCUS-NAVEUR, who'd been listening in silence up to this point.

"Yes, it could, Admiral," concluded COMSIXTH-FLT. "That's why I'm not ruling out a submarine and the Italians are checking on any ship within fifty miles they don't already know all about."

"Has any evidence been found of a mine?" asked the CNO.

"I would think if it was a mine then the torpedo element would have been mounted on some sort of anchoring system or carriage to protect it from the sea bottom. So far, however, the Italian minesweepers haven't found it. Unfortunately for all of us, the Italian coast is littered with four thousand years of anomalies. Even with the best side-scanning SONAR it's going to take time to sort them out."

"Very well, Bob. I concur with both your actions and your logic."

"Anything new from Intelligence?"

"Hell no! All they're doing is shouting 'the balloon is up' and hitting one another over the head with flash memos."

"What worries me the most," concluded CINCUS-NAVEUR, "is the possibility that this business might reappear just about anywhere in the world. The Fifth Fleet in the Persian Gulf area seems like an especially likely target."

"They're already doing more or less what Bob's doing in the Med. So's the Seventh. We've raised the security level everywhere, even the three Western Hemisphere fleets."

* * *

A few miles from the Pentagon, the midsummer heat of tidewater Virginia—the air almost as damp as the nearby Potomac River—had settled over the head-quarters of the Central Intelligence Agency in Langley. Inside the sprawling, once-modern building, the atmosphere was as cool and controlled as one might expect to find in the headquarters of the world's premier intelligence operation.

"That's all we have?" demanded the Director of the Central Intelligence Agency as he looked around his beige and blue windowless conference room at the three others present—his personal assistant; Chaz Owens, the deputy director for antiterrorism, and Greta Sabbagh. "What do the Italians say?"

"At the moment, sir, nothing," reported the Director's assistant.

"And you don't have anything more to contribute, Pat?" demanded the Director, looking right into the secure teleconferencer. "I was hoping for something a little more robust from you."

"No," replied McGrath from Beirut, "I was really hoping Greta and her people had come up with something. It seems clear to me this business extends far beyond my bailiwick"

The Director looked at Greta Sabbagh. Tall, in her mid-thirties, Greta had facial features and a complexion that reflected her father's Middle Eastern origins. The Director had always felt she was really quite attractive, although the emptiness that seemed to lie within her left eye and the slight, perpetual droop that afflicted the left side of her face were a little unsettling.

"Pat's right. Whatever this is extends well beyond his bailiwick. And he's right, I *should* have more data, but I don't. Every military submarine we know of in the region is accounted for. So are all the known civilian ones large enough to pull this off. As for a mine, somebody from outside the area must have provided it, but so far nobody admits to knowing anything. I'm a little surprised Mossad doesn't know more. They always seem to."

"They say they don't." McGrath's voice had a snap to it, audible despite its electronic nature. "They hope to soon, but they don't now. As I've already said, all they think they know is that somebody code-named the Sea Hawk is running the operation."

"How good's their source?" demanded Greta.

"I've no idea. They don't generally tell me who they are. Does the name mean anything?"

"It means the operator isn't from one of the super-religious factions," snapped Chaz Owens. "If he were, it'd be something like the 'Hawk of Allah.'"

Owens was hard-core. Even when he was seated, he was ramrod straight, and he always wore a studied frown. He knew his duty and refused to let anybody or anything stand in the way of his performing it. Especially fools. He refused to tolerate fools and others who refused, or were unable, to see what was so totally clear to him. He was a man of action and loathed meetings.

"Possible, I suppose . . ." conceded McGrath.

The Director was well aware that Greta and Pat didn't like each other. It was said that Pat believed Greta was too sympathetic to some of the Arab causes. It was also said that Greta thought Pat was a moron. He was even more aware that Chaz disliked both of them. The personal conflicts highlighted for him two crucial management questions: How far should he encourage teamwork and consensus? And how far should he foster competition? It was all a matter of balance, he decided. "All right. Pat, I want you to keep digging. Greta . . ."

"I've already started analyzing the shipping that's come in from outside the Med the past ninety days. Where each ship came from and where it stopped.

Checking with the port authorities—although we all know they lie as much as anybody. If you would encourage the field chiefs to have their people work the docks, they might come up with—"

"I'm already doing that," snapped Pat defensively.

"I didn't mean only you. You're not the only field chief in the Med."

"Damnit, Pat," interjected Owens, "this is war! Get your ass in gear and sweat your sources and anybody else who might know something. If you're not up to the job, I'll send somebody who is."

"Enough" sighed the Director. "The two of you have work to do. I wish I had more robust data to take to the director of national intelligence."

"What about our friends at the Defense Intelligence Agency and the National Security Agency?"

"The DIA claims they know nothing. At least that's what they tell me. And the NSA says the only intercepts they can find so far mentioning the *Rachael Spivak* are routine communications between the ship and her owners or various port authorities. However, we all know they may be telling the DNI more than they're willing to tell me."

"What about intercepts mentioning the Sea Hawk?"

"They're starting on that now."

"I'm sure if we dig deep enough we'll find an Iranian connection," offered the personal assistant.

"Yes," replied the Director, "that would be in compliance with the model the administration's currently working from."

"The Palestinian Naval Militia can't be a very big operation," observed Greta. "They seem to have organized and conducted this whole operation face-to-face. They must be good, too. I don't think we're dealing with the usual suicidal, misguided fanatics."

"It's always possible some sort of coded intercept may yet be spotted."

"That would be helpful."

* * *

The early afternoon sun was hot and wind of passage—the breeze created by the boat's motion—felt good as Mike Chambers guided his twenty-foot Mako center console dive boat in toward the sandy shore of Eggmont Key, a few miles south of St. Petersburg, Florida. "Stand by, Kenny," he said to his fifteen-year-old son, who was standing, already dressed in a wet suit, at the boat's bow.

As the boat crept in toward the green-crested beach, Mike studied the depth sounder. When it showed forty feet, he turned into the slight current and put the outboard in neutral. "Let go," he said when the boat had drifted to a stop.

The boy lowered the anchor over the bow and started to pay out the line. "Seventy feet should be enough under these conditions for our purposes."

"Okay, Dad." There was a note of strain in the boy's voice. Fifteen-year-olds don't like excessive instructions, Mike reminded himself. He was going to have to be very careful. Not only today but for the next ten years.

Chambers—Captain Michael Chambers, USN—was the commanding officer of a special maritime antiterrorist group, SECRESGRUTWO. The group, also known as the Trident Force, was headquartered at MacDill Air Force Base in Tampa and reported directly to the secretary of defense. It specialized in dealing with especially touchy situations, ones which involved questions of sovereignty and intervention authority, for example. The Tridents were expected to operate with a very low profile and a very high level of finesse and, if at all possible, even charm.

Commanding the Trident Force was a complex and demanding job, but Mike had taken the afternoon off to attend to another job that was, in his view, equally important.

After graduating from the Naval Academy, Chambers had joined the SEALs. A few years later he chose to return to the blue water navy and spent many of the following years at sea. For some time he'd been growing increasingly concerned about the effect his long absences might be having on his son. Since he'd assumed his current position—which was nominally shore duty—he'd resolved to spend as much time as he could with Kenny. As much time as the kid could stand. Today, with school due to open soon, they'd decided to grab the chance to work on Kenny's diving skills a little. Specifically, on his buoyancy control.

"I think it's holding, Dad."

Chambers looked forward at his son, whose hand was resting on the anchor road, alert for the twitching that indicated the anchor was hopping over the bottom rather than being firmly dug in. "Good. Let's finish suiting up."

The slightest of breezes skipped across the otherwise flat surface of the Gulf of Mexico as father and son helped each other into buoyancy control devices with attached air tanks and weights. After turning on their air supplies, they slipped on their masks and sat on the gunnel, where they fitted their fins to their feet and popped their mouthpieces into place. Mike nodded, and Kenny rolled backward into the green blue water, holding his mask and mouthpiece in place as he did. Mike followed, and after exchanging okay signals, they worked their way forward to the anchor road and swam down it.

There was extraordinarily little to see as they approached the bottom. Sand, a pale, greenish white below, and green water shading darker in the distance. With the exception of an undersized grouper and a small cloud of pinfish—all of whom seemed to have very important business elsewhere—there was no sign of life except the bubbles rising from their regulators. Kenny looked at Mike and Mike nodded. The boy stopped swimming and allowed himself to start sinking toward the sand. He pressed his inflator button and a dollop of air jetted into the vestlike BC. His descent stopped, and after a second, he began to rise. He pressed the release button at the end of his mouth-inflator hose, and air bubbled up toward the surface. He started to descend again.

Mike watched Kenny struggle with one of the more frustrating parts of becoming a really first-class diver and felt more than a tinge of sympathy. Just about everybody had trouble with buoyancy control at first, and learning to master it was generally frustrating.

After struggling for several minutes, Kenny managed to float in place without the aid of hands or feet. Mike gave him a thumbs-up and then signaled for him to float flat. The slight change in the buoyancy/center of gravity equation caused him to rise gently. He vented a tiny amount of air and regained control.

Mike, feeling a certain pride now, signaled for him to sit in the water, cross-legged. Kenny complied and began to sink. He reached for the air supply button and pushed it.

He pushed it just a little too hard and too long.

Mike watched as Kenny started to rise. Then, to his growing alarm, the boy continued to ascend with increasing speed, demonstrating the first signs of an uncontrolled ascent, which even at this depth could be fatal.

Instinctively Mike kicked his fins and reached for his son's vent button, only to have Kenny twist away from him. Mike watched, a pit forming in his stomach, as the boy continued to rise, faster and faster, overtaking the bubbles venting from the BC.

Never but never ascend faster than your bubbles. One of the cardinal rules of diving. For a moment Mike didn't breathe. Realizing his own deadly error, he forced himself to exhale and inhale as normally as possible.

The incident seemed to Mike to last an eternity, although it was, in truth, over in a few seconds. The large amounts of air Kenny was dumping soon reduced him to neutral and then negative buoyancy. Before he'd risen more than fifteen feet he stopped and then started to drift down. Mike took a deep breath and gave him the thumbs-up sign again. Training your own kid in this sort of thing, he thought, was even more nerve-wracking than training other people's sons and daughters.

Following another quarter hour of drills, Mike decided Kenny had practiced enough for one day—and his own nervous system had suffered enough. He signaled for them to go up.

"I think you've got it down pretty well, Ken," said Mike after they'd dragged themselves back aboard and were stripping off their gear.

"I almost lost it once, Dad."

"But you recovered well. I'm not worried."

"Thanks."

"Your mother has a meeting tonight, so why don't we burn a steak?"

"Does that mean you don't want me to go out tonight?"

"No. Not at all. We'll get started just as soon as we get home. You should have plenty of time after that to socialize."

"Great."

Mike's cell phone buzzed. "Chambers."

"Mike, this is Alex. Alan Parker's on his way down

from Washington. He wants to see you as soon as he arrives."

Damn! thought Mike. "That Israeli container ship?"

"That's my guess."

"I'll be there in a couple hours."

"Something up?" asked Kenny as Mike snapped the phone shut.

"Yeah. I'm afraid you're going to have to fend for yourself for dinner. I'll drop you off and then come back later."

"Okay. I guess I'll just have to make do with mac and cheese."

Mike looked at the grin on the boy's face. "I thought you like steak."

"I do. I love it. But in a pinch . . ."

"Okay."

"Dad . . ."

"Yes?"

"I'm sorry you have to work. It would've been fun barbecuing, but I've had fun today. It may not have looked like it, but I did. Thanks."

Mike looked to the west, at the thunderheads beginning to form over the Gulf, then lit off the outboard. "Let's get that anchor up, Ken."

* * *

Hussein Sherif, a member of Fatah and the PLO's coordinator of Palestinian activities in Lebanon, stood on the porch of the chalet and looked at the full moon as it rose over the mountains to the east of Beirut.

The Metn, the resort area where the chalet was located, was a pleasure to visit, he thought. Scenic, quiet. Too bad he could only stay another two days. Just long enough to meet with the Sea Hawk. Then it would be back to Beirut, before the Mossad became too confident they knew where he was.

Sherif had high hopes for al-Jabbar. He was bright and energetic. He'd proven himself on several occasions in the past and seemed to be doing so on this operation. Although his dedication to Palestinian liberation seemed rock-solid, he was flexible in his thinking and not blinded by hatred as so many others were. Assuming all went well the next few days, Sherif was certain he could arrange a position of considerable authority for the Hawk. First within Fatah and then within the Palestinian Authority, the pseudo government they all hoped would, someday very soon, develop into a real government.

* * *

Alan Parker, deputy secretary of defense, stormed into Mike's office twenty minutes after the captain had managed to reach it himself. Waiting with Mike was Alex Mahan, the Trident Force's executive officer.

Alex, who was in her early thirties, was tall—almost as tall as Mike—and willowy. Despite her slender frame and fluid way of moving, she was also as physically tough as most marines. Except on days when she felt like being a girl and the circumstances allowed the indulgence.

Unlike all the other members of the team, Alex had never been in the navy. She'd been recruited from the CIA—partially because she was smart, mostly because she'd spent her career making countless friends in the intelligence community, and remarkably few enemies. While many of her friends wouldn't talk to one another, most seemed willing to tell Alex things they perhaps shouldn't.

"Mike . . . Alex," said Parker brusquely as he slammed the door behind him, hoping to shut out the Tampa summer night, "SECDEF is very concerned about this attack on the *Rachael Spivak*."

"I gather from what Alex has dug up that nobody

knows whether it was a mine or a submarine," said Mike.

"That's all too true. All we know is that some new group calling itself the 'Palestinian Naval Militia' has claimed credit and suggested more's on the way," explained the secretary of defense's designated liaison with Chambers and his group. "Alex's former buddies at the Agency also say Mossad thinks the operation's leader is code-named the 'Sea Hawk,' but other than that, even *they* claim to know nothing."

"What about the fleet?"

"Admiral Simmons is keeping the carrier group at sea, in an ASW formation. The others, the amphibs and support ships, are being parked at Gibraltar and Soudha. Predictably, the insurance rates on merchant ships in the area are skyrocketing, causing all sorts of hate and discontent in the shipping and financial communities. Which means that Congress is already hearing about it."

"Alan, the Palestinians are far from stupid, but at the moment they lack the industrial capacity to field either a submarine of sufficient size to pull this off or a sophisticated mobile mine, which appears to be the other option. Either way, somebody is obviously helping them."

"That's the assumption. The smart money's betting on the Iranians. This sort of thing is not inconsistent with what we expect of them."

"What does SECDEF want us to do? We're really not equipped to ferret out the basic intelligence. Ray's fluent in several dialects of Arabic and Alex can order dinner, but the rest of us can't even ask for directions to the head."

"The secretary is primarily worried at the moment about the threat to the Sixth Fleet. He wants you and your people to work with Admiral Simmons and his people to sharpen their defenses. If the Agency, or somebody else, comes up with something and it looks as if you can be useful in an offensive capacity, then you'll already be there and will have familiarized yourself with the territory. For the moment, though, you'll be playing a defensive roll. In effect, you'll be auditing the fleet's readiness."

"When does he want us there?"

"ASAP."

"Where does he want us?"

"Initially he wants you to operate from the *Khe Sanh*. She's got boats, helos, communications and lots of spare messing and berthing facilities."

"Good choice," remarked Mike, thinking of the big, aircraft carrier–like amphibious assault ship, a sister to his last command. "I know her captain."

"Yes. That will help with coordination."

"I'll call everybody in and we'll go over the operation, not that there's much to go over yet. Then, we'll fly out about midnight. I'm afraid it won't give them much time to make peace at home, though."

"That's the fortunes of war."

"Alex?"

"I'm on it, Boss."

"You want some dinner, Alan?"

"No time. Got to get back to D.C. pronto. And I want you to get to work and kick some ass. What the people pay you to do."

3

"It is amazing, inconceivable, the way that ship was attacked right in front of our eyes, not five miles away, and we knew nothing of it until the evening news," remarked Signora Metello as her husband waved for the serving girl to bring more drinks. Then, before either Abdul or Magda could respond, she immediately went on to ask them if they'd enjoyed their visit and where they were headed next.

Once the initial satisfaction of victory had passed, a low-grade sense of unease had settled over Abdul. There were literally thousands of villas along the Bay of Naples from which the attack might have been controlled. Most, if not all, belonged to the wealthy and powerful. Some were rented to outsiders. Even if the security forces did manage to conclude that the attack was orchestrated from shore, it would take them days to interview all the possible owners and renters. And he and Magda would be gone in the morning.

Forcing his worries to the back of his mind, the Sea Hawk concentrated on enjoying the long, elegant meal the signora presented them and watching with concealed amusement as Carlo, the ancient aristocrat, devoted his full efforts to a furious but unsuccessful effort to grope Magda. The signora, after a sigh or two, had just looked the other way.

Once Abdul had managed to brush his concern about being detected aside, however, another thought emerged to challenge the glorious meal. The attack had been a technical success, and the fact that two men had died bothered him no more than the Americans and Israelis had been bothered when they'd killed British to get them out of their countries.

But how much had it really contributed to solving the problem? Would it really drive anybody to make a serious effort to end Palestinian subjugation?

It was a question that continued to nag at him.

* * *

It was shortly after eleven at night in Gaza City and the air outside the Universal Lifeline Clinic was as viciously hot as it had been at noon. Penny Arnold was rearranging the sheet covering a very sick little boy who she thought might not survive till dawn, when she felt as much as heard a rapid thudding. There they go again, she thought without even looking up.

Gaza City had destroyed her, she decided. Made her numb to the pain and suffering around her. And the death. And the hopelessness. She was beginning to believe she no longer cared if she or anybody else died. Blow everybody up, it wouldn't make any difference. She looked down again at the little boy and the pitiful little dribble of dark fluid creeping out of his closed mouth and realized that she could still feel pain. Unfortunately.

Half an hour later pandemonium erupted in the courtyard. The roar of at least one muffler-less car engine and
the shouting of many men shattered the silence that had
descended only a few minutes before, replacing the
thudding of automatic weapons. The front door of the
clinic flew open and a half dozen armed men flooded in,
shouting loudly as they came. They were dirty, sweaty
and wide-eyed, and dressed in an assortment of military
uniform parts, sweaters and torn and dirty business suit
jackets. Many were wearing knitted caps on their heads,
some were wearing kaffiyehs or had scarves wrapped
around their heads, and a few were bareheaded. In their
midst they were carrying a bleeding mass of human
meat.

"They've shot Moustafa Tibi," shouted what appeared
to be the leader, a wild expression twisting his face.
"You must save him."

"Put him on that examining table, there," directed
Penny. One glance at the bloody mess told her there was
nothing the Universal Lifeline Clinic, or any other group
of mortals, could do for the patient.

Within seconds Dr. Fayez was out of his office and
leaning over the body.

"Tibi's dead," said the doctor, straightening up and
looking at the leader.

The leader started to raise the assault rifle he was carrying, then lowered it, the wildness on his face turning
into a look of grim intensity. "Clean him up. We'll call
for him in the morning."

"How'd this happen?" asked Fayez.

"The Mossad ambushed him. They've wanted to get
him for some time."

"How do you know it was the Israelis?"

"Because we could overhear them talking Hebrew on
their walkie-talkies."

Fayez nodded. The party of enraged warriors stood a

moment, as if not sure what to do next. They all turned then and dribbled out into the night, their weapons at the ready as if they expected to be attacked right there in the clinic's courtyard.

"Do you know who Tibi is? Was?" Fayez asked Penny.

"One of the major Fatah leaders in Gaza?"

"Yes. He had many enemies. Not only the Israelis but also Hamas. Let's clean him up as best we can."

* * *

Alex Mahan was at her desk, collecting up the last few items she knew she'd need on the mission, when the secure phone rang.

"SECRESGRUTWO," she answered.

"Alex, is that you? This is Greta."

"Greta! I thought I spotted some of your data in the stuff we've received the past few hours. I was going to touch base with you."

"Well, I saw your group's name pop up from nowhere as a new client and decided to beat you to it."

"How's your eye?"

"Same as before. It looks almost normal but all I can see with it is light or dark." Who am I kidding? thought the analyst as she spoke. It looks like something out of a horror movie. "That's why I'm no longer in the field."

"Do they think they can fix it?"

"Not really. I'll be in analysis or administration for the rest of my career. At least I still have a career."

"You'll be the director in a few years."

"I'll probably be dead by his hand in a few days. Everybody, including him, is piling on me for not already having all the answers."

"We'll be working with you on this mission?"

"Not with. Remember, I'm no longer in operations, but I'll be providing most of the maritime intel you receive. Normally I wouldn't make a personal call to a client, but when I saw it was your group I decided to take the risk. Sometimes there are delays of one sort or another at this end when it comes to passing on data. One or two of these delays have proven fatal in the past, so I want you to understand that I'll be sending you a lot of stuff direct and hell with 'em."

"Thanks, pal. You're the greatest!"

"Let's not get carried away. This is just a better, more efficient way of doing the business we would be doing anyway. Right?"

"Right."

"And you promise to get directly to me whenever you come across some little bit of something I might like to know?"

"Right."

"One more thing. Two really. I don't think the Director's going to be happy when he learns I'm providing stuff directly to SECDEF's little crew of secret sailors. He's got to cooperate, of course, but some of those around him will do what they can to make him feel better."

"Roger."

"And number two. Chaz Owens. You remember him?"

"Super tough guy?"

"He's deputy director for antiterrorism now. I don't know where this is all going to lead, but watch out for him. If he gets involved, he's totally capable of deciding you're as much the enemy as the Palestinian Naval Militia."

An hour later a navy transport jet took off from Mac Dill, bound for the joint Spanish-American naval air station at Rota, Spain. Aboard was the Trident Force. Along with Mike and Alex were Captain of Marines Ramon Fuentes, a very talented linguist; Chief Boatswain's Mate and Master Diver Jerry Andrews, whose duties centered on maintaining all the group's gear and on keeping his teammates from drowning themselves; and Ship Fitter Second Class Ted Anderson, a wiry young black SEAL who was especially valued for his tenacity and quick mental and physical reactions.

As was so often the case, the group was traveling light—a few special sensors, communications gear and other black boxes along with their personal sidearms. *Khe Sanh*, their immediate destination, was built to transport and support a small army of marines. They'd have no trouble finding anything they needed there.

*   *   *

"Alex," asked Ted as their plane, its engines hissing quietly, crossed the midpoint of the Atlantic, "what's the story on this Greta who you say is going to give us better intel than the system?"

Alex looked into the past a moment then replied, "I met Greta at CIA indoctrination. I can't say CIA boot camp was in the same mud-and-misery league as Ray went through at Parris Island, or you went through for that matter, but it tore your guts out in equally emotional ways. Early on, Greta and I discovered we were there for the same basic reason, to defend the Constitution. We also discovered, along the way, that some of our classmates seemed to be there for other reasons. There were times when we leaned on each other's shoulder and cried. And then we each went off in different directions. I'm here now and she's at Langley with a left eye that doesn't work.

"Boss," asked Alex, changing the subject, "do you want Kenny to become a naval officer?"

Chambers, who'd been half-asleep, listening to the discussion in the darkened cabin, opened his eyes. "Some days I want desperately for him to become a naval officer. Others I pray he'll move on to other arenas. To be wealthy and powerful. To be a doctor. Still others, on those rare occasions when the true spirit of selfless fatherhood strikes me, I wish for him to be whatever it is that gives *him* satisfaction. You have anything to contribute, Ray?"

"It's safer for me to leave Jamie's ambitions to her, although Sandy seems to have a few ideas already."

"A wise view, Captain," remarked Jerry. "Lynn and I are both pleased with how ours turned out—one naval aviator and one MBA—but I'm not sure how much conscious effort we put into it.

"No use asking Ted," continued Jerry. "So far Hannah's managed to elude him."

Ted sat back in his chair and kept his mouth shut.

* * *

The night with Don Carlo Metello and the signora had been long and alternately amusing and boring. Shortly before one A.M. the Sea Hawk excused himself for a few moments to take a call from George Hadeed, the IT director at the Beirut and Byblos Bank in Beirut.

"Abdul, this is George."

"Yes, George."

"We've got a real problem here. Somebody's hacked into our system and made it impossible for us to access hundreds of thousands of files, and we're making very little progress straightening it out. Where are you?"

"Near Naples."

"How soon can you get here?"

"George, I'm supposed to go to Athens tomorrow to work a few miracles for the Greek taxing authorities. *Then* I'm scheduled to come to Beirut."

"Are the Greek's computers screwed up?"

"Always. Like everybody else's."

"Is it an emergency?"

"No, not really. Everybody knows time's on the tax-man's side."

"Then please tell them you'll see them later in the week. We need you here."

With the cell phone pressed against the side of his head, Abdul looked across the room and watched while Don Carlo, dressed in a very elegant dinner jacket, explained the fine points of a painting of one of his many esteemed, stiff-faced ancestors—whose seventeenth-century dress was even more elegant than Don Carlo's—to Magda. As he pointed out the use of light and shadow, and the fine brushstrokes, the aged aristocrat kept sidling up to Abdul's partner in sabotage and she kept sidling gracefully away from him, almost without appearing to be doing so.

Abdul liked George, who was an apolitical Christian in a country where even the Christians were often at one another's throat. He also felt an obligation to help George's bank—if ever Palestine was to have a solid economic footing, the Lebanese banks would have to play a role.

"Okay, George. I'll get there as soon as I can."

"Thanks, Abdul."

Seven hours later the sun was beating down again on Italy and Abdul had made his apologies to the Greeks and rescheduled. He and the Albanian then climbed into their rented Alfa and, with Magda driving, screeched north to the Naples airport. Magda, who hadn't bothered to tell Abdul her next destination, dropped him off at the terminal, shouted "See you soon" and quickly disappeared into the dense flow of slow-moving traffic leaving the airport.

As he watched her drive away, Abdul was again struck by Magda's stunning beauty and presence. It was a mistake operating with her. He could disappear into a crowd anywhere in the world and be forgotten immediately. She was remembered by everybody—man or woman—who happened to lay eyes on her. She was highly competent and energetic, but there was no way she could swim with the fish, as Chairman Mao so astutely put it. She was also ferociously dedicated to her cause. At the moment their interests meshed, but he knew that at some point his cause and hers would clash.

Fortunately for him, there were only two more phases left of this particular operation. After that he could shake her hand—he wouldn't dare try to kiss her—say "Ciao" and disappear back into the Middle East, the sand-blown hell of poverty and fear from which he'd originally emerged, before being sent to live with distant relatives in New Jersey.

* * *

"You have a call, Hussein," said Khalid, his only assistant, as the latter walked into the dining room. "It is Sayed in Gaza."

Hussein Sherif accepted the offered phone. "Good morning, Sayed."

"We've both enjoyed many better mornings, Hussein," replied Fatah's senior man in Gaza.

"What's happened?"

"Moustafa Tibi was ambushed and killed late last night."

"By whom? Do we know?"

"His companions are convinced it was Mossad. They say they heard Hebrew being spoken."

"You don't sound convinced."

"It could well have been the Jews, but it could equally well have been our devout friends at Hamas. Their control of the Strip has become almost total. There are relatively few of us left here."

"What do you plan to do?"

"I plan to continue watching my back."

"Please do. I'll forward this to the Revolutionary Council, unless you've already reported it."

"I've notified them. I notify you mainly to warn you. If Hamas is pushing to consolidate their power, then you'll also be on their list."

"You're right, Sayed. We've both enjoyed better mornings than this one."

* * *

After nine hours aloft, the plane carrying Mike Chambers and his team passed from the choppy blue and white waters of the Atlantic to the choppy blue and white waters of the Bay of Cádiz. As the plane started to bank and turn north, the old city of Cádiz sparkled in the sun under its starboard wing.

"That's where sherry started," mumbled Alex as she looked out her window at the green and brown land below, to the north of the city.

"What?" asked Jerry, who assumed she was saying something important to him but hadn't been able to hear her above the growling of the engines and the hiss of the cabin air.

"Sherry, Chief," contributed Ray Fuentes without invitation. "The stuff you drink. Not everybody drinks bourbon, you know."

"Nor rum, Mr. Fuentes." The two smiled across the aisle at each other.

"A guy I've been going out with from time to time and I have a little game," continued Alex, giving no hint of having heard the exchange. "When we go to my place, I try to cook something he's never had, and when we go to his place he tries to surprise me. Last week he made something wonderful with chicken and sherry."

"Name," demanded Ted. "What's his name?"

"Bill."

"And?"

"And nothing."

"This is really very strange," continued Alex after a moment or two of silence. "Something this big and we've absolutely nothing on it except Mossad's claim that the operator is code-named the Sea Hawk."

"We've undoubtedly got something someplace," remarked Ted. "We just don't know what we're looking for."

"Captain," said Jerry, "you did say the torpedo, whatever its source, appears to have gone under the ship and then turned up, right under the engine room?"

"Affirmative."

"Assuming that was intended, then we're dealing with a very sophisticated operation. This isn't just some misguided fool walking into a bar and blowing himself and everybody else up."

"We're looking for a very smooth, twenty-first-century operator," offered the group's one non-naval person. "A lot of these guys seem out of the twelfth century but this one's totally up-to-date, damnit!"

A few minutes later the plane whistled down the runway at Rota. The local time was three in the afternoon. It took less than half an hour to refuel. The plane took off again and turned east, bound for the shared Greek airbase at Soudha Bay on Crete.

* * *

"Why are you telling me this?" demanded Tareq ibn-Ali as he leaned forward over the small table in a nondescript restaurant in Rome, not far from the Vatican.

"Because I don't trust him and you don't either. He's not Hamas. He's not religious in any way. He has no interest in jihad and his mind seems to be wandering. I don't think he'll be able to execute the remainder of the operation."

"Jihad! You have no interest in jihad either. You're not even a Moslem. Your grandparents, perhaps, but not you. You're a Communist. One of the utterly God-less. We know better than you that he's a Nationalist and, for now, we work with him. Just as we work with you. For now."

"The difference, Tareq, is that I have every reason to want to see the operation completed. And, for that matter, every reason to want to see Palestine freed from the Zionists and their friends in America. He, on the other hand, seems to have become obsessed with electricity. Maybe he's lost his mind. Twice he remarked that with enough electricity the Palestinian desert could be made to bloom."

"After the rule of the Koran is restored, such things may be possible."

"He has no interest in God's rule. He's thinking about how to get electricity, and I'm certain he's trying to come up with ways to do it that don't involve the Koran."

"There are other Nationalists in the PLO. We work with them."

"And the minute you don't trust them, you try to blow them away."

Tareq scowled at her. Godless whore, he thought. Just like my mother.

Indeed, Tareq ibn-Ali had no right to the surname by which he was known. He'd been born to a prostitute in Gaza City and thrown out into the streets at an early age to survive on his own.

Or not, as Allah willed.

His future had seemed bleak, but his will to live had

been strong and he'd survived. His strength and his clev-
erness, his ability to dominate and intimidate the other
urchins, whom he'd organized into a gang, had been
noted by officials of one of the Hamas madrasas. Suspicious at first, Tareq had allowed himself to be taken to
the school of radical religion—attracted primarily by the
prospect of food. Within a month or two he was a model
student, the Koran and terror having become for him the
two absolutes of life. As part of his enlightenment he
also learned that women who showed too much of themselves, or dared to challenge the wisdom of men, were
shameless whores. And if they happened to be impossibly attractive, the sin was all the worse. As should be the
punishment.

"Think about it and remember that I'm as well qualified as he to complete the operation."

"I don't even know where he is right now," lied Tareq,
knowing that Abdul was going to Athens then on to Beirut to meet with Hussein Sherif.

"He's on his way to Beirut."

Ibn-Ali lifted an eyebrow.

"You thought he was going to Athens, didn't you?
He's changed his plan and is going to Beirut to bail out
some banker friend."

"What do you want?"

"Only to warn you. To ensure that the rest of the operation succeeds."

Tareq nodded, knowing she wanted something more
than that. Perhaps she even wanted to complete the operation herself. Why? Probably to make some point to
the Chinese. Or to prove that Godless whores are as
good as men. Her reasons didn't matter at the moment.
Al-Jabbar had been given the mission because of his
technical skills. Nobody in Hamas viewed him as anything more than a necessary tool. Tareq doubted the

Hawk had much personal backing among Fatah members, either. He was a certain liability. He knew too much.

Whores have their uses, too, he thought with grim satisfaction, and this one's charges might very well help him justify doing what he planned to do anyway. Not only to al-Jabbar but perhaps even to the whore. He would keep the movement pure and he would enjoy doing it.

Inshalla.

4

"Looks to me like they've got the whole damn fleet there," remarked Ted several hours later, as the plane flew over Soudha Bay, then banked on its final approach to the NATO airbase on the Akrotiri Peninsula. Both the bay and the peninsula that defined it were located on the north side of the large and fabled Greek island of Crete—home of the legendary King Minos, the ferocious Minotaur and perhaps even the site of the lost city of Atlantis.

The sun was now close to the western horizon, but the sight was spectacular. Set on the bay's deep blue surface were at least twenty ships, including four huge, blocky gray amphibious assault ships, each as large as most of the aircraft carriers used in World War Two. Anchored around them were several equally large underway replenishment ships and a collection of escorts. Swarms of small boats were visible patrolling around the floating gray buildings. Each small boat was undoubtedly armed with boxes of concussion grenades to use on any suspected hostile swimmers. Meanwhile, several small Greek minesweepers and mine hunters continued to plod around the bay looking for any threats they might have missed the first time.

To the north of the anchorage ran the high cliffs of the sun-baked peninsula. To the south, set in an equally sere background, sat the smallish town of Soudha, its stone and whitewashed plaster buildings burning like gold in the dying day. At the mouth of the bay three destroyers searched, their sonarmen undoubtedly more alert than they might normally be as the ships' high, sharp bows cut through the same waters parted by the bows of half the great navies of ancient history—from Minoan through American. Four helos darted here and there in the twilit sky, scouring both the shore and the darkening waters.

"You don't think they're overreacting, do you, Captain? Hiding like this," continued Ted.

Chambers took a moment to frame his answer. "Think of this as if it were a hurricane, Ted. If there were a good reason to keep the ships at sea, I'm certain Admiral Simmons would have them at sea. But under the circumstances, why not find some secure parking lot for a day or two until we know what we're up against?"

"That makes sense, I suppose, but I really hate the idea of hiding."

"So do we all. I'm sure it'll only be for a day or two."

The plane touched down so softly that none of the Tridents realized it at first. The five poured out of the jet, desperate to stretch their long-cramped bodies, only to find a helo from the assault ship USS *Khe Sanh* waiting for them, its rotors swishing gently.

"You've got five minutes to breathe deep a few times

and touch your toes," said Mike, "then we load the gear into the helo and hit the road again."

Within a few minutes the helo was descending toward the gray deck of the big amphib, swaying slightly as it did. Along one side of the flight deck were lined up five or six other helos. On the other were four short takeoff-and-landing aircraft, carried to provide close support when the marines were put ashore. Standing in the large open area between them were two figures in white.

As soon as the helo had landed, the pilot secured the engines and the door opened to reveal Captain Henry Pierson, the ship's commanding officer, and his executive officer, Commander Stanley Banks.

Pierson saluted as Mike jumped out, and Mike returned the courtesy. "Welcome aboard, Mike. It's been ages."

"Sure has, Henry" replied Chambers, grinning. "You greet all your guests this way?"

"Just the ones I want to. Or have to."

Pierson then introduced his XO and Mike introduced the Trident Force as, dressed in blue coveralls and ball caps, they emerged from the helo.

While Mike made the introductions, he noticed out the side of his eye that the sun's lower limb was fast approaching the horizon. At the same time he noticed Captain Pierson glance off to starboard, at another assault ship, *Bastogne*, which was flying a rear admiral's flag along with the yellow and green "prep," or preparative, pennant.

"He's SOPA," said Pierson, nodding toward *Bastogne* and referring to the senior officer present afloat.

Chambers nodded while Pierson glanced aloft at the prep flying from *Tonkin Gulf*'s yardarm, indicating that she was also ready to execute sunset.

The haze gray ships around them, some huge, some

small, were all facing precisely into the light wind—as if under the direction of a marine gunnery sergeant.

A police whistle sounded over the PA system. Then, "Now attention on deck!"

They all turned and faced aft, where the ensign was flying. All motion on the fight deck ceased—except for that caused by the wind—and, while no living ship is ever totally silent, a near total silence descended on the huge amphib. The whistle sounded again, twice, then "Now execute Sunset." As the words were still echoing, the prep pennants flying aboard every other ship in the anchorage were yanked down.

Alex removed her ball cap and placed it over her heart while the rest saluted as a marine detachment lowered the ensign. Forward, behind their backs, two cooks performed one of their few on-deck duties by lowering the jack, the blue flag with white stars displayed on all anchored United States ships.

The whistle sounded three times. "Now carry on."

"Mike," said Pierson as he dropped his salute and turned back to Chambers, "as you requested, I've had Stan rig up one of the empty embarked officers' berthing bays with some messing facilities, and he's assigned two mess cooks to come up with food for you. That's what you wanted, isn't it?" Before Chambers could reply, Pierson continued, "I considered letting you have the flag suite, but somebody would've noticed."

"Roger, Henry. To be honest, I'm not totally sure what we're going to be doing, but I suspect it'll involve a lot of coming and going, so I'd like to keep my people right with me, where I can grab them by the earlobe when they don't move fast enough."

Alex grimaced slightly. Ray Fuentes smiled.

"Needless to say, all our aircraft and boats—remember, we've got everything from hovercraft to HBIs—are at your disposal. And so are we."

"Thanks, Henry."

"You eaten recently?"

"Not well."

"While Stan gets your people settled in, you come on up to my quarters and my steward will come up with something quick. Rear Admiral Wolf, he's commander, Task Force Sixty-two, wants to see you aboard *Bastogne* as soon as you've caught your breath."

"Roger"

"Why don't you take my gig?"

"I knew there was some good reason I saved your butt so many times at the Academy."

"One good turn deserves another."

Mike took a deep breath. The hints in the air of petroleum and stack gas and still-warm steel suggested the presence of a fleet. Mixed in with that navy smell was the faint, dry odor of thyme and goats carried to him by the breeze as it blew from the shore. It was the eternal smell of the Mediterranean, a smell that had wafted over tens of thousands of years of civilization. Tens of thousands of years of stunning artistic achievement and cultural greatness. Tens of thousands of years of deceit and treachery, murder and bloody mayhem.

While Chambers ate and chatted with Henry Pierson, then headed off to report to Admiral Wolf in *Bastogne*, the rest of the Trident Force settled into their Spartan quarters. To the east the horizon turned a deep, brownish purple, highlighted with gold, a motif promptly reflected by the bay's waters. The high cliffs of Akrotiri turned jet black as one half of the United States Sixth Fleet settled in for a night that nobody expected to be truly restful.

* * *

Thanks to an equipment failure in Athens, the Sea Hawk's flight from Naples didn't arrive at the Rafic

Hariri International Airport in Beirut until after eight in the evening.

While standing in line for Immigration, Abdul became increasingly aware of the tension in the air. He looked around a little more carefully than he had when he'd first stepped out of the Jetway. Beirut was always tense, but tonight it seemed even more tense than usual. Most of the car rental counters were unmanned and there seemed a shortage of baggage handlers. The soldiers on guard were even edgier than usual. They seemed far more interested in keeping an eye on the exits than on the arriving travelers. Nobody was standing around chatting or waiting. All were completing their business and leaving.

Lebanon—the land of the ancient Phoenicians—was, in Abdul's view, an experiment that might have worked—that almost did work—only, in the end, to fizzle in a cloud of shrapnel.

During the middle of the twentieth century, Lebanon had returned to its Phoenician roots and reached out to the world, opening itself and becoming *the* commercial and banking center for much of the Mediterranean—the "Switzerland of the Middle East." Beirut, its capital, had blossomed into one of the most cosmopolitan of cities. Money from around the world flowed in and out. The fashionable and wealthy could be found seated along the Corniche—a great, curving boulevard that flowed along the city's rocky western and northern coasts—looking out over the Mediterranean, chatting in French, Arabic, English, Greek—you name it—indulging themselves and negotiating. From the outside, everybody seemed to get along.

But then it turned out they didn't. A civil war broke out between Christians and Moslems. It was a matter of religion, centuries-old feuds, money and money. With the breakdown of the central government, the southern part of the country became a launching ground for attacks on Israel, and the Israelis found it necessary to seize control of the region. The Syrians—to the north and east—didn't feel they could just stand by and watch, so they moved back in and took control of what Israel didn't.

Syria, the Lebanese government, Israel, Hezbollah—a powerful Lebanese Shiite party—and the Christians of various sects all continued to scheme when they weren't shooting. Beirut, and the whole country, was once again caught between more than just the mountains and the Mediterranean.

Abdul's cell phone buzzed. It was George.

"Yes, George, I've landed and am about to go through Immigration."

"Good. Hurry. More and more files keep disappearing into that black hole those bastards made in my computer."

"As soon as they let me in your country, I'll go to the hotel, drop off my gear and continue right on to the bank."

"I'll have a car waiting for you at the Phoenicia."

"Why don't I just use a cab?"

"Because there's trouble developing and our car can get you through both sides. A cab may not."

"Passport," said a voice directly in front of him.

Abdul realized he'd reached the head of the line. "Okay, George, I'll use your car," he said as he handed the immigration officer his documents. "Is there some sort of trouble in the city?" he asked.

"There are rumors," said the official. "Your reason for visiting Lebanon?"

"I'm a computer consultant. I'm here to fix a problem that has developed at the Beirut and Byblos Bank."

"Very well," said the officer, after checking the computer monitor on his desk. "Next!"

The Sea Hawk collected his one bag and cleared Customs, then found he had to hunt to find a cab to take him to the InterContinental Phoenicia Hotel, considered by many to be the most splendid of the city's several splendid hotels. He'd never have selected it for himself, but his employers, Lindley-Roberts, wouldn't think of having their representative stay at anything less than the best.

As the cab sped toward the glittering lights of downtown Beirut, Abdul's thoughts returned to Magda. Not to her beauty but to her role as a watchdog for the Chinese. And perhaps for others. It nagged at him. He had no real proof, none at all, but he was increasingly convinced she had him in her sights and he doubted she often missed her shots. There was no doubt she'd spotted his waning devotion to the concept of armed struggle. That was more than enough to make him an enemy in the eyes of many.

What would she do about it?

He looked out the cab's window and realized there was almost no traffic. Even at this late hour there should have been more.

"There's talk about trouble the next day or two?" he asked the cabdriver.

"There's talk," replied the driver carefully.

"Can you guess when?"

"By dawn. You're my last customer for the night."

"Hezbollah?"

"It's said they feel the government is leaning on them too much."

Not knowing the driver's position on the dispute, Abdul didn't bother to ask any more questions. To do so might just get him into some sort of difficult position. Whatever the cabbie's political position, his main interest was probably to get home as soon as he could, shut the door and turn out the lights. Either that or get home, grab his gun and head back out the door to hunt down and shoot the other side.

The Sea Hawk sat back in the seat and stared into himself. It was discouraging that Lebanon might be self-destructing. Again. If the Lebanese couldn't get their act together, what hope did the Palestinians have?

When he reached the Phoenicia's soaring, extravagant lobby, Abdul found himself looking carefully around at the faces filling the glittering space. Did he recognize any of them? Did any of them seem to recognize him?

He registered, took his bag to his room and, shortly before eleven, returned to the front of the hotel, where the car George had sent for him was waiting.

* * *

Mike Chambers returned to the Trident Force's quarters in *Khe Sanh* shortly after 2200. The bulkheads were white and the decks a light gray. The bunks, tables and bolted-down chairs were stainless steel. The only decoration, if they could be called that, was the various labels and instructions stenciled in black or red on the bulkheads. Fresh air whispered in through the vents in the overhead.

"What's up, Boss?" asked Ted, who was sitting at one of the tables reading a sports magazine.

"Admiral Wolf understands that we're essentially in a holding pattern, waiting for something to happen. He's asked us to audit the various ships' antiterrorist bills and readiness ship by ship until somebody tells us to do something else."

"Excellent," Ray Fuentes said and grinned. "Are we going to stage a few 0200 visits, just to keep them on their toes?"

"Not right away. There's a lot of nervous people here at the moment, and I don't want to complicate matters by triggering an accident. Once we've reviewed their procedures and discussed it all with them—reminding them the objective is to discourage and, if necessary, kill terrorists, not to create more—then we can decide if any, or all, are ready for a midnight visit. So, until further notice, Alex and Ted will work as one team and Ray and Jerry as the other. I'll be coordinating and liaising."

"That means drinking coffee with the captains and telling war stories while we heckle their crews, right?" asked Alex.

Yes, thought Mike with scant pleasure. While the ships could undoubtedly benefit from a little more training, what we're really going to be doing is simply killing time, waiting for something to happen. Probably something bad.

* * *

"Who's going to be at this meeting?" demanded Moshe Goren, shouting into the phone.

"I don't know."

"Where's it going to be?"

"I don't know. In the mountains someplace."

"In the mountains! The PLO is holding a conference in the Metn?"

"In the mountains, although you can believe, if you wish, that he's going to go all the way to Jordan. I don't know where the meeting is to take place."

"You know perfectly well. You're just not telling me."

"I'm telling you where and when you can grab the Sea Hawk. That's worth the usual to you."

"We're not paying you anything unless you tell me more about the meeting."

"We've been through this before. You'll accept what I offer or you'll get nothing."

Goren snarled to himself. Dealing with this particular informant was infuriating. It was possible, of course, that he really didn't know more—he was, after all, nothing more than a low-level thug—but Moshe always suspected that he did. "Okay, where and when?"

"He'll be in a white, 2005 Jeep Grand Cherokee, license COY427Z. He'll be passing the entrance to the White Fields ski resort—the bankrupt one on the road just outside the town of Ras al-Metn—at between eight thirty and eight forty five tomorrow night. He'll be headed east."

"What does he look like? How'll we recognize him?"

"I've never seen him. It'll be just him and a driver. Don't hurt the driver."

"I've heard Hezbollah has positions in that area, despite the Christians. Sounds like a perfect place to ambush us."

"You talk like an American sometimes. We at Hamas are Palestinian Sunnis. Hezbollah is Lebanese Shia."

"That's a ridiculous thing to say."

"Their nearest position is about three kilometers away, but they know nothing about his passing that way, assuming they even know he exists. On the other side of the road is a big field, a perfect place for you to get a helicopter in if you don't trust the roads. If they ambush you, then I no longer have a customer."

"Okay."

The phone went dead.

"Did you get all that?" Moshe asked his assistant.

"Yes."

"We're going to need three cars—six men—and a chopper on standby. I want this bastard."

"I'm on it."

"And I want you and three others on your way out there right now to secure the area. A bankrupt ski resort is perfect for our purposes. It's also perfect for Hezbollah—or Hamas or anybody—if their purpose is to grab a few of us. You ski, don't you? You should know your way around."

"I ski farther to the north, but I know my way around."

"You like the skiing here?"

"I prefer Vail or Aspen."

"In the States?"

"Yeah, there's nobody shooting at you there."

"Screw you."

"Why do you put up with that damn Arab?"

"Because I get more out of him that way than I would if I told him to fuck off. He thinks he's going to be able to retire to Switzerland in a few years. Problem is, neither we nor the PLO are ever going to *let* him retire in peace."

The assistant smiled.

"I also want three more cars and six more men. I want to track that white Jeep Grand Cherokee just in case there's a change in plan."

"Where is it now?"

"How would I know? We know the license plate number. Find it!"

* * *

Penny Arnold scrunched up in the high-backed desk chair and tried to relax. She shifted her head from side to side, moving the pillow as she did. The lights in the office were out but she was not. She lay there, listening to the not-so-distant gunfire, smelling the thick stench of pain and death and shuddering. They were at it again, practicing what they called politics in Palestine. Hamas and Fatah trying to kill each other. Or maybe it was the Israelis. Or maybe some other gang of thugs. So far, all she'd seen professionally were Arabs. The Israelis took care of their own wounded.

Yesterday there'd been fifty cholera victims jamming

the clinic to overflowing. Today there were another fifty, suffering from tattered limbs, gunshot wounds and God knew what else. And then the blasted remains of that Fatah chieftain. If there was any humor in the situation at all, and there was precious little, it was that once they had a hole in their stomach—or a missing leg—nobody cared if the guy in the next bed was Shia or Sunni. At least not until the sedative wore off.

There was a knock at the door, then it opened.

"Ms. Arnold?"

"Yes, Dr. Fayez?"

"Ah, good, you're resting."

"Is there anything you want, Doctor?"

"No. Only that you rest."

She must have been tired, very tired, because later she couldn't explain to herself why she had let it slip out. It was the sort of question you learned not to ask in the Middle East. "Doctor, you knew something was about to happen, didn't you? This is the second or third time since you've come here that you knew."

Fayez sighed. "Yes, Ms. Arnold, I knew something was going to happen. I didn't know what, but I knew there would be trouble."

"But Dr. Awad never knew in advance."

"Dr. Awad was an excellent doctor and an even greater human being. I miss him greatly. But he didn't practice in Gaza as long as I have. And in Lebanon and Jordan. During all those years I've met many people. On all sides. Some professionally, as you have. Some socially. And a few of them, from time to time, have chosen to give me advance warning so I can prepare. No military secrets. No political secrets. Perhaps it's an effort on their parts to convince themselves they're still human."

"Then you're part of it?"

"We're all part of it. I like to think those of us here are

the good guys, but it's possible I've compromised myself. You, I assure you, remain uncompromised."

Penny winced inwardly. More than once she'd told herself that he—or she—who patches up a warrior so he can fight another day is serving on that warrior's side.

"Ms. Arnold, I want you to try to get at least four or five hours of sleep. If you can, in that miserable chair. I'll look after your patients. I seriously doubt I can match your bedside manner, but they'll simply have to make do."

"Yes, Doctor," responded Penny, closing her eyes.

Gaza, she thought, how I hate you. A hundred-plus square miles of sand and rocky soil jammed against the Mediterranean. A narrow band that butts against Egypt to the south and is surrounded by Israel to the north and east. A godforsaken hole stuffed with almost two million people. People with no food. People with no jobs. People with no hope. People nobody wanted sixty years ago. People nobody wants now.

Shit, she sighed. Will I never be able to sleep?

5

The very slight zephyr wafting in from astern guaranteed the stomach-wrenching stench of the old fishing boat's diesel exhaust would settle over the three young men gathered in the boat's tiny pilothouse. None paid much attention to the fouled air. They were all too excited, and nervous. Ahead, in the misty distance at the east end of Soudha Bay, they could just make out the glow of the anchor and security lights of the massive U.S. armada that was anchored there. To the right, on Akrotiri's southerly shore lay the NATO supply facility, its piers and the two supply ships berthed at them wrapped in the diffuse light of their floods.

If asked, the three young men might have admitted that what they were about to do was very wrong. Especially Miklos, who at sixteen was the youngest and already well through his second pack of cigarettes. But, wrong or not, they were determined to do it. If they succeeded, things would change for them. Things would change very much for the better.

* * *

Abdul stood in front of the Phoenicia and paused, both hearing and feeling the *thump, thump, thump* of a heavy weapon being discharged within a few blocks of the hotel. As he listened, his eyes searched the surrounding road and sidewalk, alert for he-wasn't-even-sure what.

"Sir?" asked the driver of the black Mercedes George had sent for him.

A stiff offshore wind had developed, he thought. Blowing through the city and on out to the west, undoubtedly roiling the generally placid summer Mediterranean.

"Hezbollah?"

"Most likely the army."

"Where?"

"Downtown for the most part," said the driver as Abdul and his briefcase settled into the backseat.

"Do you anticipate any difficulties?"

"No, sir. It's all been arranged."

Although the distance from the hotel to the bank was only a little more than a kilometer, they had to pass through two roadblocks. The first, composed of five cars spread across the road and the sidewalk, was a hundred yards from the Phoenicia's drive. The driver halted, and one of the heavily armed masked men manning the blockade came to the door. "You can't pass through here," he said, holding his weapon at his side while several of his associates aimed theirs directly at Abdul and the driver.

The driver handed him a sheet of paper.

"Very well," said the man finally, after studying the document with a skeptical expression. He waved, and one of the cars was pulled aside to let them through.

Five hundred meters farther on they came to a second block—this time composed of army trucks and armored vehicles.

The Lebanese Army lieutenant who commanded the roadblock was, initially, a great deal more hostile and suspicious than the Hezbollah commander. He clearly assumed that if the other roadblock had allowed them to pass then they were no friends of his.

As the army officer read the driver's pass, the Sea Hawk could hear the sharp, thudding chatter of automatic weapons somewhere out in the dark. The officer and his men all looked briefly over their shoulders, then returned their attention to the car and its occupants.

Abdul studied the Lebanese soldiers and decided they looked nervous and uncomfortable. So, in retrospect, had the Hezbollah. None seemed truly fired up for his cause. Maybe it was just because it was still early in the morning. Or maybe he was projecting his own confusions.

"Very well," said the officer. "You may proceed to the bank."

Three hundred meters later the Sea Hawk was walking up the steps to the glass-and-stone entrance of the Beirut and Byblos Bank. The glass, he knew, was less than a year old. The stone almost one hundred.

He looked around him quickly. At the towering buildings and the narrow streets. Towering like in New York, he thought. And narrow like in downtown New York, too. He'd never for a moment considered himself a man of the desert, but for the first time in his life, he felt a city was closing in on him.

"I'm Abdul al-Jabbar," he said to the two armed guards at the door. "I'm with Lindley-Roberts and I'm here to see George Hadeed."

The guards eyed him suspiciously. One raised a walkie-talkie to his lips and whispered into it. He waited, never taking his eyes off al-Jabbar, while the other fingered his assault rifle. There was more firing in the distance as the wind wound its way, whistling slightly, around the buildings and out to sea.

The guard held the walkie-talkie to his ear. "You may enter," he said with no sign of welcome as he unlocked the door and opened it.

George was standing right inside the door.

"Abdul! Thank you for coming. My God am I glad to see you. I can't tell you what a mess these cretins have made of our systems."

Abdul took George's offered hand. "I'm surprised it's taken them this long to get to you."

"This isn't the first time. Not by a long shot. But this is the first time we haven't been able to fix it ourselves."

"Okay."

"Have you eaten?"

"Not recently. I haven't even showered. A friend asked me to come running."

"Come on into my office. I'll have something sent up from the kitchen."

George then led him across the dimmed lobby, past a row of tellers' counters, to a bank of elevators and on up to his sixth-floor office. For the rest of the night, and into the next day, Abdul and George struggled to undo the damage they increasingly came to suspect had been caused by some pimply-faced delinquent who probably didn't even understand how much damage he—or she— had caused.

Outside the bank's stone walls, the people of Lebanon practiced muzzle-blast politics.

* * *

"What's that!" mumbled the officer of the deck aboard USS *Bastogne*. He stopped pacing in the pilothouse and

walked through the door out onto the open bridge wing.
There it was again.

"Sounded to me like gunfire, sir," offered the boatswain's mate of the watch. "I think it's coming from the
other end of the bay."

The OOD scanned the waters around them—the other
shadowy ships and the even more shadowy patrol boats,
floating through the night like fireflies in the dark haze.
He returned to the pilothouse and notified the admiral's
duty officer of what had sounded like gunfire at the eastern end of the bay. He then notified his own captain and
his ship's CIC, directing them to alert *Bostogne*'s patrol
boats.

* * *

It was shortly after two A.M. local time, when Pat Mc-
Grath in Beirut placed a call to Greta Sabbagh at her office
in Langley, Virginia. "It's happened," he said, "as I told
you it would. Hezbollah's taken to the streets again."

"How extensive?"

"They're just starting to move now. Downtown as
usual. My sources aren't sure how far or how fast they'll
go. If they can reach an agreement with the government
quickly, it may be over in a few hours. Or weeks."

"Casualties?"

"None so far. Not that I've heard of."

"Pat, I have to give you credit. You picked the precise
day." She hated to compliment the guy, but fairness required it. "What have you told the embassy?"

"I suggested they advise all Americans to stay in-
doors until the situation resolves itself a little. I don't
think we're the prime target this time—the Lebanese are
going after each other—but shit happens. They're trying
to arrange a deal with both sides to allow buses to run to
the airport unhindered. The Brits, Germans and French
are all in on the bus plan."

"What about the Syrians?"

"They haven't said a word, unless you've picked something up."

"They really don't have to say anything, do they?"

"No, though I doubt Hezbollah would make a move like this without clearing it with them."

"If the Sixth Fleet starts to move ships in that direction?"

"You mean to evacuate our nationals?"

"I sure as hell hope nobody in the District wants to invade Lebanon again," remarked Greta. "It never seems to work out for us."

"I'm not sure it's going to be necessary, but I suppose it wouldn't hurt. Especially if they can avoid the temptation to tell the whole world they're doing it. With luck they'll keep well offshore unless the shit really hits the fan."

"Okay. Thanks again."

"Roger."

* * *

The phone in the Trident Force's quarters whined and buzzed. Mike Chambers rolled over, stood and pulled the handset off the bulkhead. "Captain Chambers . . ."

"Mike, this is Henry. There's been an incident and Admiral Wolf wants you and your people to get out there and take a look at it. See what you think it's all about, and how much of a threat it represents."

"What happened?"

"Two men have been shot and killed in a little cove about three miles from the anchorage. From what I can tell one of the patrol boats manned by civilian contractors came on them, challenged them and, when they didn't feel their responses were satisfactory, opened fire."

"God damn it! When?"

"Less than an hour ago."

"I didn't even know the admiral was using civilian contractors to patrol."

"I don't think he is. It wasn't in the last OPORD I saw for this drill. They seem to be attached to the support facility."

"Where are the gunslingers now?" Mike had never liked the practice of using civilians for combat. On several occasions he'd tried to convince himself he was being foolish—that whatever worked worked and they were no threat to him. His efforts to restructure his thinking to conform to the thinking in Washington had never quite succeeded. As far as he was concerned, they were just one more band of illegal combatants—outlaws—in a world filled with illegal combatants.

"They're still at the scene. One of the fleet's patrol boats is there but the contractors won't let the sailors ashore. The admiral wants your opinion on whether or not there really are terrorists involved. And he wants it pronto."

"What else do you know?"

"That's it, I'm afraid. What kind of transport do you want, Old Buddy?"

Mike scowled as he looked around the space, which was illuminated only by one dim red light. "Two armed HBIs," he replied, referring to hard-bottomed inflatable boats.

"They'll be rigged and ready in fifteen minutes."

"Roger."

Mike replaced the phone then turned toward the darkened compartment. "Reveille! We've got work to do."

"So who screwed up?" asked Alex. "Did somebody screw up or has World War Three broken out?"

"You were eavesdropping again, XO."

"I thought that was part of my job."

The rest of the team, still in their racks but clearly awake, chuckled.

"Now listen up. Some civilian contractors have shot and killed two men at the other end of the bay, and the admiral wants us to look around a little before everybody else does."

"They have us playing cops again," remarked Anderson.

"If they were terrorists, then they're our type of guys and we've got to find out what they had in mind and if they had backups. If not, it's still our business because the hired hands are only supposed to shoot real terrorists."

"I just hope we haven't made any more enemies . . ." remarked Ray Fuentes, yawning as he spoke. "The Cretans have a reputation for being very proud and a little . . ."

". . . touchy," concluded Mike. "Now everybody up and brush your teeth."

* * *

Tareq ibn-Ali was wide awake at three A.M., Rome time, because he was unable to sleep. He was also angry, which was probably related to his insomnia. He'd never trusted al-Jabbar and he'd never trusted Fatah. Cooperation of a limited sort was necessary with them, at the moment, but in the end Hamas would crush them. Fatah was weak and corrupt. Hamas was strong; it had the strength of God. The death of Moustafa Tibi in Gaza had been a necessary act of housecleaning. As would be the death of Abdul al-Jabbar, with or without Fatah approval. He would see to it.

* * *

It was just before first light when the big gate across the *Khe Sanh*'s stern opened and the Trident Force's two HBIs shot out into the darkened bay and turned east toward the site of the incident. Each boat was equipped with a fifty-caliber machine gun and the crews were also armed with assault rifles, sidearms and a riot gun.

As the two boats screamed over the dark waters, Mike looked around him. Astern, through the haze, he could see the floodlights of the commercial port—and the fuzzy outlines of the docks and cranes and warehouses. To starboard lay the Greek naval station, while slightly ahead and to port the snowball-like floodlights on the NATO docks and the two supply ships berthed there continued to burn.

Chambers didn't like the feel of this "incident." Two men were dead, and it sounded as if Admiral Wolf didn't really believe they were terrorists. It was a situation in which he had even less data than he usually did. The details—even the other players—were as hazy as the night.

"Captain," shouted Ted over the scream of the twin outboards when they were about a mile from the fleet, "there's an armed Whaler off to port challenging us."

Mike glanced to his left and caught the end of the boat's signal lamp flashing. Whoever was driving the Whaler—probably a nineteen-year-old third-class boat-swain's mate—was following to the letter the instructions reviewed and approved by Mike Chambers.

"Very well. Reply to the challenge before they decide to open fire. There're a lot of edgy sailors around here at the moment."

"Aye, aye, Captain," replied Ted, who had been checking and rechecking the fifty-caliber machine gun behind which he was seated.

Five minutes later, as the very first evidence of a less-dense black began to appear to the east and the haze began to thin slightly, Mike throttled back and used the walkie-talkie to instruct Ray, in the other HBI, to do the same. He then grabbed a thermal imager and studied the little bay they were now off.

His first reaction was that the cove was something of a gem. A nearly perfect beach shadowed here and there by whatever those trees were. Three thousand years ago it probably looked the same as it did right now. He then focused on the small fishing boat pulled up on the beach. There were two men near the boat—they seemed to be on all fours, looking for something in the sand. And there were three bodies—they could only be bodies—lying in the boat's shadow.

Three bodies?

Floating between him and the fishing boat was another navy patrol boat. He pulled alongside. "What's the story here, Boats?"

"There was some sort of firefight here, sir," replied the second-class boatswain's mate skippering the boat. "At least three people seem dead, but those fuckers won't let me ashore. When I approached, they fired a warning shot. They say they're waiting for their supervisor to arrive."

"I can see the three bodies, but you only reported two," said Mike, a little surprised at the petty officer's timidity. But then, he knew even less than Mike did and had considerably less freedom of action. He was probably right to call for help and stand off until somebody with more authority showed up.

"Yes, sir. When I arrived there were only two next to that fishing boat. Then they dragged out the third from behind that rock a few minutes ago."

"Very well. Stand by."

After signaling to Ray in the other boat to move off to one flank, Mike gave Alex the helm and directed her to drive slowly toward the rocky little beach. As they got closer, he could see a total of four hired guns, dressed in splotched, tan and black desert camouflage. The two who'd been searching had now stood and been joined by two more who were standing under a tree, their weapons in their arms.

Alex throttled way back on the engines. "I'm a United States naval officer," bellowed Mike through cupped hands. "I am coming ashore."

One of the contractors walked down to the water. "Stay off. We're securing the site. Do not land or we will open fire."

Mike studied the cove carefully for a minute or two. They'd already fired at the patrol boat, so he had to assume they were stupid enough to shoot at him. "Stand by the fifty, Ted," he said quietly. "Your target will be the cliff just above our friends there. I want a five-second burst on my command." Then he picked up the walkie-talkie. "Ray, you see their boat? It's beached just to the left of the fishing boat."

"Roger."

"When you hear Ted commence firing, Jerry is to open fire and trash it. If they return fire, you're to shoot them."

"Roger."

"Commence fire," he said quietly to Ted.

The SEAL's weapon exploded to life and small portions of the light-colored cliff flew in all directions. Almost simultaneously, Jerry's fifty exploded into barking life. As the two machine guns pounded and thundered, Mike watched the contractors carefully. At first they all reached for their weapons, but then they hesitated. The one who seemed to be the leader started to raise his, then seemed to think better of it.

"Move on in and beach the boat, Alex," said Mike after the thundering had stopped. Once the HBI was up on the beach, within a few feet of the remains of the contractors' boat, Mike stepped ashore. As he walked past the fishing boat, he looked inside it briefly. When he heard a sound behind him, he turned. It was Ray, who'd just climbed out of the second HBI.

"Very well," said Chambers to the contractors. "Now all of you place your rifles and sidearms in a pile and step back twenty feet."

"Shit, Captain, this is ridiculous. We're all here for the same reason—to defend the nation and keep America great," said the contractor who appeared to be the leader, a short, almost bald fellow with a ratlike face.

I'd be more inclined to believe that if you were in uniform, or at least under oath, like the rest of us, thought Chambers. "Put your weapons in a pile and step back," he repeated.

Grumbling, the contractors did as they were told. With every passing beat of his heart, Mike was more and more convinced that something was seriously wrong.

"Jerry and Ted, secure those weapons."

While the pile was being cleared away, the walkie-talkie in Alex's hand mumbled and Alex mumbled back.

"What was that?" Mike asked quietly.

"The admiral's chief of staff. He wanted to know what the shooting was about. I told him we'd had a minor difference of opinion with the contractors but that everybody's on the same page now and there're no casualties."

"What did he say?"

"Roger."

"Very well," said Chambers as he turned back to the contractors, "now you," he pointed at the rat-faced spokesman, "step forward to where that pile was and strip. Everything. Throw it to one side and be quick about it."

"You're out of your mind, pal. There's going to be big trouble about this."

"Do it."

"Jerry, you and Ted examine all that. Boots to ball cap."

The search turned up a knife and a small pistol.

"Dress," ordered Chambers. "Then step over there, sit down and keep your mouth shut. Now the rest of you, you're each going to strip, and if we find anything like we found on your leader I'm going to be very unhappy. So toss anything else you've got over there."

Two more knives, another pistol and a blackjack appeared.

"That's not standard antiterrorist patrol gear," remarked Alex when she saw the blackjack.

"It's not," agreed Mike. "Something else is going on here. Alex and I will chat with these fellows while Ray, Jerry and Ted check out the boat and the bodies. Try not to foul up the evidence too much. You know what we're looking for."

"Aye, aye, sir," replied the trio as they turned toward the wreckage.

"Now," continued Mike, facing the rat-faced one, "tell me what happened."

"Not much to tell. We were patrolling when we spotted this boat headed west toward the anchorage with no lights. We flashed the recognition signal and they failed to respond. We hailed them and they failed to respond. They were in a restricted area so we had to assume they were preparing to attack our ships. We opened fire. They ran for this cove and drove their boat up on the beach. We followed and neutralized them all."

"Who fired first?"

"We fired when we had reason to believe they were about to."

"What was that reason?"

"Instinct. When you've been in the security business long enough, you just know."

"Were they still in the boat?"

"No, they were jumping ashore."

"So you got them all on the beach?"

"Two of them. One made it about fifty yards into the brush. We dragged him back out."

"Did the fleet security officer assign you this area to patrol?"

"No! We work for the support facility, not the fleet security officer. We patrol when and where we think best."

The sun was now beginning to creep above the horizon, adding a golden tint to the gray scene around them.

"Captain?" It was Ray. "Would you please come over here?"

"Sit down," said Chambers to the contractor. "Alex, make sure they all stay seated." He then walked over to the remains of the fishing boat.

"These guys"—Ray pointed at the bodies—"were not terrorists. At least they weren't doing that last night. Except for one old pistol there's absolutely nothing aboard the boat that would indicate it and I'm certain those civilians knew it." As he spoke, he opened his fist, revealing a dozen red capsules.

Mike stiffened. "Are there more?"

"Yes, sir. Mixed in with the sand and in the bilges of the boat."

"What is all this shit!"

Mike turned to find the rat-faced contractor standing about twenty feet away with an M-16 in his hand. "I told you to turn in all your weapons."

"When you're in security, you learn to take precautions."

Aggressive son of a bitch, thought Chambers. But then that's what they're hired to be.

"Drop that weapon and go sit with your associates,"

said Mike, bestowing on the contractor the sort of look he normally reserved for palmetto bugs—the Southern version of roaches.

"Bullshit! We had every reason to believe these guys were terrorists."

"Go and sit down!"

"We don't work for you. We're employees of the Branchwater Corporation and we ain't attached to or embarked in any United States ship." Mike noted that the M-16 was aimed very close to him and the contractor's hand was very near the trigger.

"Drop that weapon and sit down," said a quiet voice. Alex was now standing off to one side, about twenty feet from Mike, the riot gun aimed directly at the contractor's chest.

Mike glanced at the other contractors and was delighted to see Ted and Jerry standing behind them, their Glocks also drawn and aimed. He was even more delighted when rat-face placed the M-16 on the sand and rejoined his men. Then Mike heard the sound of another boat approaching the cove. He turned and watched as a Greek naval patrol boat pulled up to the beach and a not particularly young Greek naval officer jumped into the knee-high water then up onto the beach.

The officer looked around at the shot-up fishing boat and the bodies then glanced at the eagles on Mike's collars and saluted. "Lieutenant Diamantis, Greek Navy, Captain."

"Michael Chambers, Lieutenant."

"We received reports of gunfire here, Captain."

"So did we. We assumed at first it was terror-related, and that's what these civilian guards claim, but I now have my doubts. Ray, show the lieutenant what you have in your hand."

Ray stepped forward and opened his fist.

The Greek officer looked at the pills, then at the fishing boat and bodies again and finally at the contractors.

"I think they were doing some sort of drug deal," explained Mike. "I'm not sure who was doing the buying and who was doing the selling, but I think both parties were involved and something went wrong."

"And what do you suggest? These fishermen were obviously Greek nationals and they've been killed on Greek soil. And please remember that Greece is not one of those countries where you make all the rules."

Mike understood perfectly what was on the officer's mind and decided to try a little charm. "Lieutenant, this is Captain of Marines Ramon Fuentes." As he made the introduction, Mike nodded slightly to Ray. Normally he wouldn't want the marine officer to reveal his ability to speak and understand Greek—vast amounts can be learned from eavesdropping—but in this case he wanted to establish as much rapport with the Greek officer as he could.

"Good morning, sir," said Ray in Greek.

"Good morning," replied the Greek officer a little sullenly. Diamantis frowned, as if to say, *This guy just sat down with a phrase book and is now trying to snow me*.

Fuentes understood the expression and immediately launched into a flowing appreciation of the beauty and history of Soudha Bay and the widely recognized nautical prowess of the Greek people. And especially that of the people of Crete.

Lieutenant Diamantis listened, then started to laugh. "Captain Fuentes, your Greek is better than mine. Except for the accent."

"That is a Puerto Rican accent, sir."

"Ah! Another island people. Just like the Cretans."

"Lieutenant," said Mike quickly, before the smile left Diamantis's face, "my people and I are in the antiterror-

ist business, not the drug business. I've no idea who was
selling what to whom, but they weren't here to blow up
ships. As far as I can tell, no naval personnel are involved in this matter, so I suggest you take custody of
these civilians. I also suggest that a careful examination
of the area will turn up more of these red capsules, or
something like them."

"Yes, Captain, I'll take custody of them and we'll
conduct a standard police investigation. We will, of
course, need a report from you."

"I'll prepare that just as soon as I finish explaining
the matter to Admiral Wolf. You'll have it in your hands
by noon. I also assume you'll be hearing from their employer."

"Without doubt."

While Diamantis and his men took custody of the
contractors, Mike wandered over to the bodies of the
dead Greeks. Two of them had clearly been young men.
At first glance the third looked to be of about the same
age, but then Mike looked more closely. In death he
looked just as old as the others—drained—but in life
he'd been little more than a boy. Roughly Kenny's age.

Kenny. Drugs. Jill worried about it. He worried about
it. He had a terrible feeling there was only so much they
could do about it at this point. And even less when he
was running around the Mediterranean, thousands of
miles away.

"Boss," remarked Alex as the HBIs skipped back
across Soudha Bay, toward the anchored fleet, "we were
damn lucky those clowns didn't open fire when you
started decorating that cliff and obliterating their boat."

"We were, weren't we?"

6

Once, thought Hussein Sherif as he watched the sun rise over the rocky, light brown mountains that surrounded his rented chalet, these were all covered with cedars. Two thousand years ago. The Cedars of Lebanon. Now they're all gone, have been for millennia. All except two or three patches. Felled for the construction of ships and buildings. Burned for charcoal. Gone during the earliest phases of man's march toward mastery of his world. Now, he took a deep breath, and he could only smell them—faintly—when the wind was blowing strongly from the south. Or maybe it was just his imagination. Wishful thinking.

That march, he thought as he walked in from the deck and sat down to breakfast, was inevitable. As were many things.

The phone rang.

"Hussein, this is Tareq."

Sherif winced visibly. He knew all too well that Tareq was one of Hamas's most active agents of discipline. Also one of those who failed to recognize the inevitable march of technology.

"Good morning, Tareq," replied Hussein.

"I'm about to fly out of Rome right now. I must meet with you early this afternoon. It's about the man you will be meeting with later."

"Oh?"

"Yes. I'll be there before four."

"Very well."

What else could Sherif say? A phone call from Tareq or one of his associates was bad enough. A visit was even worse. And he could imagine why one with a mind like ibn-Ali's might latch on to Abdul as a less than solid citizen. Abdul was able to imagine the future. Tareq was only able to imagine the past. For the disciplinarian, the future was an ungodly lie. The work of the devil.

Tibi in Gaza. Now Abdul. It was open season on Fatah. Was Sherif next?

*   *   *

"Come in, Mike," said Rear Admiral Jerold Wolf as Mike was shown into his quarters by the admiral's chief of staff, Captain Peter Ramsay. "Sit down."

"Thank you, Admiral," said Mike, not totally certain how the interview was going to go.

"I never expected to have you working this soon after your arrival. Tell me exactly what happened."

Mike went over the "incident," starting with his being called and ending with his arrival at *Bastogne*.

"Then you're certain the three fishermen weren't terrorists?"

"Yes, Admiral."

"Is it possible the patrol had reason to believe the

fishermen were dealing drugs and stopped them for that reason?"

"In my opinion they did know, yes. They were the second party to the transaction. If they were innocent, they would've reported that they'd engaged a drug vessel, but they claimed they were terrorists."

"It does sound like a case for the Greek authorities—although there's going to be a lot of screaming and shouting in Washington. Their employer has a large number of influential friends."

"Then you don't object to my turning them over to the Greeks?"

"Not at all. They're civilians, as they kept reminding you. I'll need a written report from you ASAP. As you know, Pete and I are heading off to join the *Bill of Rights* formation. We'll be at sea, where sailors belong, right?"

"Right, Admiral. My XO is already preparing a first draft. She, as you know, was also there."

"Good. I'll forward the report to COMSIXTHFLT and make every effort to focus my attentions on Lebanon. Admiral Simmons, who has already been informed, will have somebody read it and then forward it to CINCUSNAVEUR. From there it will move up the line. I have no idea where it will end up, since I really don't understand who controls the contractors, if anybody, but I'm beginning to wonder when they're going to outsource the whole Department of Defense. Then, to save the taxpayers even more, they'll tell our successors to pillage for their pay and ransom all prisoners. Put it all on a more businesslike footing. Just like in the good old days."

"Yes, sir."

"I must tell you that when I heard you'd taken this job I thought you were out of your mind. I already have my flag and I think you deserve one, too, but a lot of people don't see things the way you and I do."

"I'm beginning to get that impression myself, sir."

"As for you and your people, I suppose SECDEF wants you to hang around here until somebody comes up with something more about whatever sank the *Rachael Spivak*. Or something more on this 'Sea Hawk.'"

"That's my understanding, sir."

"Very well. Thank you for coming by."

"Have a good trip, Admiral."

"Thank you."

* * *

Mike returned to *Khe Sanh* after his interview with Admiral Wolf and checked on the team. Alex was working on the report, and the others were snatching an hour or two of rest to make up for what they'd lost the preceding night. He considered catching a few winks himself but decided he wasn't tired. Instead, he took up Henry Pierson's invitation to visit the bridge anytime he liked.

"Good morning, sir," said the boatswain's mate of the watch.

"Good morning, Boats."

"The captain's already on the bridge, sir. He's out on the starboard wing."

Mike stepped through the door and out onto the wing. "Good morning, Captain," he said to Henry.

"Good morning, Mike. Isn't this just one of the most magnificent sights? Few people except sailors like us ever get to see it."

Mike couldn't agree more. The surface of the bay and the sky above were a uniform darkly burning purple, except for the gold to the east. The cliffs of Akrotiri to the north were bathed in shadows, and there wasn't a breath of wind. The only motion appeared at first to be the patrol boats gliding from shadow to shadow. Otherwise, the stupendous gray armada of which *Khe Sanh* was just a part lay quietly at anchor, waiting for the day to develop.

Only after he'd stood for several minutes did Mike hear the quiet *thunk, thunk* of an anchor chain being heaved around on. He looked off to starboard, at the shadowy form of *Bastogne*, then heard a distant police whistle. Admiral Wolf's flagship was under way, bound for Beirut. Actually, she was bound in the direction of Beirut with orders to loiter over the horizon—far over the horizon— to avoid complicating matters. A second whistle sounded as *Corregidor*, the second assault ship in Admiral Wolf's force, also housed her anchor and started to turn toward the entrance to the bay.

Mike continued to watch as the two huge ships turned slowly and headed to the east, out of the bay. As they maneuvered, their four escorts twisted and turned to take station on the flagship. Thanks to their soaring, muscular bows and relatively low waists, the destroyers always made Mike think of great mastiffs, lunging and yanking at their leashes.

A whistle sounded on *Khe Sanh* as *Bastogne* passed nearby to starboard. Then there was a second whistle and all hands on deck aboard *Khe Sanh* saluted, rendering passing honors to Admiral Wolf's flag as they would to any other ship whose commander was senior to Captain Pierson. After the flagship had returned the salute, two whistles sounded. Then three—carry on.

Long before *Bastogne* had reached the entrance, the escorts had taken station and were searching intently above and below the surface for threats.

"The admiral's taking four escorts," remarked Mike. "That doesn't leave the rest of you many."

"No. If we all have to get under way, we'll be doing it naked, but I agree with Wolf. This is the first time in a

long time—hell, it must be twenty, thirty years—that
we've had to face a real torpedo threat, and he's headed
in just the direction to need cover. Anyway, COM-
SIXTHFLT told him to."

"I'm sorry, Henry. I agree with everything you've
said. I object to the shortage of escorts."

"They're hoping to send some from Norfolk in a few
days.

"Mike," continued Pierson, a slight grin on his face,
"you *do* realize you almost became SOPA when Wolf
got under way, don't you?"

"Somebody must be senior to me."

"Archie Hart aboard *Chesapeake* is twelve numbers
senior to you. But it would still be an interesting situation."

"I suppose I should forward him a copy of this report
Alex is working on," said Mike. "With Wolf gone, Archie's probably going to be involved."

"That makes sense, though I'm not sure Archie will
appreciate it. He won't be able to plead ignorance if the
Greeks get on his back."

"I don't think they will, but he may be hearing from
the support facility."

"And Washington, without doubt."

"And Washington."

"I know you hate to separate yourself from your people, but I'd love to buy you a late breakfast and a cup of
coffee. And you can tell me what really happened."

"They can do without me for an hour or two. Let's
head up to your penthouse whenever you say."

* * *

When Tareq ibn-Ali's flight reached Beirut, he was still
angry. He always got angry, and stayed angry, when he
thought of traitors, and he was now convinced that Abdul
al-Jabbar was a traitor.

"Where's the trouble?" he asked at the car rental desk after determining that cars were still being rented but not to everybody. He had business to attend to and didn't want to get caught between Hezbollah and the army.

"Downtown. The port area. If you want to go there, find a cab. We can't help you until this is cleaned up."

"What about the mountains? The Metn?"

"Okay. But stay out of the city," insisted the woman behind the counter. Obviously she had no idea who she was talking to.

After finishing the paperwork and finding his car, ibn-Ali drove out of the airport and, constantly alert for danger, turned east, toward the mountains that cradled Beirut. Perhaps thirty kilometers from the airport he turned off onto a smaller, twisting road. Then another until he came to a very plush resort.

It was wise of Sherif to choose to live here, he thought. The area was filled with Christians, perhaps, but it was quiet. A location where it was possible to conduct business in an orderly manner. It was also more than a little too plush. Sherif, like much of the Fatah leadership, was, in ibn-Ali's opinion, far too interested in his own comfort. And his own bank account.

He followed a narrow, unpaved track—one which served as a cross-country ski path in the winter—to a handsome chalet that overlooked one of the trails, which were now a splotchy brown highlighted here and there by a little green.

"You picked a bad time to come visiting," said Hussein Sherif as the bodyguard showed Tareq into the comfortable living room.

Tareq suppressed a smile. For most people, any time Tareq ibn-Ali came to visit was a bad time. By definition. And he was proud of his reputation.

"We must talk before your meet tonight with the Sea Hawk."

"Yes? Sit down. Would you like refreshment?"

"Ice tea, please."

"What then is so important it could not wait?"

"Al-Jabbar is a traitor."

"What!"

"I had a very disturbing discussion with the Albanian girl last night in Rome. The one working with the Hawk."

"Yes?"

"She believes he's preparing to deal with the Israelis. You notice there were only two casualties in his last attack. And the ship did not sink even though the charge was very large."

Sherif pursed his lips. It was possible. It was also possible ibn-Ali was just making one more lethal move in the continuing internal warfare that had marked the movement for decades. Secular nationalists versus devout Moslems. Shia versus Sunni. And then within and around each faction still more. Druzes . . .

"He's always been too much of a freethinker," continued ibn-Ali. "He thinks he knows the answers. His fidelity has never been totally clear."

Sherif started to remind his guest that one of the major reasons Abdul had been given the operation was precisely because he did have a modern, reasonably flexible mind. Sherif resisted the temptation, however, because he felt sure ibn-Ali would interpret it as a slur against the faithful. "Why are you prepared to trust the girl more than the Hawk? She's not only a girl, but she's not one of us."

"Normally I wouldn't, but in this case it's very much in her interest for the operation to be successfully completed. She may have no true interest in our cause, but she has every reason to want to kill Americans and Israelis and destroy their ships."

And, thought Sherif, she will also want to please her

current masters, the Chinese, by providing a string of successful tests of their little toy.

"I am not convinced, Tareq. You have very little to go on."

"I'll talk with him when he arrives here tonight. Then I'll decide." In fact, his mind was already made up.

Sherif didn't remember inviting him to the meeting, but he knew that was irrelevant.

"You really believe he's betraying us to Mossad?"

"It's my job to suspect everybody and then deal with those who merit it." As he spoke, Tareq glanced around at the chalet's plush furnishings and found himself wondering just how much Hussein was paying per month. How much, that is, the PLO was paying.

Undoubtedly too much.

"We'll see what happens this evening," said Sherif, wondering if he should warn al-Jabbar not to come. No, that would just make it worse for everybody. "In the meantime, rest. You've already had a long day. All the way from Rome to Beirut."

* * *

Mike was sitting at the stainless-steel-and-laminate table in the team's quarters, reading over the draft of the incident report Alex had prepared and starting to doze off, when he felt a hand shaking his shoulder. He opened his eyes and saw a messenger standing a few feet from him. "The officer of the deck's respects, sir, and you have a call from Deputy Secretary of Defense Parker in the teleconferencing center."

Mike studied the speaker a moment. He was probably about eighteen. A few years older than Kenny. Thirty years ago, he thought, waking a full captain would have been an unsettling experience for a young seaman. Today, he honestly didn't know. The kid seemed almost bored. Did captains impress them? Did admirals? Or was it only actors and rock stars who did?

"Thank you, I'm fully awake. Please inform the OD I'm on my way to the teleconferencing center."

"Aye, aye, sir." The messenger waited a moment, perhaps to be sure Mike was really awake, then turned and left.

"Mr. Parker picks the damnedest times to call you, Captain," remarked Ray.

If Ray was awake, then they all were awake. That was how they seemed to operate.

"Yes," replied Mike noncommittally as he stood and headed toward the door.

Ten minutes later he was seated in the teleconferencing center looking at the video display of Alan Parker seated at his big desk, with flags flanking him and his necktie knotted perfectly. The lighting was perfect, too, as was the makeup that Mike suspected Alan had someone apply whenever he was going to teleconference.

"Damnit, Mike, I keep telling you, no incidents! And you keep causing them! Only this time you've gone over the top. You're not in compliance. Roughing up some loyal government employees and then turning them over to the Greeks."

"They're goddamned lucky Alex didn't shoot them!"

"What?"

"Alex was about to shoot one when he threatened us. When drugs are involved, she and Ted almost explode. I can understand Ted, he's from a part of L.A. where you either love drugs or hate them, but I've never totally figured out Alex's motivation. It's probably in her record someplace."

"Look here, Mike. Those guys were defending the fleet. Your fleet! And their employers are damn mad.

They've got senators, congressmen, you-name-it calling SECDEF."

"They weren't defending the fleet, they were doing a drug deal. They work for the Branchwater Corporation, don't they?"

"Affirmative."

"And who do *they* work for in this particular case?"

"That's far from clear. The base is nominally a NATO base and then their contract includes a number of 'hold harmless' clauses."

"Does SECDEF pay them?"

"That's need-to-know."

"Did SECDEF tell you to ream me out?"

"He didn't have to, especially after your buddy in blue, Admiral Wolf, said he was off for Beirut and bucked it up to COMSIXTHFLT."

"What did Admiral Simmons say?"

"His chief of staff said Admiral Simmons does not exercise operational control over civilian contractors."

"Is SECDEF unhappy with our performance?"

"Mike, there are times when I honestly don't understand why he picked you for this job. You, and your crew, are developing a serious reputation in some circles for being loose cannons. And even worse."

"You mean Captain of Marines Fuentes? He should be a little more careful when he makes his Puerto Rican nationalist statements. The fact is he's really a commonwealth man. He personally thinks the current deal is better than either independence or statehood. That it all just needs a little fine-tuning."

"Not just him. All of you."

"Alan, if our mutual boss should wish to relieve me, I will bow graciously and say 'thank you, sir' for the opportunity. In the meantime I have a very busy schedule. I was informed not long ago that I'm twelve tiny lineal numbers from being SOPA of this anchorage. All that's necessary is for an officer I happen to like to have a heart attack or fall overboard or resign in disgust."

The screen in front of Mike went blank. Admiral Wolf had been right. Mike wasn't making many friends in his current position. He hoped the admiral did better. Those support operations off Lebanon didn't always work out quite the way they were supposed to, either.

* * *

Take almost any road east from Beirut and you find yourself in first hills, then mountains, almost before you know it. By the time Moshe Goren reached the town of Ras al-Metn, he'd been twisting and turning on mountain roads for twenty minutes, much of the time between the long lines of tall resort condominiums along both sides of the road.

Goren passed through Ras al-Metn and continued on until he spotted the sign for the White Fields resort, where his informant had said the Hawk would be passing around eight thirty. He slowed but didn't stop as he noted what had to be a security guard seated inside the gate. Undoubtedly employed by the resort's creditors, he concluded.

About a kilometer past the gate, and out of sight of the guard, he pulled off the road and looked around in the dying light. His advance people had been right—the informant's description had been less than perfect. The field onto which he'd pulled was, as advertised, empty, but there were several condos within sight. The location would do, but he wished he'd managed to locate the Jeep so he could have it followed—or that he knew where the meeting was. Then he could have picked the location most suitable to him rather than the one most suitable in the informant's eyes.

He picked up his walkie-talkie from the passenger's seat. "Report your positions."

The first two cars to report were those located between the White Fields gate and Ras al-Metn. The remaining three were spread out along the road on the other side of Ras al-Metn, where they could alert him of the target's approach. He'd join the nearest two cars and grab the son of a bitch a kilometer or two before he reached the gate. He certainly didn't want to have the security guard as a witness, and there was no reason to follow the informant's advice to the letter.

He got out of the car and leaned on the hood, watching as the sun continued its slow dive into the distant Mediterranean.

* * *

Abdul and George spent over fifteen continuous hours struggling to recover tens of thousands of pages of records that the hackers had—perhaps intentionally, perhaps accidentally—managed to hide in various far corners of the computer. As they worked, they discussed who might've done it and how they'd gotten in. Abdul did finally find what he thought was the entry method— a defective firewall between spaces to which some of the bank's bigger customers had access and some of the bank's own archival spaces—but that told them little about who'd done it and why.

"So far," observed George as he sipped a cup of coffee, "there's no evidence anybody transferred or withdrew any funds. It might still be political, but I'm beginning to suspect it was just some computer freak having fun on a Friday night."

"Possibly a bored employee at one of your bigger accounts or possibly anybody else in the world clever enough to gain access through one of the customers' sites."

"Which means millions of messages and tens of thousands of servers . . ."

"Unless you're under pressure to do so, I don't think it's worth your while to try to track this guy down. I can install a good, solid patch on the hole and I think that will end that."

"Until they find another way in."

"I'm glad you're not expecting any miracles . . . at least with respect to computers."

"All right."

By five thirty, the two had managed to recover about forty percent of the data and to develop a procedure by which George and his staff could recover the rest.

"Can I buy you something to drink, Abdul?" asked George after he'd returned from washing his hands and face in the men's room. "Some dinner?"

"What's the situation outside?"

"My Lord," groaned George. "I'd forgotten about that. Let me check." He picked up a phone and called the bank's security department.

"Same as before," he reported after listening a few minutes. "They're negotiating but there's still no solution. Maybe we'd better not . . . unless we get something at the Phoenicia."

"Normally I'd love to, but I'm scheduled out—back to Athens—in the morning, and I have some old friends I have to see tonight."

"How do you plan to get around in this?"

"They live in the east. In the mountains. I'm hoping the trouble is still here."

"That's what they say. For now, anyway."

"Okay. Can your driver get me back to the hotel?"

"Yes. As I told you, at the moment nobody wants to damage the banks. Keep your head down."

With the sun fast advancing toward the horizon, the Sea Hawk walked slowly down the bank's front steps.

Fighting cyberterrorists was just as draining as being one, very possibly more, he thought as he settled into the backseat of the black Mercedes. Then he started to worry about how, without the safe conduct the bank had been able to provide, he was going to get through any new roadblocks that might have been put in place between the Phoenicia and the mountains. Hopefully, Hussein had taken care of that.

Tareq ibn-Ali watched the fall of the same sun whose demise Moshe Goren had observed. In many ways, his thoughts were very similar to those of the Mossad agent. One way or another, he would have Abdul al-Jabbar.

Although Tareq had told Hussein the Hawk was dealing with Mossad, he didn't really believe it. Not yet. Al-Jabbar, thanks to his undisciplined way of thinking, was a traitor in the making and, therefore, as much of a threat as one already made. The only important question that remained was whether to allow him to execute the second and third attacks before he met his fate. Or should Tareq let the Albanian whore do it?

He sniffed the air. What was that? Was it the vaguest hint of cedar? Would the smell carry all the way from the Reserve—one of the national parks that contained some of the few remaining stands of cedars in Lebanon? Perhaps it wasn't that far after all. Hussein was certainly living well. High on the hog, as the Americans said.

* * *

Abdul al-Jabbar showered and grabbed a quick dinner and was standing on the Phoenicias' front steps when the white Jeep pulled up and stopped in front of him. It was right on time.

The doorman ran down and opened the door for him, receiving several Lebanese pounds as a reward. "Good evening" said Abdul to the driver as the doorman closed the door.

The driver grunted but did not turn around as he pulled away from the curb.

The Sea Hawk wanted to settle back in the seat but was unable to relax. The gunfire had died down several hours before, and the TV seemed to think a compromise was in the works, but something felt very, very wrong, and it wasn't just his own personal doubts. He looked at the back of the driver's head, which was nothing more than a black shape, outlined by the glow of the headlights. He didn't know the man; not that there was any reason he should, but it was possible he could be on his way to just about anywhere. Where just about anything might happen to him.

While Abdul started to sweat, the driver sped east, away from the towering skyscrapers that had grown out of the ground plowed and fertilized by the civil war, then through older, only partially reconstructed areas and finally out of the city and into the mountains. Soon he was twisting and turning through the night along narrow, poorly lit, winding mountain roads. A few kilometers south of the resort town of Beit Mery the driver slowed to take a particularly tricky turn. As they came out of the turn, a small hamlet appeared, along with a mass of army vehicles which blocked the road.

"I thought this business was ended," shouted Abdul to the driver as he became aware of a rapid thudding

sound that seemed to make the windows on both sides of
the car vibrate. Looking to the sides and rear, he spotted
shadows moving in the darkness, then the blue white
flashes and pounding thuds of automatic weapons
erupted on all sides, tearing the darkness to pieces.

Shit! he thought. We've driven right into the middle
of a battle.

Without responding, the driver slowed further, just in
time to receive a face full of AK-47 slugs as the Lebanese troops returned the fire of the gunmen hidden along
the road, behind and around the Jeep. Then the entire
windshield exploded.

If he'd been in the front passenger's seat, he'd be as
dead as he assumed the driver was, thought Abdul. And
that was his last coherent thought for some time.

The car shuddered then swerved violently to the right.
The still-speeding vehicle then forced its way over the
curb and through the closed door of a decrepit, three-
story concrete block building, its steel screaming as it
enlarged the building's doorway.

Abdul al-Jabbar slumped in the seat, stunned, as the
engine stalled. All around, the firing continued. He felt
tired and wanted to stay right where he was until he had
more energy. He wanted to lie there in the dark, removed
from whatever the madness was outside. Then a sym-
phony of aches began to grow as the plaster on the walls
around him disintegrated from the gunfire now coming
in the building's shattered door and his instinct for survival told him he couldn't stay. Not in the middle of the
war around him.

Vaguely conscious of the shooting still going on just
outside the shattered store, Abdul forced himself to
crawl out of the car, which was lying on its side. As he
stumbled clear, he paused a moment, fascinated by the
great clouds of white steam—faintly visible in the er-
ratic light—geysering out of the radiator. He looked

quickly at the driver—or what was left of him—and then smelled gasoline. A world of gasoline, its fumes tickling and biting his nostrils at the same time. Again, instinct screamed at him.

Then he heard voices. Backing away from the Jeep, he looked in the direction of the recently enlarged door and saw shadows moving around and then through it. He had to get away!

Still operating more on instinct than thought, he crawled through the wreckage of the building—which had been some sort of store—and out the back, away from the fighting and the approaching shadows.

Five minutes before, Abdul al-Jabbar had known more or less where he was. As he crawled out of the building's rubble, he no longer had the slightest idea. The knowledge had been lost to him in the shock of the wreck. But he did know he had to get away, away from the shooting and the shadows. As he emerged from the rubble, he saw open fields off to one side. There was no shooting there. That was where he wanted to be.

* * *

By nine thirty Moshe Goren was beyond impatient. Repeated calls to the cars to the west of Ras al-Metn had resulted in no news of the target. Nobody had seen the white Jeep. Was his informant wrong? Had the bastard fucked him? Had the target taken another road? Had something happened to him? Moshe cursed. If he knew where the meeting was being held, he'd know better what to do now. By eleven he was almost certain the operation had failed.

"So much for your fucking Arab source," remarked his assistant, who was sitting beside him in the car.

Yes, thought Moshe, so much for my fucking Arab source. Except the source had never been wrong before and had no reason to be wrong now. Unless he'd been turned or had been a double agent all along. Unless he was setting them up while they thought they were setting up the Sea Hawk.

He climbed out of the car and looked carefully around him into the dark. The dry wind carried the faint perfume of cedar, of goats and of sun-baked rocks. The perfume of the mountains.

Were there twenty Hezbollah gunmen hiding out there in the dark? Mixed in with the rocks? If so, what the hell were they waiting for? Some sort of signal? What a triumph it would be for them to capture or kill him and the five others with him. He'd had the area reconned even before he'd arrived, and he still had two men out there somewhere in the dark, but some of the enemy were very good and his people might have missed them. Or Hezbollah might have found his people and done something about them.

"Prophet One," he whispered into his walkie-talkie, half expecting to receive nothing but silence—or static—in reply.

"Prophet One here."

"All quiet?"

"All quiet."

"Prophet Two?"

"Prophet Two, all quiet."

He looked around him again. It wasn't a setup. If it were, either he and his men or the attackers would all be dead by now. There was no reason for them to delay. Something must've happened to the target. "Let me see that map again," he snapped to his assistant as he climbed back into the car.

He had no idea where the target had left from— though he had to assume that since he was to be headed east, it was someplace in Beirut. He had no idea where he was headed, although clearly someplace in the Metn. Had the Jeep's driver chosen a different route for some reason? What other roads might serve the same purpose?

He studied the map, tracing the shortest route from the city center to Ras al-Metn. If the meeting was in or near Ras al-Metn, then there was really only one reasonably direct route. If the meeting was farther east, then there was a second road. And if the meeting was even farther east, the first two roads offered access to at least four more.

"Shit!" he mumbled. The roads were all mountain roads with few interconnections, except maybe goat paths. It would take him hours to check all the possibilities. He'd never find them.

"Prophet One and Two," he snapped into the walkie-talkie, "return to your cars."

"Understood."

"Understood."

"Prophet Team, we're going to backtrack to the highway, looking for signs of the target."

"Understood."

"Prophet, Prophet Four," grumbled Moshe's walkie-talkie half an hour later. "We're stopped in a hamlet a couple kilometers south of Beir Mery. There's a Lebanese Army roadblock about three kilometers ahead of us. As we approached, we saw firing, but all seems quiet now."

Shit, shit, shit, thought Goren. I could always go home and grow citrus with my family. The absolute last thing he wanted to do was explain himself to a Lebanese Army officer.

No, that wasn't true. Explaining himself to a Hezbollah officer would be even less attractive. He studied the map then gave directions to each of the cars to follow routes that seemed to lead around the roadblock and back into Beirut.

When the first rays of light began to appear over the mountains, Moshe was back in his office. The Sea Hawk must've been scared away by the roadblock. Or the Lebanese government, Moshe fumed, must've taken him.

He wondered if they even knew who—or what—they had. And how much Moshe wanted him.

* * *

Tareq ibn-Ali looked at his watch. "It's almost midnight, Hussein, and he's not here."

"I assume something happened to him. Perhaps he had an accident. Perhaps the army got him."

"Perhaps he never intended to come."

"The driver would have contacted us."

"If he were still alive. It's my job to assume the worst. One way or another I'll find him and he can tell us himself what he's doing. I'm heading back to Beirut now."

"Why not wait until it's light? You might see something on the way back."

Ibn-Ali glowered at him. "No. I'll return to Beirut now. There's work for me to do."

Hussein Sherif had a sick feeling as he watched Tareq storm out the door. It was a condition that did not improve when he heard the disciplinarian speed down the gravel driveway. He wasn't ready to condemn Abdul yet—there were too many possible innocent explanations—but his confidence was shaken. More to the point, Tareq's attitude and actions made clear that Hamas was, once again, ratcheting up the pressure on Fatah. Tareq was clearly hoping the Hawk was up to something, something that could be used against not only al-Jabbar but also against any who might think at all like him. And when Tareq ratcheted up the pressure, blood usually ended up flowing.

* * *

"Somebody finally did their job," said Alan Parker as he pounded on his desk and shoved his face into the video camera, the flags of the United States and the Department of Defense clearly visible behind him.

"I'm glad to hear that," replied Mike Chambers as he sat in the secure teleconferencing facility aboard *Khe Sanh* at two A.M., local time, and wondered if his liaison person with the secretary of defense was talking about the attack on the *Rachael Spivak* or the situation in Lebanon or something entirely different.

"The Defense Intelligence Agency has a resource who reports that the Chinese have sent at least three recently developed, highly programmable, self-propelled mines to the PLO as an expression of 'people's solidarity.' He thinks the *Spivak* was hit by one of them. He also thinks one of the others was headed for the Strait of Gibraltar."

"Does he think it's on its way or it's already there?"

"The implication is that it's already there."

"But where?"

"We're checking the satellite shots looking for anything odd the past few weeks. Big ships stopped where they shouldn't be, that sort of thing. Of course there's no requirement that a very large ship be involved."

"What about the third?"

"He says he doesn't know."

"How'd they get them into the Med without anybody noticing?"

"We're working on that. Most likely they loaded them in China and then transferred them to other, local ships in small ports. There must have been a little razzle-dazzle involved."

"Or in some port where the authorities would be willing to look the other way."

"Yes."

"Does he know how they're put in place?"

"We have to assume they're just dropped overboard. They're only a ton or two."

"They must be controlled—or is the programming so good that they can pick out particular ships?"

"We don't know for sure that the *Spivak* was a specific target or just the first to attract the device's attention."

"Any hint about when the second's going to be used?"

"Soon."

"I have a feeling we're headed for the Strait of Gibraltar."

"Unless you have a better suggestion. There are two frigates patrolling there, the *Abernathy* and the *Lines*. For now you can operate from them, until we come up with something else. Remember this resource is very sensitive and the intel is severely limited distribution. COMSIXTHFLT knows we're dealing with mines and not submarines, but for now nobody else is to know there aren't any subs."

"Anything else we should know?"

"Apparently there're two operatives involved, not just the one code-named the Sea Hawk, who's a man, by the way. The other is a woman. Other than that we know nothing."

"Nothing? Think hard."

"Nothing. Now get your asses back to Rota and rendezvous with those two frigates. I want some butts kicked. I'd be especially happy if you could find a way of pinning it on the Chinks. And I don't want any more incidents."

"I'll keep you posted."

"You'll do more than that. These goddamned things are a disaster. If you don't neutralize them before they kill some Americans, there's going to be big trouble on the Hill. The media's already screaming for somebody's blood. What you're going to do is find the mines and catch the bastards, too. That's what the American people are paying you to do. And if a few of the less enlightened of the world get in your way . . ."

"Roger, Alan."

Whenever Mike became even a little infuriated with Parker, he ended up feeling slightly sorry for the fellow. The deputy secretary of defense lionized the armed forces, and insisted on talking like the toughest son of a bitch ever to sleep with a loaded M-16, but somehow he'd never actually served in uniform. Doing so might have interfered with the accumulation of academic and political credentials necessary to get a high-level job in the Pentagon. The result, it seemed to Chambers, was that Alan was desperate to convince himself he was in control at all times. The problem for Parker was that SECDEF had made it clear to Chambers that Chambers had the final say, except, of course, for the secretary himself. Alan was liaison, not command and control.

* * *

Watching the sun rise over the mountains failed to give Hussein Sherif the pleasure, and the sense of hope, that it usually did. He was faced by a mystery and the last thing in the world he wanted was mysteries. Especially mysteries that might prove fatal. When you're conducting a guerrilla war, the objective is to create mysteries for the enemy, not to suffer them yourself. Not when Tareq ibn-Ali is out for blood and viewed the mystery as a sign of weakness or betrayal and an excuse to act.

After some arm-twisting, Hezbollah had reported that a white Jeep was caught in the cross fire at a government roadblock on the route from downtown Beirut to Sherif's chalet. But they claimed to know nothing about the car, its driver or any possible passengers. They assumed they were either dead or in the hands of the Lebanese Army.

The phone rang. It was, unfortunately from Sherif's perspective, Tareq.

"You've heard about the roadblock," stated the Hamas disciplinarian without preamble.

"Yes."

"Hezbollah says they know nothing about either the driver or the passenger, and the Syrians say the Lebanese have the driver but not the passenger."

"They could be lying."

"Why would they do that?"

"The Syrians may have their own plans for him. It's also possible the Lebanese aren't telling them everything."

"It's much more likely that he's managed to elude all of them. I warned you about al-Jabbar. If the government has him, it's because he turned himself in to them. Or Mossad may have him. But I'm inclined to believe he's taken advantage of the situation to play some sort of game. The bastard spent half his life in America. Obviously some sort of sickness rubbed off on him."

"If he has turned, then the remaining mining operations are dead. He'll have told them everything."

"Not at all. I don't like working with the Albanian woman, but we must. I'll tell her al-Jabbar's been killed and she's to complete the operation immediately. This is just what she wants. She's a fanatic. She'll do it."

"But if they have him, they'll have no trouble stopping her."

"He hasn't been captured by anybody, yet. I can feel it. He's still trying to make a deal with them. Even if he *has* told them, we've nothing to lose. The woman is not one of us. Until somebody proves me wrong, I'll assume he's still free in Beirut—or nearby—and that's where I'll track him down and interrogate him. Then kill him."

Nobody, thought Sherif, would dare to prove Tareq

wrong about anything. The man's belief in his own
hunches would be laughable if they weren't so often accurate.

Before Sherif could say another word, the phone
went dead. He turned back to the window and watched
the shadows of the trees in a nearby copse start their
slow retreat back to the forest. As soon as he could, he'd
also retreat back into the forest—the Fatah Forest at Ra-
malla, the unofficial "capital" of the PLO in the West
Bank, where he had a little more protection from Hamas
than he did here.

* * *

Abdul al-Jabbar awoke with a splitting headache. He
groaned and rolled over, then looked around in the early
morning light. He was lying in an open, rocky field.
Judging from the smell of the soil, sheep had been oc-
cupying the field recently. Or maybe goats.

Al-Jabbar rubbed his temples and sat up. At first he
hadn't the faintest idea where he was or why. Then, for
better or worse, he knew. It all came back. Or most of it.
He was someplace near the resort town of Meit Mery or
maybe near Ras al-Metn. He also remembered exactly
where he had been ten hours ago—in a white Jeep caught
between two warring armies in a hamlet someplace near
his current location.

Stumbling and feeling woozy, he stood and looked
around, holding his head as he did. He seemed to be
alone, although several expensive-looking condos were
visible in the distance. Fortunately, they showed absolutely no sign of life, despite the cars in their parking
lots. Hoping he was safe, he allowed himself to collapse
and then crawled up onto a large rock.

He sat on the rock and watched as the morning light
flowed around the peaks and ridges to the east, bringing
to life the wild beauty the Metn still possessed, despite

the real estate developers' best efforts. He could still see no sign of life in the condos, even though he heard no more firing. He had to assume that the locals would soon be sticking their heads out. It wasn't as if they'd never been through this before.

He felt in his pockets. He had his wallet and his cell phone. All was not lost! He had his Jordanian and international driver's licenses, his credit cards and a means of contacting friends. All he lacked was his passport, which was in his briefcase in the Jeep. He considered going back for it.

That, he assured himself, would be a fool's errand. By now, whoever had won would have examined the car and found it. If the winner had been Hezbollah, he'd probably be okay, but if the government had won, he was in trouble. The driver was Hamas, and it would take the Lebanese Army no time at all to determine that fact—in Lebanon, everybody knew practically everybody else's thugs. And they might well ask what a Jordanian computer guy working for a big American firm was doing riding around the mountains in the middle of the night with a known Hamas thug.

He looked again at the phone. If somebody was serious about finding him, they could locate him anytime the phone was on, so he'd be taking a big risk. But he didn't see any other choice. He'd be quick. Maybe they hadn't had time yet to put a watch on his number.

The Sea Hawk opened the phone and punched in Hussein's number.

"Yes?"

"This is the Hawk. My car was caught in a firefight between the army and Hezbollah last night and—"

"Say no more. You're alive. The Lebanese have your passport, so they may already be monitoring your phone. We must be quick. Tareq ibn-Ali is convinced you're a traitor, and no explanations will change his mind. You're a hunted man. You must fend for yourself, my friend. There is nothing I can do for you at the moment. You must disappear." With that, the conversation ended. Fifteen minutes later, leaving all his clothes and taking only a few crucial documents, Hussein Sherif climbed into his car and headed for the Jordanian border, hoping he could get across before Tareq, or anybody else, decided they had a better idea.

Abdul looked at the cell phone in his hand. At the moment it was his only contact with the outside world, and it'd been twenty years since he'd been without one. He'd feel naked without it. But it was also deadly poison. Not only could they use it to locate him, but it also contained names, addresses, and appointments in its memory. He'd have to utterly destroy it.

With a sigh he placed it on a large rock and then smashed it with a smaller one. Again and again. He then picked out the larger chips—those that probably had a memory function—and ground them into a dust with the same consistency as your grandfather's ashes. He then collected up the remains and spread them across the field, as if he were fertilizing it.

A sharp pang of loneliness swept over him. Not that he wasn't always lonely, but at that particular instant he felt even lonelier than usual.

He had to get himself back to Beirut and he had to do

it without going to Hezbollah for help. Hezbollah, Hamas, Fatah, the rest of the PLO and Abdul al-Jabbar were all on the same side, right? Except when, for any of a thousand reasons, they were trying to destroy one another.

He had no doubt that if he did go to Hezbollah, Tareq would know about it almost immediately. And nobody in the PLO—Fatah, Hamas or any of the splinter factions—would be so stupid as to intentionally bring himself to ibn-Ali's attention by trying to shelter or defend Abdul al-Jabbar. Especially if the disciplinarian had already tagged him as a traitor.

The worst part of it was that the bastard was right not to trust him, Abdul admitted to himself. He could no longer follow the path followed by Tareq and many others. He had to find a new one.

He looked at his trousers. They were dusty, but he couldn't find any blood or grease. Nor were they torn. He removed his shirt and scrutinized it. A little dirty, a small spot of blood on the sleeve, but no rips. His arms were bruised and dirty, but it was his head that worried him the most. Was there blood? Where had the blood on the sleeve come from? He felt his face and discovered he needed a shave, but he couldn't find any fresh blood. Where had the blood on the sleeve come from? There had to be dried blood somewhere, unless the driver's blood had splattered on him. He noticed a small stream, little more than a rivulet, about fifty yards away. Walking carefully, he went to it and was able to scoop up enough of its cool water to rinse his face and arms. In the process he found a small cut on his neck. He cleaned it and assured himself it was no longer bleeding.

He brushed off his clothes and, hoping he could come up with a good story, set out for the road that led back to Beirut.

* * *

Tareq ibn-Ali looked around on all sides as he twisted and turned through a maze of narrow, dusty streets lined with low concrete-block buildings. The tired walls on either side of him had been decorated with a riotous mixture of graffiti and posters, some new enough to have been placed there yesterday, others many decades old and faded to illegibility. The only sign of life was two very small and very naked children running from building to building, hitting each other with sticks.

Time was wasting, he thought acidly as—under the eyes of lookouts posted in buildings on both sides of the street—he pulled into an alley between two exceptionally worn buildings. Once out of view from the street, he stopped next to a small door, slid out of the car and, after knocking once, opened the door and stepped in. Two guards, their automatic rifles aimed right at him, greeted him. He nodded and continued through another door into a room whose walls were peeling and whose odor, if not exactly rancid, was still far from fresh.

"Did you have trouble, Tareq?" asked a small man seated at a rickety card table in what had once been the living room of the now-abandoned apartment.

"No," said ibn-Ali to Faud el-Khodery, the chief of Hamas's operations in Beirut. "I'm late because I took extra precautions. I apologize if you've been inconvenienced," continued the thug not caring in the slightest whether or not el-Khodery had been inconvenienced.

"I'd be more inconvenienced if the government had ended up with you as a guest."

"That's how I saw it," replied Tareq as he took the seat offered to him.

"What, then, is this emergency?"

"You've heard of the Palestinian Naval Militia and its successful attack on a Zionist ship off Italy?"

"Yes, of course."

"The man who executed the attack is a traitor. He's disappeared here, between Beirut and the Metn."

"A traitor? To us?" asked el-Khodery, a slightly perplexed look on his face as he lit a cigarette.

"Yes."

Like Hussein Sherif, Faud knew better than to ask how the man could be a traitor if he'd just blown up a Zionist ship. He also knew better than to ask what made Tareq think so.

"Has he been taken?"

"I doubt it. He was headed for a meeting with Hussein Sherif when he managed to get caught between a force of Hezbollah and a government roadblock. The car was shot up and the driver killed, but our friends at Hezbollah have been unable to find any sign of the Hawk."

"The Hawk?"

"The Sea Hawk. That's his code name."

"I didn't know."

"You had no reason until now to know. He hasn't been operating out of Beirut."

"Yes, of course."

"His name is Abdul al-Jabbar. He's a young Jordanian computer expert, said to be brilliant. He's PLO, although definitely not one of us. He's nonreligious."

"The Movement contains many factions, not just Hamas."

"I've never trusted him," said Tareq, by his expression challenging el-Khodery to dispute the matter further, "and neither does the woman who's been working with him."

"A woman?"

"An Albanian Communist."

"You trust her?"

"For now. Sherif still seems to believe al-Jabbar is injured or something and will reappear. Whether or not

Hussein's correct about his loyalty, I intend to find and kill him. He can't be depended on."

"Has Hussein agreed to any of this?"

"He wants the woman to complete the program," lied Tareq, confident that when his job was completed nobody would trust Sherif any more than he trusted al-Jabbar.

"What about killing this al-Jabbar?"

"He'll accept it as necessary. There are times when we must act on our own. The Revolutionary Council will see the wisdom of our actions later."

"Should we discuss it with Hezbollah?"

"No. They're Lebanese, not Palestinian. It's none of their concern."

El-Khodery studied ibn-Ali a moment. "You do have a photograph of him, don't you? Plus any known contacts in the Beirut area."

"Of course."

"And if he slips out of the city?"

"You and your people will prevent that, and I'll be right at your side to help you do it."

"Very well."

"Good. Remember, Hamas is to take him. Not the PLO, not Hezbollah. Hamas."

* * *

"Abdul al-Jabbar."

Moshe Goren looked up from the monthly report with which he was just starting to struggle. "Abdul al-Jabbar?"

"Yes," replied his assistant. "The guy who got away from us last night is named Abdul al-Jabbar. He's Jordanian, although he spent ten or twelve years in the States. He's an IT consultant for an American firm."

"How do we know all this?" Goren's juices were beginning to flow at warp speed.

"Because the Lebanese Army found his briefcase in a white Jeep that got caught in the cross fire at that army roadblock in the Metn that Hezbollah decided to attack. It contained his passport and a number of business papers."

"So that's what happened to him. Do we know anything else useful?"

"He was scheduled to work at the Beirut and Byblos Bank bank yesterday. With a George Hadeed, the IT manager. And he was, or is, staying at the Phoenicia."

"Was our source also able to provide a photo of the target?"

"He made a copy of the passport photo. It's not great but it's a start."

"Let me see it."

Goren studied the grainy copy and decided he could be looking at any one of five million men in the world. Still, it was a start. "I want somebody to talk to George Hadeed. And I want the Phoenicia checked. Has he been seen there? Who knows, we might be incredibly lucky and find him there, still in bed."

"Or maybe he's back in Jordan now," offered the assistant.

"Or maybe he's back in Jordan now," agreed Goren. "Or on the moon for that matter."

There was a pause.

"Without a passport?" Goren asked himself out loud. "It's possible. Check with our people in Amman. Check with our people everywhere. Find out anything we can about him. Remember, this isn't some illiterate fanatic. This guy's a real threat."

"Okay."

"What about his cell phone? He has to have a cell phone. Was it in the car?"

"I'll check."

* * *

The Sea Hawk paused beside the road and watched as a Honda Accord—trailing a cloud of dust—rocketed toward him. Even in the still-early light he could see blond hair streaming out one window. Blond hair, he thought, probably meant American or European. If the owner of the blond hair had any sense at all, she'd tell the driver to floor it if Abdul tried to wave them down. In fact, he often found it amazing that any tourist with half a brain would even set foot in much of the Middle East. But he had nothing to lose, so he closed his fist, extended his thumb and waved it in front of him, hoping he wouldn't be mistaken for some local shepherd or goat tender.

The car stopped and the passenger with the blond hair leaned out the window. "Are you all right?"

British, he thought. And the driver, too. Both were blondes. Neither was wildly beautiful, but both were attractive. Dressed in jeans and T-shirts. Had to be students.

"I seem to have been in the wrong place at the wrong time last night. There was some political violence in that village." As he spoke, he pointed.

"Yes, there isn't much left of it now," said the passenger, "but they say the trouble's all going to be over soon. You speak like an American."

"I was raised there. I'm in the computer business. I was headed back to Beirut after visiting friends in the mountains and managed to drive right into the action. Now I'm trying to get back to my hotel."

"Which one?"

"The Riviera," he lied, hoping they weren't staying there.

Of course they weren't staying at the Riviera! Footloose students couldn't afford the place.

Either way, assuming Lebanese intelligence had connected him with a Hamas thug, they'd be waiting for him at the Phoenicia, so he couldn't go back there.

The girl studied him for a moment. His clothes, he knew, were right—even if a little dirty—and hopefully his story would explain his beaten-up condition. "Do you have identification?"

He pulled out his wallet and extracted his driver's license and a selection of credit cards, all of which he handed to the passenger. "As you can see," he said hopefully as he slowly turned around, "I have no weapons."

"All right," she finally said, now smiling, after examining the cards and talking with the driver. "Get in the back. We'll give you a ride."

The Sea Hawk's initial reaction was of shock. There was a civil war going on! How could they possibly consider picking up a hitchhiker? Only because they were a couple girl tourists, he decided, out to experience the real thing. Somebody had probably told them the Metn was safe because it was essentially a resort area. He doubted they'd care even if he explained that, in the past, the fighting here had been just as bloody as anyplace else.

Abdul opened the back door and climbed in. He would've liked to settle back and nap, but he didn't dare. "You two just here to visit or are you studying?"

"We're taking the semester off from university and giving ourselves a tour of the Middle East. As much of it as we can get into, anyway."

"It's a rough place at times," he agreed. "Most of the people are just as nice as the people anywhere, but religion and poverty keep causing problems. That and the fact that anybody with even a shred of power has his own personal agenda and won't hesitate to use that power to advance his own interests."

"That makes it all the more exciting, now, doesn't it?" remarked the driver.

Abdul was tempted to say that yes, it was all very

exciting if, thanks to your passport, both sides were willing to give you the benefit of the doubt and you could jump on a plane anytime the "excitement" got on your nerves. He resisted the temptation, not wanting to irritate his hosts and get himself tossed back onto the road. Rather, he did his best to give them a guided tour of the countryside as they passed through it, a tour which continued as they entered the suburbs. For several minutes he became so involved in the performance he almost forgot about his unfortunate position—although he did remain alert for roadblocks.

"Do you know how to get to the Riviera?" he asked as they approached West Beirut.

"It's on the Corniche, isn't it? And what happened to all the roadblocks everybody said we'd run into?"

"Yes, at the eastern end. Turn right here. They must've reached some sort of agreement, just like you said a while ago."

"Abdul," gushed the passenger as they pulled up in front of the Riviera Beirut Hotel, "you're a great guide. How about tonight? Will you show us the hot spots?"

The Sea Hawk laughed. What could he say, even though he had every intention of disappointing them? "I'd love to. How do I get ahold of you?"

"Here's my cell," said the passenger as she handed al-Jabbar a slip of paper. "All of a sudden," said the driver, a big smile on her face, "Beirut's turning into one of my favorite places."

"It does have its charms," said Abdul as he climbed out of the car and closed the door. "I'll give you a call as soon as I get my schedule organized."

He watched the Accord pull away from the curb, both girls waving enthusiastically at him, then walked quickly into the lobby to a public pay phone.

"Robert," he said quietly when his call was answered. "This is Abdul."

"Abdul! What's up?" demanded Robert Saleh.

"I'm in Beirut for a day or two and hoped to see you while I'm here."

"Great! When?"

"Tonight."

There was a slight pause, as Abdul suspected there might be. He frequently visited Robert when he was in Beirut, but he always provided a day or two of warning. And Robert—who essentially stuck to his duties as a professor of business administration and steered well clear of politics of any sort—knew Abdul was into something more than fixing people's computers. A last-minute visit was bound to raise his suspicions.

"Good, at my place. About seven?"

"I'll be there."

Relieved that he had a place to go, at least for the night, Abdul decided to try Hussein Sherif's number again. He deposited more coins and dialed.

There was no answer, not even a message. He had to assume the Fatah liaison had not only abandoned the phone number but probably also destroyed the phone and moved out of the chalet. He had no proof, but it seemed both possible and likely. He also had to assume his disappearance would cause major defensive moves by the PLO—both factions. And if Lebanese intelligence had ended up with his briefcase, then his enemies would be without limit.

He ambled across the Riviera's lobby, nodding at the desk clerk as he did, exited the hotel by a side door and tracked down a taxi. "The Phoenicia," he directed the driver. "When we get there, I want you to drive slowly by. Don't stop."

The driver looked at him over his shoulder but said nothing.

As they passed the Phoenicia, Abdul carefully scanned the sidewalks and cafés on both sides of the Rue

Fakhr ed Dine. With the first hint of a cease-fire the prosperous part of Beirut had returned to its most common
pleasures—socializing and negotiating. He didn't recognize anybody, but then why would he? There were
countless people sitting around looking either at each
other or at nothing at all. Any one of them could be
watching for him. He desperately wanted to go into the
hotel to collect up this luggage, but he knew if he did
he'd deserve whatever evil fate befell him.

"Thank you," he said to the driver, "I guess she's not
there. Will you now take me to the Café Pepe on the Rue
al Maarad?"

The driver nodded and turned east toward the downtown area, several kilometers from the Hawk's ultimate
destination that evening.

* * *

"What is it, Beth?" demanded Pat McGrath as he rubbed
his aching forehead. It wasn't just his head, he thought.
It was all of him. He simply wasn't feeling well. Perhaps
it was the tension—having Chaz Owens snarling and
snapping at his butt. Perhaps it was a bug of some sort.

"I think we've identified the Sea Hawk."

"Really?" McGrath perked up. "Who is it?"

"A Palestinian with a Jordanian passport. A computer
specialist named Abdul al-Jabbar. He works for Lindley-
Roberts, the big IT consulting firm."

"What makes you think so?"

"Last night, during the 'disturbances,' a Jeep Grand
Cherokee got caught in a firefight between a Lebanese
Army checkpoint and a band of Hezbollah. The driver of
the Jeep—who's been identified as a Hamas thug—was
killed, but it also seemed to have a passenger who es-
caped but left his briefcase and passport behind."

"You mean Hezbollah thug."

"No, Hamas."

"Go on."

"The passport shows that he was in Italy several days ago, for a week."

"Doesn't prove he blew up that ship. Consultants get around."

"He certainly does. Barcelona twice in the past three months. Athens twice. Rome, Cairo, you name it. He was even in Tripoli a few weeks ago."

"And he was riding around two nights ago in a Hamas SUV in Beirut."

"In the mountains, not in the city."

"Okay. It's slim but it's something. See if our people in Naples can find out what he was doing."

"They've already asked the Italians to see what they can find out."

"Why don't they do it themselves?"

"They're trying to keep a low profile. Some of the Italians still consider it open season on us."

"Prissy bastards. How'd we get this?"

"From the Lebanese Army."

"Officially?"

"Yes. We didn't have to steal it. They're telling us for some reason of their own."

"Did they give us a picture?"

"Yes, here."

McGrath studied the copy of the passport photo and wasn't impressed. Even with it, he doubted he could spot the man on a crowded Beirut sidewalk.

"Computer jock, eh? Was his cell phone in the car?"

"The Lebanese didn't mention it."

"Find out. And find out his number and have the NSA put a watch on it."

"Roger."

"Anything else?"

"Al-Jabbar lived in New Jersey for twelve years after his parents were killed in a car crash someplace near

Amman. He went to junior high school and high school
in Jersey then went to Florida and got a bachelor's and
master's in computer science."

"Who'd he live with?"

"Some relatives also named al-Jabbar."

"They rounding them up?"

"They plan to talk to them as soon as they find
them."

"The guy lived in our country for twelve years and
then he becomes a terrorist! We should hang him by his
balls."

"Maybe he thinks Palestine should have democracy
like they have in New Jersey."

The woman's a real smart-ass, thought McGrath. I've
got to get rid of her just as soon as possible.

* * *

"So, my friend," said Moshe Goren into the telephone,
acid dripping with every word, "there we were, in the
middle of the night, waiting for some phantom you
dreamed up in your drug-addled mind and the phantom
never arrived." He knew perfectly well what had really
happened, but he loathed the informant. Not only was he
Hezbollah, but he was disloyal.

"That, you Israeli scumbag, is because his car was
caught in the middle of a firefight between a government
roadblock and a Hezbollah team. As you undoubtedly
know by now."

"Oh?"

"Yes. If he hadn't stumbled into that situation, he'd
be in your hands now."

"In whose hands is he now?"

"Nobody knows. The Syrians say neither they nor
Hezbollah have him. Perhaps the government has him,
but nobody's mentioned that to me. He may be dead
someplace or he may be in bed with a beautiful woman."

"You are a worthless bastard. I want solid information. I want to know where he is right now and where he's going to be when I grab him."

"I've always given you what I have, and don't you think to not pay for what I have given you."

"It didn't do me any good. You'll have to do better."

"Just remember, I know more about you than you do about me. I can always set you up for real if you fuck with me too much."

"Then I'll let it be known that you have a personal retirement fund in Europe."

"How? You'll be dead."

9

"Good work Greta!" gushed Alex into the secure sat-phone. "The old firm comes through!"

"Alex," said Chambers, who was standing at the door into the superstructure, a note of irritation in his voice. "The helo's all packed and your friends are waiting for you."

"Give me a few more minutes, Boss. You're going to love what Greta's got for us.

"It's true," she continued, "that she got it with the help of the Lebanese and/or the Syrians, whose motivations in this particular case remain hazy, as usual."

Mike sighed and nodded for her to continue the conversation with Greta.

"So we think the guy's name is Abdul al-Jabbar," said Alex into the phone. "He's a computer guy, went to school in New Jersey and Florida and was in Naples at the right time."

"That's it, pal."

"Any place else interesting?"

"All over. Barcelona, Rome, Athens and Tripoli. Tripoli. That kind of jumped out at me."

"Tripoli? Interesting. You sending his picture?"

"Natch."

"What about the chick?"

"Nothing yet, but the Italians are working on it."

"Tripoli. Sounds like a damn good place to transship things somebody might not want us knowing about. I have a feeling we may end up heading for Libya. You have any good ideas how we might get in without being noticed?"

"Into Libya? You must be kidding! They can smell Americans there. Of course, they can smell Americans everywhere. Off the top of my head the only thing I can suggest is to dress up like oilmen, but that might take time to arrange."

"You know who might have an idea? Mariano."

"Gomez?"

"Yeah. The Spanish do a lot in North Africa."

"Good idea."

"If Mike wants more, I'll call you back. That okay or will you be someplace you can't talk?"

"You and your friends do have an enemy or two around here—probably jealousy—but you obviously have a need to know this."

"Seems that way to me. Anything else?"

"Not really. Seems he was a hot swimmer in high school and college. Chaz Owens is trying to track down his relatives. They may be able to tell us more."

"Keep me posted."

"Say hello to Mariano for me."

"Roger."

Alex clicked the phone off and, speaking loudly to be

heard above the all the whooshes and roars on deck, summarized her conversation with Greta.

"It's a lead," Mike finally shouted back, a look of concentration on his face, "but we're going to need more before we go visit. We have to know who to talk to and where to look. Who's Mariano?"

"He's a senior Spanish officer. Buddy of Greta's and mine."

"You two find him good-looking."

"In a fatherly sort of way. They're very active in North Africa—remember, they used to be part of it until about five hundred years ago when they threw the Moorish kings out of Spain. Even if we don't know anything, he might. He might also have some ideas about how to get us in and who we should talk to. May I contact him once we're in the jet and I can hear myself think?"

"Any friend of yours is a friend of all of ours."

Having ended the conversation, Mike turned to lead the way out to the helo, only to stop and turn back to Alex. "Call Greta back. I have to speak with her. The helo's just going to have to wait."

"Sabbagh," said the phone a minute later.

"Ms. Sabbagh, this is Mike Chambers. I work with Alex."

"How do you do, Captain. It's a pleasure. What can I do for you?"

"From what you told Alex, there's good reason to believe Tripoli may be the distribution center for these devices."

"That's my suspicion."

"There're two frigates patrolling the Strait. While we're trying to decide what we can do about your data, I'm going to ask Admiral Simmons to direct the frigates to start boarding likely ships—by which I mean any ship that's outbound from Tripoli or, for that matter, any Libyan port. Throw in Algerian for good measure. Can you provide them that data quickly?"

"That's a lot of ships."

"Forget about the big tankers and the LNG and container ships. And others belonging to large, established organizations. Except, of course, hostile governments."

"I can start zapping it out to them within an hour. Pictures, too, in most cases."

"Please wait for three hours. I still have to clear it with COMSIXTHFLT and explain it to the frigates. Otherwise they won't know what to do with all the nice stuff you send them."

"Three hours, Captain. Unless you call to cancel."

"Thanks."

Fifteen minutes later the team was in the helo, which carried them from *Khe Sanh* to the NATO airbase on Akrotiri. There, in the hot air perfumed with the sweet, sharp scent of jet fuel, they climbed into a navy jet and headed out, chasing the setting sun back to Spain.

Five minutes after the jet was airborne, Mike was explaining the situation to Admiral Simmons.

"You're assuming the devices haven't all been placed yet?"

"Either way, until we have something else, Tripoli seems a good starting point."

"It sounds good to me, Captain, but you're going to have to tell the frigates what they're looking for. What about the severely limited distribution?"

"I'm sure you have the authority, under the circumstances, to define the term, Admiral."

"So do I. I'll issue the order immediately."

"With your permission I'll give them a briefing."

"I'm just the fall guy in this operation, Captain. You're running it. Very good luck."

"Thank you, Admiral."

* * *

"Good," said Faud el-Khodery into the cell phone. "You've done well. Now stay where you are." He then folded the phone shut.

"What is it?" snapped Tareq, who was seated with Faud at a café table on the Corniche. "Have your people got him already?"

"No, but we now know he's registered at the Phoenicia and spent the day working at the Beirut and Byblos Bank."

"Is he at the hotel now?"

"The clerk says no. I have two people there, watching."

"Good. What about this bank? Do we know who he was working with?"

"The manager of the computers, a Christian named George Hadeed."

"Where is he now?"

"In his office."

"Do we know where he lives?"

"We're checking."

"I want him picked up on the way home. I want to speak with him."

"I must work quickly to have him identified."

"Then do so."

"If we miss him tonight, we'll have to get him in the morning."

"We'll drag him from his home."

"This isn't Palestine, Tareq. Hezbollah might be able to do that, but I doubt we can."

"Then you'll get him on the way home."

El-Khodery opened his phone open and dialed.

* * *

"We've taken one of his cousins into custody," said Chaz Owens to the CIA Director, "and we've begun interrogating him."

"You mean the FBI got him?" asked Greta, who was the third party present in the Director's conference room.

"No. My people did."

"You're operating domestically?" She glanced at the director as she spoke.

"Of course," sneered Owens. "In accordance with the president's special executive order."

"What special executive order? I don't remember reading one that says anything like that."

"You wouldn't have seen it. You had no need to know."

"It's current policy, Greta," interjected the Director, not looking her in the eye. "What've you learned from him?"

"He's not being as cooperative as he might. He's told us more than we really want to know about al-Jabbar's school years in New Jersey, but none of the associates he's named have developed into anything, and he claims to know little about the terrorist's activities after he went off to college."

"Keep working on him."

"You better believe it! We've already explained to him that we'll be keeping him in detention until the War on Terror is won or until he cooperates. We'll keep applying pressure and he'll finally talk. Apply enough pressure and they all talk."

Owens noticed Greta was staring at him. "Don't start up on all that fuzzy moralisms crap, Sabbagh," he snapped. "When will you understand this is a war to the death against evil? Evil incarnate." As he spoke, the fury in his eyes was every bit as great as that shown by Tomas de Torquemada, the greatest of the inquisitors general during the Spanish Inquisition, or even by John Hathorne, the most inspired of the magistrates during the Salem witchcraft trials.

The Director, who was a political appointee and at times found himself intimidated by Chaz, leaned back in his chair and looked at the wall as if he were looking out the window that wasn't there.

* * *

Robert Saleh opened the door to his apartment. It was located on one of the side streets in the area of West Beirut just south of the leafy, shorefront campus of the American University of Beirut.

"Abdul, it's great to see you. What's happened?" he added after looking a little more closely at al-Jabbar's clothing. "And where's your bag?"

"It's a tangled story, Robert."

"Come in and tell me," said the professor of business management, a look of concern on his face. Concern about his friend's condition and concern about what he was about to hear.

"Abdul," smiled Juliette, Saleh's French wife, as she pecked him on the cheek.

"A glass of wine before dinner?" asked Robert. "He looks starved, Julie. Do we have anything for him to munch on?"

"I'll get something."

Al-Jabbar glanced around the living room. It was as he remembered it, a carefully thought out blend of traditional Middle Eastern fabrics and artifacts and contemporary European art and furniture. Traditional enough to be comfortable, contemporary enough to be alive. Too bad it didn't seem to work for Lebanon as a whole.

"Robert, Julie," said Abdul after sipping the glass

of wine, "you both know that I do more than fix computers."

"Yes," said Robert, his back stiffening a little. "We know you're involved in Palestinian politics, and I'm not sure we really want to know more. Life's just too difficult in that respect for most of us who live at this end of the Mediterranean."

"I apologize for coming, for taking the chance of your getting involved. I should leave." As he spoke, the Sea Hawk put down the glass and started to stand.

"You've already come, so we're probably already involved. What are we involved in?"

"Hamas, and probably Mossad and everybody else, are looking for me. I suspect Hamas is the closest."

"What about Hezbollah?"

"I doubt they have the slightest interest."

"I don't think we have enough room here for that many guests."

Julie didn't smile at her husband's joke. "What do you want from us?" she demanded in a sharp tone.

"Julie! Abdul's been a friend for years."

"I know," sighed Julie. "You two have lived your whole lives in this sort of *merde*. It's taking me a while to get used to it."

"If you can feed me tonight and give me a bed, I'll be gone in the morning. And so must you be. I *was* stupid to come to you. These Hamas bastards are good. They'll keep digging around and somehow discover that we've been friends for years. They'll want to talk to you. Get the first flight out in the morning. To anywhere."

"I have classes."

"Call your dean five minutes before you get on the airplane and tell him . . . Julie, do your parents still live in the mountains near the Swiss border?"

"Yes."

"How are they?"

"Fine."

"Good. Tell your dean Julie's father is very ill and you'll be back in two weeks. You're a full professor. You can get away with it. If your first flight isn't to France or Switzerland, get another after you land. But get out of Beirut."

"I had an offer to teach in the States, you know? Well, Jules, I guess we're off to see your parents. The weather should be a great deal better there than here."

"In every respect, Robert," agreed Abdul.

Julie sighed and headed off to finish preparing dinner while Robert got on the phone and arranged for two tickets to Ankara, Turkey.

"It's done, old friend," said Robert as they sat down to eat. "What about you?"

"You don't want to know. I'm not sure myself."

"Whatever you're going to do, you've got to let me loan you some clothes. And some cash. From the look of you, I bet you're broke."

"Thanks. I'm sorry."

"Why don't you leave?"

"I don't have a passport at the moment."

* * *

Magda sat at an outdoor table at a café in the Albanian resort town of Sarande and enjoyed the cool, offshore breeze that blew over her and past, out over the Adriatic. She sipped a glass of wine and watched the reflections of the dim lanterns that swayed in the wind as they danced over the dark water while she considered her position.

Even she was surprised at how things were working out. An unexpected message from Hussein Sherif had arrived two hours before, only a few hours after she'd returned to her homeland. The Sea Hawk had died in Beirut, caught in the cross fire of the ongoing struggle by Hezbollah to retain its rights, and since the remaining two devices were already in place, she was to complete the operation herself.

Magda looked out over the ancient waters, only visible now thanks to the lights strung along the quay. Did she really believe al-Jabbar had been killed?

It seemed all too possible. He'd never struck her as a man who could be trusted to even take care of himself, no matter how much of a technological genius he might be.

If he hadn't been killed, then why else would they ask her to finish the operation? It was obvious from the start that none of them really trusted her. She wasn't one of them and she was a woman.

Maybe he'd been captured and they wanted to use the devices before he revealed their locations. That would make sense because they'd have nothing to lose if she were taken or killed.

She smiled slightly. And then there was the reality that she was the only person on Earth, besides al-Jabbar, who knew the precise locations of the two remaining devices.

Would she do it? she finally got around to asking herself.

Yes, now more than ever, because now *she* could pick the targets, not that addle-headed Jordanian. No more merchant ships. Warships. She would destroy warships now. American warships.

She took another sip of wine and focused on a young man sitting at a nearby table. Looking at her. She smiled. He was good-looking in a rough sort of way. Just the sort who would expect to dominate her. In the end, he would learn. That was half the fun of it all. He stood and walked over toward her.

* * *

The ruined building, located several kilometers south of Beirut's center, had once been a store, until it was almost totally demolished in the civil war thirty years before. In the midst of the rubble, a stairway had been cleared; a stairway that led to the largely intact basement.

When Tareq ibn-Ali walked into the cool, dimly lit cellar, his normally cherubic face had an intense air to it. Even he was beginning to feel the pressure.

Faud el-Khodery nodded as the disciplinarian entered and gestured toward the figure—his hands and feet bound and his eyes covered by duct tape—seated bolt upright in a chair. Tareq studied George Hadeed a moment. The whoreson had information Tareq needed. And he was a Christian. Tareq hated Christians, especially Arab Christians, with the same exquisite passion that he hated Jews.

"It's nice to meet you, George," he said.

Hadeed, who'd been sitting in a terrified state of near paralysis, jerked slightly. Who in God's name were these people? Mossad? Hezbollah? The government? Why did they want him? Even as he asked himself the question, he knew the answer didn't matter. He cursed the day he'd been born.

A length of iron bar slammed into the side of his head, causing it to feel as if it were exploding.

"Be careful," said Tareq to Faud, "he must be able to think and talk.

"George," Tareq continued, "time is short and you must learn to respond more quickly. Do you know Abdul al-Jabbar?"

"Yes," grunted George, "he helps keep my computers running."

"When did you last see him?"

"Yesterday." The pain and terror were beginning to confuse George. All he really knew was that he shouldn't ask why. All he should do was try to satisfy his interrogator and hope he might survive.

"Where is he now?"

"I don't know. He left the bank . . ." The iron bar slammed into his elbow with devastating force.

"'I don't know' isn't permitted, George."

"He left the bank in the evening and said he was returning to the Phoenicia," cried Hadeed just as his other elbow exploded in pain.

"You had no more contact with him after that?"

"No."

"Who are his friends in Beirut? His business acquaintances?"

"I think he has one or two other accounts here, but he never talks about them."

George's left knee exploded, its cap shattered. His brain was fast being reduced to a mass of quivering protoplasm.

"Time is short, George. What about personal friends?"

"I never socialized with him that much." It was the last totally coherent statement ever uttered by George Hadeed.

"Bring that bucket of water," directed Tareq as he stuffed a large piece of rubble in George's mouth and then taped it partially shut. He had no time to prepare the more elaborate and effete devices of which the Americans were so fond, but he felt sure this would work. It always had.

Faud dragged the banker to his feet and Tareq slammed him in the gut, driving the air out of his lungs and forcing him to double over and fall to his knees. He then forced George's face into the bucket of water and held it there until he could feel Hadeed's body arching and shuddering.

"Do you have anything more to tell us, George?"

asked Tareq after his victim's head had been removed from the bucket and the tape and rubble removed from his mouth.

George opened his mouth and a torrent of vomit poured out. Tareq, a look of disgust on his face, slapped George hard. "Speak up, George."

"Teachers at the university," gasped George. "Friends."

"Which university?"

"American."

"Names?"

"Don't . . ."

Somebody grabbed his jaw and began to force his mouth open. "A woman, George?" prompted Tareq. "Does he have a woman who he sees?"

Although blood continued to flow through George's brain, it would be impossible to say he still possessed much of a mind. What little did remain heard "woman" and made a connection. "Nadine," he blurted out, thereby placing his assistant in deadly danger even though she and Abdul only had the most casual of office acquaintances.

"Nadine? Where does she live?"

"I . . ." Before he could finish, the rubble was jammed back into his mouth and the tape replaced. Then his face was stuffed back into the bucket.

Once again Tareq waited until what was left of George was shuddering and convulsing. The disciplinarian dragged the banker's head out of the water, but when he cleared his mouth it just fell open. The disciplinarian felt for a pulse and found it. Barely.

"We have no more time for this infidel pig. Serve him to the rats and dogs. We'll now concentrate on Ras Beirut and Hamra, near the American University."

* * *

"Alex, I'm most pleased to hear from you," said the voice of Mariano Gomez in Alex's phone.

"Mariano, you're the most elegant guy I've ever known in my life."

When it comes to getting information and cooperation out of people, that woman certainly has a way, thought Ted, who was sitting behind her, eavesdropping with closed eyes.

"You embarrass me," said Mariano, who was past middle age but not only still elegant, but also tough. "I hear you're no longer working for the Agency."

"No, I fell in with some sailors who do strange little jobs for the secretary of defense."

"Are they all handsome?"

"Terribly. Mariano, have you seen the intel on this Abdul al-Jabbar, who appears to be the Sea Hawk, the guy who was behind the attack on that Israeli ship off Naples?"

"Indeed I have. We're chewing on our fingernails, as you North Americans would say, trying to ensure that he doesn't do it again off Barcelona. Or anywhere else."

"Then you noticed that among the places his passport shows he's visited recently is Tripoli?"

"Indeed?"

"Mariano, for this to make sense I have to tell you something that, for the next few days, has severely limited distribution."

"I've never been able to decide which of you—you or Greta—would make the best director of national intelligence. But please, proceed. I'm a most loyal subject of the king of Spain, but I also understand the value of discretion."

"We know the ship was attacked by a mobile mine— a combination mine and torpedo. There was no submarine, but apparently this al-Jabbar and a woman arranged and triggered the attack. We also know that at least two

other such devices were delivered to the PLO somewhere in the Med."

"By whom, Alex? I understand this is sensitive, but
whatever you're about to ask of me has its risks to my
people and my nation."

"The Chinese."

"What will you allow me to do for you?"

"We're tempted to go into Tripoli, but we're not sure
where to begin looking, and Greta has no better idea
than we do. We're also not sure how to get in without
upsetting Colonel Khaddafi. We really don't have time
to establish a proper cover."

"Where are you now?"

"About thirty thousand feet in the air just south of
Greece, headed for Rota."

"Excellent! I'll meet you at Rota. If I'm not already
there when you land, enjoy some coffee. I'll be along."

10

Magda rolled over in bed, and the sun coming through the window hit her full in the face.

Shit, she thought. I'm late. Very late. She jumped out of bed then turned and looked at the guy still lying there, asleep, in the bed. He hadn't been as tough as he'd looked, but he'd still been fun. Better than nothing. "Up!" she said as she slapped him. "Get up and get out. I want you gone by the time I get out of the bathroom."

Dazed, he opened his eyes and started to speak. "Out," snarled Magda again as she slapped him for a second time and turned toward the bath. When she returned, he was gone. He wasn't that smart, she thought, but he was smart enough.

The Albanian terrorist packed quickly, checked out of the ancient guesthouse and grabbed a taxi. Five minutes later she was hurrying down the dock to the high-speed ferry that ran across the Corfu Channel to the island city of Corfu. She was just in time—the seaman at the gangway waved at her to hurry. As he waved, he was also giving her the look—leering, hopeful and disappointed at the same time. It was the look men often gave her when they were smart enough to realize that, dream though they might, she would never be theirs. In his case, he was too pretty. As she showed him her ticket and stepped aboard, she gave him the obligatory look of contempt with just the hint of a smile—as false as all her smiles. It was a game, and while she wasn't normally into games—except those of the most serious sort—it was one she enjoyed playing.

Even before she was totally settled into her seat, the ferry's engines, which had been pulsing throatily as they idled, revved up. The dock lines were cast off, and the ferry backed from the pier and turned toward open water. At first she advanced in a staid, civilized manner, but once clear of the harbor, the captain shoved the throttle forward and the boat's twin red and white hulls lunged into and over the brilliantly blue, slightly choppy waters.

The run across the channel was a trip she always enjoyed—the speed, the spray flying from the boat's bow, the sense of being on the move. Today the sensation was even stronger because she was confident that on this mission she would shake the world and, in the process, savor the sweet taste of revenge.

In all too short a time the ferry slowed and approached the dock in Corfu. Magda stepped off the ferry and looked around. The city, as she had expected, was filled with tourists. Germans, French, a few Americans and more Germans. When she realized that one or two young men had already noticed her and started to move toward her, she picked up her bag and hurried to a taxi. She didn't have time to screw around with them today.

An hour later Magda was settled into her seat on the

fight from Corfu to Barcelona. As the plane rolled down the runway, she closed her eyes and took several slow, deep breaths. While she wasn't really tired, she firmly believed that adequate rest was essential when one was about to blow up an American warship or two.

* * *

"Robert," said Abdul as the two stood in Saleh's kitchen having a quick cup of coffee before the professor and his wife dashed off to catch the first flight out of Beirut, "I can't tell you how sorry I am that I've gotten you and Juliette involved in this."

"It's the world we live in, Abdul. You've always been a good friend and companion to both of us, and I don't want to know what you're doing. Just tell me that what you are doing stands some chance of making things better."

"Robert, I've wondered for some time if what I've been doing is right. I can now say that what I'm doing now is right. Does that make sense?"

"More or less, but then it's still dark outside."

"I'll be leaving just before dawn."

"Please don't tell me anything now. Juliette, we should head down to the lobby. The taxi will be here any minute. Good-bye, Abdul, and God be with you."

* * *

The sun was just waking up in Spain—although it was hard to see through the overcast—and the wind was blowing when the Trident Force's jet landed at the joint Spanish-U.S. airbase at Rota. Yawning and stretching, they climbed out of the plane. While Jerry supervised the unloading of their limited gear, the others walked into the lounge in a small building off to one side of the field.

"Mariano!" Alex called enthusiastically as they walked into the room.

A distinguished-looking man with silvery gray hair, dressed in a polo shirt and slacks, put down his coffee and stood. "Alex!" he replied as he walked forward and, taking her gently by the shoulders, kissed her on the cheek. After returning the compliment, Alex made the introductions and they all sat down at the table.

"Have you eaten?" asked Gomez.

"Yes, Mariano. That's one thing the navy's good at. Feeding its sailors."

"Coffee, then?"

Everybody nodded, and the Spanish intelligence officer waved over a waitress and ordered coffee for everybody.

"I've been considering your problem, Captain," said Mariano after the waitress had left, "and I think I have some very good news for you. First, I have a source who thinks he saw this al-Jabbar fellow aboard a ship called the *Ameer Badaweyy* during the right time period. The ship, which is a grubby coastal freighter of about four hundred tons, is in Tripoli right now. What you might learn from visiting her I can't guess, but it's a start. I also think I have a way of getting you into Tripoli and out again without causing an incident that will embarrass everybody."

"You've been very busy during the past six or eight hours," said Mike after taking a sip of his coffee. "How do you plan to get us in?"

"There's a Spanish general cargo ship on its way there right now with a cargo of bagged Portland cement. I'm sure we can find a helicopter to get you aboard this afternoon. You and your gear. Getting from our ship to your target and back is up to you to plan."

"What about the crew? Can they be trusted?"

"Some are Spanish. The others are not, but they live in Spain and wish to continue doing so. Few want to

return to where they came from. And the captain is a true
patriot."

"How diligent are the Libyan Customs and Immigration?"

"This ship makes this run once a week, and no matter
how paranoid Colonel Khadaffi is, the average Libyan
official knows there's very little money to be made
smuggling people into their country. The profit is in getting people out. Our captain will be able to hide you
with no trouble."

"What about port defenses?"

"Yes, they do worry about other people's terrorists.
They almost certainly have anti-swimmer SONAR in-
stallations. Primarily passive. And patrol boats. And
some cameras—both normal and infrared—here and
there. They've also strung barbed wire under some of the
piers and have guards on top of them And some of the
larger, more modern ships in port will have their own
anti-intruder systems."

Mike, deep in thought, watched as Jerry walked in
and Alex introduced him.

"I'm sure we can find a way to get aboard that little
coaster," he said finally. "Do you happen to have any
charts of the harbor?"

"Of course." Mariano beamed as he opened his briefcase. "Navigational charts, tidal current charts, satellite
images. What would you like to start with? And, by the
way, I've already suggested to your people here that they
line up a jet to get you back to Sigonella and the helicopter there to get you out to our freighter."

Mike glanced at Alex. "Your friend's a warlock, isn't
he? Well, I guess that's the kind of friend we'd all expect
you to have."

"I'm sorry," said Mariano an hour later, after two or
three possible plans had been worked out. "You must go
and so must I. I'll keep you supplied with any new infor-

mation that may come my way, and if you need anything, Alex knows my phone number."

"I can't tell you how much we appreciate what you've already done," said Mike, standing as Mariano stood. "We owe you big-time."

"You owe me nothing. Spain has enough trouble with Basque crazies—the ETA. We have no need for further trouble with the Arabs. We thought we solved that problem a long time ago."

* * *

Not long after Robert and Juliette had left for the airport, Abdul finished collecting the toiletries and two changes of clothing that Robert had insisted on giving him. He said a cheery "Good morning" to the half-asleep security guy in the lobby and walked out onto the still-dark street.

The morning was cool—there was even a hint of dew on some of the cars parked along the street—and there was little pedestrian traffic. Abdul turned right after coming out the door of the Salahs' building, and started to walk slowly. With so few other pedestrians, he felt totally exposed, certain he was standing out like a sore thumb to whoever might be looking for him. After eight or ten blocks he came to a small commercial hotel—one that didn't always insist on full documentation of its guests—and checked in.

For the first time in many years Abdul al-Jabbar was at a loss about where he was heading and what he was doing. An almost paralyzing sense of dread had started to creep up on him. Hussein wasn't taking calls, which meant he'd probably left Lebanon—or that he was dead—leaving the Hawk on his own. He considered reporting directly to the PLO Revolutionary Council in Ramallah, but hesitated. Hamas was hunting him, not with the best intentions, and he had no passport, so it would be very difficult to leave Lebanon. He simply had to know more.

If he didn't have his passport, who did? Hezbollah? Hamas? The Lebanese government? Mossad?

He lay down on the lumpy bed and tried to rest. Short of standing in the middle of the street and waiting to see who shot at him, the only way to learn who was after him was to look for their trails, which would not become clear until at least the afternoon. In the meantime he would attempt to settle, in his mind, his vision of his own future.

Blowing people up simply was not working. But how likely was it that some of the other options, the ones championed by Hussein Sherif and others—their voices low but hopeful—would ever be possible? And what might his role be?

He held his head, which felt as if it were splitting. How'd he gotten here? Why hadn't he stayed in the United States? Or, if not, at least avoided the insane, vicious rat-pit his Palestinian countrymen called politics?

He'd liked living in the United States. His cousins' house had a green lawn in front and there was always enough food. They'd lived in a suburban town. Not a swanky suburban town, a modest but comfortable one. The people, most of them, had been nice. Especially when it turned out he was a natural swimmer. A butterflier. The local YMCA team. High school. College.

Yet, he had to admit to himself, there'd always been a nagging undercurrent. A-rab. Camel jockey. Bomb thrower. At first he'd barely noticed, but as he grew older it did begin to nag at him. Nobody had ever said anything to his face, but there'd been occasional strange looks and mumbles. America was supposed to represent great ideas, but it didn't always act that way. Even the presidents broke the rules—or made up their own—and then laughed about it.

And then there was always the Palestinian factor. He'd lived in a Palestinian family in America, one that had a house and a green lawn and food and jobs and could walk the streets with reasonable safety thanks to a government that, if far from perfect, was pretty damn impressive by historical standards. None of his relatives wanted to go back to Palestine, but, like the Irish, they couldn't let the old country go. The dust and dirt, the hunger and pain, the hopelessness. A people caged in their own land, imprisoned by the disinterest and self-interest of the peoples around them and the greed and fanaticism of their leaders.

Early in college Abdul decided he had to do something. He didn't know what, but something. By the end of his junior year he knew that something was to be a Palestinian minuteman. A Nathan Hale of the desert. But he knew better than to run out and join the local mosque or stand on a street corner shouting about liberating Palestine. From the very start he imagined his role as infinitely greater, and more effective, than that of a simple soldier. The precise details of this role, however, didn't become clear for another year or two.

* * *

"Tareq," said Faud, closing his cell phone.

"What?" demanded ibn-Ali without taking his eyes off the morning crowds passing through the Place d'Etoile. He had no good reason to assume Abdul would pass by him, but he felt certain the traitor would not try to disappear into one of the dirt-poor districts. He was a man of commerce and he'd lived a privileged lifestyle. He wouldn't feel comfortable among the impoverished Arabs. He wouldn't fit in. No, he was here somewhere. Not far from the banks and the water.

"The 'Nadine' mentioned by Hadeed has been located."

"Who is she?"

"She's Hadeed's assistant. Hers must have been the first name that came into the Christian's mind."

"Pig's testicles. People do sometimes provide less than valuable information when they are under stress."

"It is possible, though, that al-Jabbar and this Nadine may have done more than just work together. Even if they didn't, people talk at the office. She may know something useful. Get her. I want to talk to her."

* * *

The Mediterranean is a relatively small body of water, totally surrounded by very large continents, so it should be no surprise that its weather is the plaything of the air masses that spin and swirl and pound over the surrounding land. By the time the sun was high over the Strait of Gibraltar, the area was being pummeled by a levanter—a fierce wind blowing from the east; the spawn of a conspiracy between a high pressure area over Europe, which drove its winds in a clockwise direction, and a powerful low over Africa, which drove its winds in a counterclockwise direction. The result was gale force winds which blew directly into the prevailing current—which flowed from the west, in from the Atlantic—to form treacherously high and confused seas.

Commander Arthur Nichols, commanding officer of the frigate USS *Abernathy*, watched the razor-sharp bow of his command slice into the tumultuous seas and felt her shudder as she did. Tricky weather for calling away boarding parties, he thought as the ship rolled and he had to grab a stanchion to avoid making a spectacle of himself. He braced himself against the rail and turned his glasses on *Lines*, cruising several miles to the east, while he considered the special instructions promulgated by that Captain Chambers. He still didn't really know who Chambers was, but COMSIXTHFLT had said he was the man, so he was the man.

They were looking for a mobile mine, or evidence of one. There were believed to be two left—in addition to the one that had damaged the Israeli ship—and nobody knew if they'd already been planted or not. It was also assumed that they were controlled devices—that somebody somewhere had to activate them—and that they had a range of at least five miles, if not more. The CIA's Mediterranean Maritime Section was providing names, positions and even photos of ships they considered worthwhile targets for boarding. Of course, Nichols was expected to use some discretion. If something looked odd, board it.

When they boarded, they were to take a look at the ship's papers, but what they were really looking for was the device. And assuming the bad guys were on their way to lay it, it would probably be on deck or near the top of a hold. Think of it as an SUV, Chambers had said. If a space is so inaccessible that it would be difficult to get an SUV out in a few minutes, then it's not worth looking into.

All reasonably straightforward, he thought as the ship shuddered from the impact of a stray wave—one of many—attacking from a direction different from that of the majority. Where the real delicacy was required was the special rules of engagement.

"You're to tread very carefully," Chambers had repeated several times. "Remember, you're absolutely not to open fire on anybody or anything unless they've already opened fire on you. Or are about to ram you. Or you're convinced they're about to trigger a device. Also remember that every ship but one will be innocent—of what we're looking for, anyway. You'll be well within your rights as a warship to board any merchant ship in international waters for any reasonable reason. But also remember that people tend to resent being boarded and we're not out to make new enemies. Tactful and even cheerful boarding officers may help prevent a certain amount of hate and discontent from people who might know—or have seen—something useful and who might possibly be able and willing to help."

The logic, thought Captain Nichols, was impeccable. It was the execution that was difficult, especially for the boarding parties.

* * *

The late afternoon shadows were already beginning to descend on the Hamra district, south of the American University campus, as Abdul hurried along the Rue Sidani, trying to blend in with the flow of students. He should, he thought, feel totally at home here. He'd spent half his life, or so it seemed, at universities, and the students here looked and acted just like students everywhere. It could almost have been Boston, or more likely Paris. But it wasn't. There were enough Arabic signs to remind him that it was Beirut. And mixed in with the students were hunters. Hunters who must by now know what he looked like even if he had no idea what they looked like.

As he walked, he tried to study everybody without seeming to do so. Suspecting that he was failing in both respects he turned into the Café Continental as soon as he came to it. Predictably the café was jammed with students—those who hadn't quite made it home yet and those that had done so and now returned to start their evening out. He took a table and ordered a glass of red wine then walked as casually as he could to the phone and called George Hadeed's office.

"Abdul," wailed Nadine, George's assistant, "George is missing and everybody's assuming the worst."

"What happened?" asked Abdul, holding his hand over the mouthpiece to try to shut out some of the background chatter of the café's other patrons.

"He never got home last night. Security says he left the office about six, got in his car and headed off. His wife called at ten to see where he was. Nobody knew then and nobody knows now."

"What about the police?"

"They say they're looking, but they haven't even found his car. They also said something about talking to you."

"He wasn't involved in politics, was he?"

"No. If he were, I'd have known."

That's it, thought the Hawk as he glanced nervously around the crowded room. They're working backward, whoever they are. Trying to find me.

"You'd better go to the police," suggested Nadine.

"Yes, of course, I will."

"If we learn anything more, I'll give you a call."

"No!" he almost shouted. If somebody was watching his cell phone number, then the incoming call would register, even if the phone itself was fertilizer. And that call might draw the watchers' attention to Nadine. "I'm afraid I've lost my cell phone. That's why I'm using a landline. I'll have a new one tomorrow, but for now I'll have to call you."

"What's going on, Abdul!"

"Nothing you want to know about, Nadine. Forget I called."

He hung up, returned to his table and downed the glass of wine in one shot, his hand shaking as he did.

He had to get out, he thought. But nobody just gets out. If you want to get out, you have to change sides and then go into hiding for the rest of your life. Not to the Israelis—he'd never survive the pleasure. The Italians, the French, the Spanish? The Greeks, even? He stood a chance with all of them; they'd lived in the Mediterranean world long enough to have a historical perspective, despite the bad reputations some had developed over the centuries. But he worried if they could protect him. In the world as it stood, finesse and subtlety seemed to be losing to brute force.

Which left the Americans. He'd been very happy when he lived there. They were far from perfect, but some might understand his position. He'd been fighting a war, and he'd always limited his attacks to targets that were clearly strategic.

Then again, many Americans wouldn't understand his position. The shattering image of the World Trade Towers melting, evaporating downward, had seared untold numbers of minds, burning away flexibility and any chance of understanding.

Did he know anybody, anybody at all, who might help him?

A smiling face with big eyes popped into his head. A blond girl he'd known in graduate school and seen not six months ago in Cairo, where she was picking up medical supplies. A girl who desperately wanted everything to work out the best it could for everybody. A girl who'd mentioned that a year or two before she'd treated a very badly injured American who had seemed destined to, at the very least, lose her left eye. Under sedation the injured American woman had not only rambled on about being an employee of the CIA but also spilled her guts about her own feelings about life and politics and the universe. When the American regained her sanity, the girl had naively repeated her drug-released confessions. The American said that everything the girl had heard was true and that the girl and the team she worked with had saved her life and that she would remember.

Could the blond girl's one-eyed friend be the contact he so badly needed?

He'd noticed a cybercafé a block or so away. Thanks to the hordes of students, there were hordes of cybercafés. He paid for the wine and hurried out onto the street and around the corner to the Café Cosmic.

Now, what was her address? She'd reminded him in Cairo.

Crazywithhope 101. That was it. Who else but Penny would have come up with something like that?

After edging his way through the door, he twisted and turned through yet more students—and the clouds of cigarette smoke in which they were all swimming. He somehow found an empty table with a computer. He staked his claim to the table and waved down a waitress and ordered a coffee. He then set to work, using another of the hard-to-trace addresses he'd set up over the years at certain ISPs that charged a fortune to ensure your account was virtually untraceable.

His e-mail to Penny was short, but the contents would've filled a book. He was already working quickly when, out of the side of his eye, he spotted a face at the door, looking in, looking around. It wasn't the face of a student. It wasn't the face of somebody who he could believe would idle away his free time in a cybercafé. It wasn't even the face of a dirty old man who might be hunting young girls. It was the face of a man who might be hunting somebody like him.

When the face came through the door, followed by a body, Abdul quickly signed off and cleared out a side door, hoping the searcher hadn't noticed him.

Hamas or Mossad? It didn't matter. They'd reached the obvious conclusion that a computer jock would gravitate to computers. Somehow he was going to have to get his own computer and a new lodging where he had access to the Internet.

* * *

"Captain," said *Abernathy*'s XO to Commander Nichols, "if ever there was a classic terrorist ship, that's it."

Nichols studied the coastal freighter through his binoculars. *Al-Zahra* was about a mile away off the port bow, wallowing in the schizophrenic seas. She'd once been painted blue and was now adorned with a multitude of rusty, weeping lesions. Otherwise, she was just a mess. It was late afternoon and they'd already boarded two ships, both of which turned out to be innocent of carrying mobile mines. At least at the moment. "Is she on the list, XO?" he asked his second in command as he propped himself against the control console.

"Yes, she is, Captain."

"Very well, pass the word for the boarding party to assemble on the fantail and for the interpreter to report to the bridge." Nichols then turned the ship and headed for the coaster.

While the interpreter—a Moroccan who worked for Spanish intelligence—rushed to the bridge, and the boarding party checked over their armed HBI, *Abernathy* slowed and approached her target, pitching and rolling more and more as she slowed. The haze gray warship, which was bigger and infinitely sleeker than a World War II light cruiser, soon towered over the 120-foot, 300-ton cargo vessel.

When the frigate was about two hundred yards downwind from the target, the interpreter pressed the button on the loud hailer and directed the ship to stop for boarding and inspection—first in Arabic and then in French—while Nichols sniffed the air.

"XO," he said as a puff of black smoke erupted from the funnel of the little ship, "do you notice anything odd?"

The other officer stared hard through her binoculars a minute, then wrinkled her nose. "Smells like cows, Captain."

"Yes," replied the captain. After turning to the interpreter and asking her to head aft and join the boarding party, Nichols turned the ship slightly to starboard in an effort to create a lee for launching the boat. He then instructed his XO to maneuver to hold that position.

"Away the boarding party," ordered Nichols after the boarding officer had reported he was ready.

Nichols leaned out over the lee bridge wing and watched as the seven-person party, all dressed in wet suits and carrying weapons, struggled down the Jacob's ladder and into the HBI, which was hopping and jumping and bouncing off *Abernathy*'s hard, gray side.

Once loaded, the HBI was cast off and turned toward the *Al-Zahra*, pounding and at times flying over the choppy blue waters of the Mediterranean. Nichols checked one more time to ensure that all hands were at the modified General Quarters he'd set. He then returned his attention to the HBI. He watched as it turned, rolling wildly in the chop, and pulled up alongside the rusty blue mess of a coaster, right beside the worn-looking rope ladder her crew had lowered for his boarding party.

Up went the boarding officer, followed by all but two of his party. They were met on deck by six men, probably the ship's entire crew, except for the piratical-looking old fellow on the little bridge and perhaps one engineer down below. From the distance, the coaster's raggedy crew didn't look in the slightest hostile. A fact which Nichols interpreted as threatening in its own way.

"Welcome, Americans, welcome to our little ship," said one of the poorly dressed sailors in English to the boarding officer. He turned out to be the ship's one mate. "We have nothing out of order. Nothing but cows and us."

As invited by the mate, the boarding officer marched up to the bridge, where the piratical captain showed him both the ship's papers and a brotherly smile. Satisfied, the boarding officer and his party prowled around the deck. While they were, Nichols noted that the HBI was being beaten to death by the coaster. Before he could make the suggestion, the boarding officer alerted him that he'd instructed the coxswain to get under way and stand off the coaster's side.

"*Abernathy*," squawked the speaker on the pilothouse bulkhead ten minutes later, "this is *Abernathy One*."

"Roger, *Abernathy One*," responded Nichols after clicking his microphone.

"There's nothing of interest on deck."

"Roger."

"And there are two hundred cows in the hold. This gem only has one. They're taking them to some small port in Morocco."

A small ship with a hold full of cows, thought Nichols. What a perfect place to transport a mine. "*Abernathy One*, go on below and take a good look inside that hold. And be alert, god damn it! This is just the sort of situation where we get in trouble."

"Roger." Was there a hint of dismay in the boarding officer's voice? "Captain, these cows don't look happy. They're sliding all around, crashing into one another, mooing, stamping and bellowing and knocking down their stalls. And whether or not they're really cows, most of them have horns."

"Roger. Leave one person—Chief Stendahl—on deck to keep an eye on the crew and take the rest below. I can't think of a better place to hide a weapon than in the middle of a herd of seasick cows."

"Roger."

Nichols watched as the boarding officer and three of his people, with the help of the coaster's crew, disappeared over the hatch combing and down a ladder into the hold. One armed American and the interpreter remained on deck. As far as Nichols could see, the Algerian crew, who were leaning over the combing, were laughing their asses off at the circus that must have been taking place before their eyes.

Suddenly, Nichols spotted motion. Water was churning at the coaster's stern and she was swinging. He tensed, then relaxed again. He had to keep maneuvering *Abernathy* to keep her head more or less into the seas—the pirate in command of the cattle boat would have to do the same.

Nichols later learned that the interpreter had finessed her way out of going below by pointing out to the boarding officer that the cows understood English just as well as they did Arabic.

Once the inspection of the coaster had been completed and a dozen packs of cigarettes had been passed out among her crew, the boarding party returned to *Abernathy* and *Al-Zahra* continued on her presumably lawful way.

While the boarders were still being hosed off on the fantail, a small tanker appeared. One that was on Greta's list. Nichols decided to send the same party out again since they were already wet.

"Are you sure the CIA didn't think up the idea of giving those guys cigarettes?" asked the XO. "If we can get them to smoke enough, we'll never have to worry about them."

"It was Captain Chambers's idea. From what I know of him, I think his objective was goodwill, not genocide."

11

The Spanish freighter *Crepusculo Ardiente* was south of Sicily and abeam of Malta, about two hundred miles from Tripoli, when the gray U.S. Navy SH 60 helo hove into view to the north, hissing at first and then clattering and roaring through the slowly dying breeze.

Although the ship was far from new, she was equipped with a small helo pad on her fantail. The pad, however, was far too small for the big, two-engine machine that was approaching. So the Trident Force arrived by wire, as it so often did.

"Welcome to *Crepusculo*, Captain Chambers," said Captain Manuel Sarmiento just as soon as he thought his voice could be heard above the roar of the helo, which, having deposited its passengers and their luggage without incident, was heading north back to Sicily.

"Thank you," said Mike, shaking the Spanish captain's hand.

"Let me show you your accommodations for the next

few hours. Shortly after midnight, I fear, you'll all have to move to a very-difficult-to-reach void near the engineering spaces. It's far from comfortable, and very noisy, but the port officials will never bother to look there. We're frequent visitors to Tripoli and they know us well. In the meantime, why not shower and rest up? Have something to eat and ask me anything you need to know about the harbor."

"Sounds good to me," said Mike as Sarmiento led them down a ladder to the main deck and then forward toward the superstructure.

As they went, Ted studied the half dozen crew members who were visible. They all seemed normal—mildly curious about the new arrivals and nothing more—but on this sort of an operation any one of them could be dangerous. All that was needed was a wink or a nod to a Libyan official. One in particular bothered him a little. An Arab-looking guy whose face seemed twisted in distaste, if not outright hatred. Ted considered mentioning it to Chambers but decided not to. Alex's friend Mariano seemed convinced they'd all keep their mouths shut, and Ted would simply have to go with that.

* * *

Magda awoke instantly, fully alert, when the pilot announced the plane was preparing to land. She sat a moment, listening for any unusual sounds, glancing around to ensure that none of the other passengers was showing too much interest in her, sensing the air for anything that might be wrong. All seemed well.

She looked out the window and saw Barcelona, shrouded in a light golden brown veil of dust and smog as it so often was in the summer. If she concentrated, she could even see the low-lying sun glint off the glorious, outrageous ceramic sunflowers with which Antoni Gaudi had crowned his giant, unfinished, schizophrenic church, the Templu de la Sagrada Familia. For Magda there was nothing glorious about either the sunflowers or the church. They were both just foolish. Preposterous. The work of a man whose brain had been addled with superstition, and the fact that the Spanish continued to work on it was proof that Gaudi wasn't the only one with a soft head.

After the plane landed, the Albanian terrorist joined a mob of German tourists on the jammed airport bus. Her destination was a commercial hotel near the airport, where she would spend the night before going on to Málaga. Their's, she hoped, was one of the fancier resort hotels.

Yes, she thought as she tried to disregard the impossibly noisy Germans, it'll be an American warship this time. I have no interest in sinking Israeli ships. It may take an extra day or two, but I'll get something worth getting. The Chinese will love it; it'll prove their device can overcome even the most advanced defensive systems. Tareq and his band of fanatics will love it, too. With luck, I might even get two.

Just as the bus took a sharp turn, an incredibly fat German on the other side of the isle, clearly drunk, stood and landed on top of Magda. The temptation to break his neck was almost overpowering, but Magda restrained herself and settled for levering the drooling bastard off her and into the isle before he got sick all over her. He was so drunk that he didn't even seem to understand what had happened.

Pigs! They could all pass for Americans.

* * *

Abdul al-Jabbar lay in the lumpy bed and watched the glow of dawn slowly transform the window from black to splotchy gray. He shuddered slightly, not at all sure that he wanted the approaching day to arrive. The dark had been sleeplessly nerve-wracking—listening tensely for a sound that was out of place or the crash of the door being broken in; constantly, achingly alert for a light at the door or the window—but the daylight would be just as nerve-wracking and even more dangerous. Once the sun rose, anybody could see him; his every move would be exposed. To his badly strained mind only the gray, semi-obscure dawn seemed to offer any refuge, any chance of being able to see without being seen.

How long would it take them to find him? Hamas? Mossad? How close were they? He didn't think he'd slept for more than a few minutes all night, and now he felt like hell. Despite the sensation of painful numbness in his head, his every nerve was even more painfully alert. He wanted to jump up and run back to the Café Cosmic, to see if Penny had replied to his call for help. He knew that was idiotic. The café would still be closed, and the nurse had probably not even had time to look at her latest e-mail. Of greatest importance, the Cosmic Café was being watched. Very possibly by more than one group. All the cybercafés were probably being watched by somebody. If he was going to survive the next few days, he'd need a computer and a hotel that had an Internet hookup of some sort. Unfortunately, the hotels with Internet were not the sort that would overlook the lack of a passport.

He dragged himself out of bed and walked across the tiles, which felt cool on his bare feet, to the opened window. The breeze was cool, from the mountains. It must be an early hint of the approaching Mediterranean autumn, he thought. He saw no sign of life at first except the breeze. Then a small army convoy—a truck and two jeeps—grumbled down the road. He didn't know whether to take comfort from that or to fear even more.

Of all the possible hunters, the Lebanese government appeared the least likely. What interest could they possibly have in him? They had more than enough home-grown problems. Not to mention those imposed by the Syrians and the Israelis. He walked back to the bed and, after taking a deep breath, lay down and forced his eyes shut. The act of will failed to shut down his mind.

* * *

It was shortly after dawn when the *Crepusculo Ardiente* drifted to a stop at the entrance through the seawalls that protected Tripoli Harbor. There the pilot boat came alongside, and the harbor pilot, along with the Customs and Immigration officials, made the long climb up the ladder Sarmiento had lowered for them.

"It's a pleasure to see you again, Captain," said the pilot.

"It's a pleasure to see all of you," replied Captain Sarmiento as he led the Libyan officials to the bridge.

While the freighter's arrival was a pleasure—a profitable pleasure—for both the Libyans and the Spanish, it was a thoroughly uncomfortable experience for the five Tridents jammed and bolted into the oddly shaped void beside the house-sized, diesel main engine. It was impossible to stand in the space and impossible to sit comfortably, due to a mass of pipes and cables that criss-crossed the deck. It was also hot, smelly and incredibly noisy.

Fortunately, the period of torture did have a limit. Within an hour of stopping for the pilot boat, *Crepusculo* was moored at her usual berth, the paperwork was completed, and the hatches were being opened. Captain Sarmiento's ship ran on a tight schedule—all ships do these days—and was scheduled to be under way early the next morning.

There was a clanking on the other side of the plate that sealed the void as the bolts were loosened and removed. Then the plate itself dropped down.

Damn! groaned Mike inwardly as he crawled out of the void and stretched. I shouldn't be this kinked up, but I am. He then turned and gave a hand to the others as they followed him out of their miserable accommodations.

* * *

Unable to stay in bed any longer, Abdul got up at about eight, showered and counted his money. Enough for three or four more days, if he was careful. Not enough for three or four more days plus a computer. He looked at his credit cards and wondered if they'd been cut off.

No, he told himself. Using them was not a good idea. It would tell any pursuers precisely where to find him. Assuming they were looking for him, both Mossad and the Lebanese government—not to mention the Americans—could trace him if he used a card. Instantly. For that matter, if they were as clever as they were supposed to be, they'd probably made a point of *not* cutting off the cards. In the hope he would be stupid enough to use one of them to, say, check into a hotel.

But what if he only used one card once to buy a computer? All that would tell them was that he was in Beirut, which they already knew. And if it was declined? So what! It happened to people all the time.

But he still didn't have a place to use the computer. So, for the moment, he was going to have to risk a cybercafé. At least once more. But not the Café Cosmic. He'd noticed another a couple blocks from the Cosmic.

A truce had been arranged at some point the proceeding night between the government and Hezbollah, and the streets in the vicinity of the American University were already beginning to fill with their normal traffic. As were the umbrella-shaded tables along the sidewalks. Abdul tried to blend in. No frantic looking around or turning suddenly to look behind him. All the same, every nerve in his body tingled as he worked to spot, or sense, somebody staring at him. He wondered how career terrorists could live this way, year after year. Certain they were being hunted day and night. Maybe they didn't care. Maybe they really believed God would protect them.

When he was within a few doors of the Maison Electrique, he stopped at a small store and bought a newspaper. He looked over the front page, scanning the street as he did. Did anybody seem to be loitering?

It was hopeless! He had to take his chances. Get in and get out quickly. With the paper in his left hand, he continued on to the ornate wood-and-glass door with "Maison Electrique" and a riotously colored lightning bolt pointed on the glass. Forcing himself not to look around as if he were a felon, he walked in.

Even before nine the Maison Electrique was crowded. Students mostly, with what looked like a few young tourists mixed in. All were wearing Western clothing, which meant nothing. Some were sitting staring intently at computer screens as they pounded on the keyboards. Others were slurping coffee and talking. A few were sitting staring into the cloudy air as they got started on their day's pack or two of cigarettes.

What if he ran into the two English girls? he asked himself in alarm. He hadn't seen a laptop in the car, so they probably used places just like this to keep in touch with family and friends. How would he explain his failure to call them?

He sat at an empty table and ordered a coffee and a pastry. To reestablish his self-discipline, he took several deep breaths of the tangy, nicotine-flavored air and ate the pastry slowly before opening the e-mail account to which he'd instructed Penny to reply.

Nothing. No new mail, except, incredibly, a half dozen servings of spam. He knew a number of spammers on a professional basis and well understood their techniques, but their ubiquity, and their ability to identify addresses that even the United States government hadn't spotted yet, continued to amaze him.

He sat for five minutes slowly drinking his coffee and looking at those around him. What was he going to do now? What was his next step? Did he have a next step? He couldn't hide forever in Beirut, and he had no way of getting out. He didn't even have enough money for an airplane ticket—or a bus ticket to Jordan. Not that he could ride either without a passport.

He wondered how many of the young students so busy at this moment talking to one another had, during the past few nights, been carrying rifles for one side or the other. Some were undoubtedly foreigners. How many were Palestinians? Hamas or Fatah? Moslem or Christian? How many were atheists and willing to admit it? How many were terrorists? How many had orders to track him down?

"Excuse me," said a voice in Arabic. "Are you finished?" The voice, although soft, had a sharp edge.

Startled, Abdul stopped staring into space and looked at the girl standing next to him. Judging by her dress— sloppy jeans and a baggy sweatshirt—she had to be either a student or a suicide bomber, and she was looking more than a little impatient. Rather than replying immediately, he looked around the hazy room. During the few minutes he'd been here, the population had doubled, and there wasn't an unoccupied chair in sight. "I'm sorry," he replied as he wondered if she was in a hurry to complete some academic assignment or to see if her boyfriend still loved her or what. "I have to check one more thing then I'll be out of your way."

She nodded slightly, not really smiling, and moved a couple steps back.

He opened his mailbox one more time. Still nothing.

"I understand there's some sort of cease-fire," he said as he signed off. "Do you think it will last?"

"Maybe. Until the next round of brainless stupidity. Animals, they're all animals."

"Why do you stay?" he wondered aloud. And immediately wished he hadn't.

"Because it's my country," she replied, seeming to take no notice of his incredible rudeness.

He looked at her and wondered whether she and her generation would do any better than the current herd of "leaders."

Feeling totally out of place now—and totally exposed—he stood, smiled at the girl and worked his way through the crowd toward the door. Once out on the street, he was surprised to realize the air was still cool and fresh. It was developing into a beautiful day, not that it really mattered to him. He was in no position to amble along the Corniche enjoying the breeze, or even to sit in a park. There was nothing else for him to do but return to his hotel room. The more he wandered around, the more likely it was that somebody would spot him. He hurried back to the hotel, stopping only to pick up cheese and bread for lunch.

Despite the risk, he knew he'd have to find another cybercafé that evening. It wasn't until he'd almost reached the door to his hotel that his brain started working again. Students, thousands of students in the neighborhood. Students. Computers. WiFi. The university undoubtedly had a number of WiFi networks, which were probably protected. But with all these students

there were bound to be some unprotected networks—
dozens of them, in fact, since so many people never
bothered to defend their home networks. He was probably surrounded by them right now.

Abdul continued on up to his room. He placed his
lunch in a cupboard that looked reasonably rodent- and
insect-proof then screwed up his courage and went out
shopping. For a WiFi-enabled PDA. He could use that to
text Penny and never have to go near a cell phone circuit
or a cybercafé.

* * *

The late summer sun was beating down fiercely on Tripoli Harbor, and the sky was a pale, very slightly brownish blue. Outside the pilothouse the air carried a hint of
baked sand combined with the sharp-sweet smell of petroleum volatiles.

"So far so good," remarked Mike as he stood with the
rest of his team in the middle of *Crepusculo*'s pilothouse,
well away from the windows. He glanced down at the
chart of the harbor displayed on the ship's plotting system then looked up and out again, at the large tank farm
built along one side of the harbor and the rows of warehouses that dominated the rest. He couldn't help but notice that the perimeter of the port was flat, open and
totally devoid of vegetation, right up to the lightly traveled highway that encircled it. "Is that open area a security measure or do they plan to build there?" he asked, as
much out of curiosity as anything.

"Some of both," replied Manuel Sarmiento, who
Mike was now certain was more than just a freighter
captain. "A true patriot," Mariano had said.

Chambers then redirected his glasses toward the target ship, *Ameer Badaweyy*, which was moored—along
with several other sorry, rust-streaked coasters—to a
smaller pier about half a mile away.

"Aside from the harbor's defenses, how many of these ships will have their own anti-intruder systems?"

"Only the larger ones. The tightest security is around the petroleum facility. This section of the harbor is watched but not with the same enthusiasm as the tank farm and tankers."

"And the tide turns at midnight?"

"Inside the breakwaters, closer to one."

"I almost feel Mariano arranged it all for us."

"Please don't become overconfident, sir. The Libyan leadership often appears insane, but they're not fools."

"No. We'll be careful."

* * *

"Don't stop," snapped Tareq ibn-Ali as Faud el-Khodery slowed the car in front of the Café Cosmic.

"I wanted to make sure our man is there, where he's supposed to be," replied Faud, trying to disregard the chorus of horns that had already erupted behind them.

"Check with him on the phone and continue around the corner. I'm sure he's here somewhere."

"There!" hissed ibn-Ali twenty minutes later. "Stop now. I just saw the son of a whore walk past. Where else would he be? That miserable little Christian banker said he has friends at the university."

El-Khodery had slowed, looking for a parking place, when a policeman appeared from nowhere and angrily waved at him to keep moving. "That cop's mother is a whore," snarled Tareq as he jumped out of the car. "Find a place to park then come find me."

Both angry and excited, the disciplinarian strode up onto the sidewalk between two occupied café tables, slamming against one of the chairs as he did and forcing the elderly man sitting in it against the table. Without responding to the angry shouts of the diners, he contin-ued on, forcing his way through the crowds on the sidewalk, elbowing aside students, old women and children of all sizes and barely aware of the shouted insults his grace elicited.

It was him, he told himself. They'd met several times. It wasn't a matter of trying to match a shitty photograph. He knew the pig.

Now, where the devil had he gone?

Tareq stopped suddenly and studied the faces around him. Those he'd forced aside a minute or two before were now compelled to walk around him.

Al-Jabbar must've speeded up, he thought. He must be up ahead.

He hurried along the sidewalk, once again assaulting those ahead of him. He stopped at the corner and looked in all four directions and saw nothing of interest. Could he have walked right by the traitor? Could the son of a whore have been one of the cattle he'd shoved aside? And where was Faud?

He turned and started back slowly over the track he'd just covered. Some of the pedestrians he'd forced his way past were now encountering him for the third time. Two had the temerity to not give way, forcing him off the sidewalk into the street. Then he realized the cop who'd told Faud to move on was watching him. He forced himself to conform more carefully to the crowd's movements as it flowed up and down the sidewalk. To give himself time, he stopped every now and then to study the storefronts.

There was a woman's clothing shop that displayed just the sort of clothes—Western and tight-fitting—that students might buy. Whores in training, he reminded himself. Next to it he found a small food store and then two cafés, both jammed with young people. Then he found himself looking into an electronics store.

Yes, he thought with a mild sense of shock, that makes perfect sense.

Tareq stormed into the store. There were several customers present, milling around and playing with various
computers and TVs, but none was al-Jabbar.

"Did a man just come in here?" he demanded of the
clerk.

The young girl looked at Tareq's baby face and then
glanced around the room as if to say, "Look around
you." She also considered asking just what sort of cop he
was. Then she noticed his expression, and sensed the
waves of violent fury radiating from him, and thought
better of arguing. She could guess who he meant. The
young guy who'd rushed in, bought the new PDA and
hurried out again. "Yes."

"Is he still here?"

"No. He left about five minutes ago," she reported,
her unease growing by leaps and bounds.

Tareq felt somebody move rapidly behind him and
spun, ready to defend himself. It was Faud. "Give me
that photo," Tareq snapped.

Faud reached in the pocket of his jacket and handed
the blowup of the passport photo to the disciplinarian,
who shoved it in the girl's face. "Is this the man?"

"Yes," replied the girl. Her eyes were growing bigger
by the second and she was beginning to fidget with a pen
on the counter.

"What did he do while he was here?"

"He bought a PDA."

"A what?"

"A personal digital assistant. A little computer you
can use to send messages to other people."

"Did he give you an address to deliver it to?"

"No. He took it with him."

"How did he pay?"

"With a credit card."

"Let me see the slip."

A large and powerful middle-aged man walked out

from a door behind the counter. The girl turned and looked at him, an expression of relief on her face. The man looked at Tareq and nodded at his daughter. He hadn't managed to stay alive as long as he had in Beirut by arguing with psychopaths.

Tareq grabbed the slip and read it. Abdul al-Jabbar. There it was, clear as it could be.

"Where did he go?"

"I have no idea, sir," said the girl, hoping desperately that the thug would just disappear.

"Come, Faud," ordered Tareq. "He must be living around here somewhere. Your people will take the photograph to every pension and hotel and restaurant. We'll have him by dawn."

"Perhaps Nadine can tell us something."

"Yes, I'd forgotten about her for a moment. I want her, Faud. And I want you to take personal charge of her capture. You're to ensure she doesn't get away."

Faud had planned to send Achmed and three others to handle the job, and resented being told to handle it personally. He was the head of Hamas operations in Beirut, not some brain-damaged thug from the desert. But despite the affront, Faud had no intention of disagreeing with Tareq ibn-Ali.

* * *

If Penny had received Abdul's e-mail three years before, it would have knocked her senseless. It was short and to the point, she thought as she read it again:

Penny—

I need your help. I've been a PLO activist for some time and have even killed a few people in the process of attacking strategic targets. I've come to doubt the wisdom of trying to achieve liberation by blowing people up and wish to go to the Americans. Hamas is after me for my heresy. You once said you have a friend at the CIA who is honest and respectful. Will she help?

Abdul the Water Camel

The consummate nice guy on campus, the quiet computer jock who still loved to swim, she thought, even though he'd spent half a lifetime inhaling chlorine.

Now he tells her he's been going around killing people!

Three years before it would have taken her breath away, but now she was numb. So many people were dying and so many people were killing. Night and day, everyplace she looked. Try as she might to avoid it, she was beginning to think of the patients as numbers. Units to be processed. Nothing more. And she was sure some were terrorists. Or war criminals. Or something. And the rest were what? Victims? Somehow, the word seemed inadequate.

Was any of it justified? The fighting? The agony of patching up the participants? She no longer knew and had even begun to not care. But now she found she'd been jolted back to caring. It was personal again.

Abdul was a person, a real person who'd once meant something to her. Maybe he still did. What did he mean when he said he'd only attacked strategic targets? Did that mean he'd never killed, or even attacked, the innocent or the helpless? Is that what he meant? Did it make it all any better? What did he mean when he said he wanted to find a better way? Did the phrase even mean anything? Was there a better way?

She hadn't the slightest idea. But she had to find out—she had no choice—because she was involved. Abdul was—had been—a friend, and as Dr. Fayez had said, they were all involved, whether or not they wanted to be.

She'd make no decision now. She was simply too wiped out. Instead, she'd try to take the nap Dr. Fayez had ordered and sleep on it. As she tried to doze, she thought that Abdul, the Abdul she'd known, had never wanted to hurt anybody. All he'd ever said he wanted to do was end the suffering. Had he been lying? Had he been too immature to understand his own passions and true motivations? She didn't know. One thing she did know was that one of the main reasons she was drowning in this hellhole of Gaza was that she'd paid far too much attention to his words in the past. He'd convinced her that even she could do something to end, or reduce, the suffering that continued to blossom from over three millennia of almost continuous hatred and warfare.

Sleep didn't come easily to Penny, but it did, in time, arrive. There was no alternative. She'd enjoyed less than four hours of true sleep in the past forty-eight. The other forty-four had been filled with the incessant horror of the disease and warfare that surrounded her.

* * *

Magda enjoyed the sixty-mile drive from Málaga down along the coastal highway to Algeciras, brief though it was. The levanter had finally disintegrated, leaving a deep blue sky and warm but not hot breezes; the traffic was light, allowing her to force more out of the Miata than its designers may have intended, and the sense of anticipation of what was to come was almost erotic. Of course, the infestation of off-white high-rise condominiums did nothing to improve the view, but she was willing to overlook them, knowing that someday it would be the workers, and not the parasites, who enjoyed their comforts.

The Albanian terrorist arrived in Algeciras in mid-afternoon. After returning the car to the rental agency, she found a small café, where she had a bite to eat, and then took a taxi to the ferry pier. Twenty minutes later the ferry pulled away from the pier, setting out on the fifteen-mile run across the Strait of Gibraltar to the Spanish enclave of Ceuta, located on the most northern tip of Africa, surrounded by Morocco and facing on the narrowest point between the Pillars of Hercules.

From there it was possible to observe practically everything that passed through the Strait.

* * *

Abdul, carrying his gym bag of clothes and a new PDA, grabbed a taxi that was cruising down Rue Sidani. "Place d'Etoile," he said to the driver, referring to the center of the downtown area several kilometers from the American University. The driver nodded and the Hawk tried to settle back into the seat.

He'd initially planned and hoped to remain in Hamra—where he was certain a blizzard of carelessly secured WiFi circuits filled the air around the university—but further thought had made it clear that was nothing more than wishful thinking. Everybody who might be after him had access to credit card records. Certainly the Lebanese government and Mossad. They already knew he was in Beirut. Now they knew he was in Hamra, so he couldn't stay there. He had to make it harder for them. To gain a little more time until he was ready to do . . . To do what?

He leaned forward and glanced at the newspaper lying on the front passenger's seat. There, on the front page, was a photograph of George Hadeed. "Beirut Bank Officer Found Mutilated and Killed," read the headline.

Abdul al-Jabbar continued sitting forward and felt sick. Sick with fear. Sick with self-contempt. Would he be reading about Robert and Juliette tomorrow? And Penny the next day?

The driver squirmed, as if uncomfortable with Abdul's head being so close to his. The Hawk sat slowly back, a great wave of terror and disgust breaking over him.

12

"Hamra," said Moshe Goren to his assistant. "Al-Jabbar used a credit card in a store near the American University to buy a PDA. For a bright guy he's stupid. He must know the risk, so why did he take it? To confuse us or is he really that desperate? Why does he need a PDA? He must be communicating with somebody. If we just knew exactly where he is, or which ISP he's using, we might be able to join in his conversations."

"How do we learn all that?"

"I don't know. Even the Americans with their big, hairy ears will probably need more than just this."

* * *

"What do you think of the Old Man's plan?" asked Ted, who was sitting in his bunk examining the super-low-profile dive mask he'd be wearing in a few hours.

"It's logical," replied Jerry without turning away from the porthole he was looking out. "With a little luck it'll work just fine. I'm more comfortable with it than with some he's come up with, and they've all worked out. More or less."

"I hear the jails around here really suck."

"That's why we send terrorists here to be interrogated."

"There's one thing I don't understand about that. These people don't really like us, right?"

"That's what they say."

"So if they do the interrogating and none of our guys are there, how can we be sure what they tell us the terrorist said is what he really said?"

"I'm a boatswain's mate, Ted. Ask Alex, although even she may be out of the loop about things like that."

"You think she'll ever go back to the Agency?"

"I doubt it. She's picked up too many bad habits from us."

* * *

Abdul paid the cabdriver and walked quickly across the Place d'Etoile, picking his way through the forest of well-attended outdoor café tables, and headed south and east on side streets.

Thanks to great efforts by the Lebanese, the Place had been totally rebuilt after its near-total destruction during the last great civil war. Now its stone and concrete buildings and broad sidewalks radiated a sense of solid grace and prosperity, a prosperity they'd not yet managed to extend to the rest of the city. Rebuilding on such a scale is a major project, one made especially difficult if the rebuilders continue sniping at one another—both politically and literally.

After walking half an hour, Abdul found himself in an area that had been at least partially resuscitated—cleaned up, patched and painted—but which projected neither the glitz that bathed the soaring towers along the

Corniche nor the dignified elegance of the Place d'Etoile. He stopped in front of the open gate into a courtyard that fronted a four-story stone-and-plaster house. It had once, he suspected, been the home of some prosperous merchant. Now, according to the sign, which was in only French, it was "le Pension Marrakech."

He was tired and depressed and certain it was only a matter of time until he was spotted, so he decided this was as good a place to try as any. Crossing his fingers mentally, Abdul walked through the gate, across the courtyard and up the stairs to the big double wood doors. Both were scarred with long grooves and a smattering of round holes—undoubtedly lingering evidence of the civil war so many years ago.

Inside the doors he immediately came across Madame deVine, the elderly and somewhat portly proprietress, who was sitting behind a small table doing her accounts.

"Do you have a room available, madame?" he asked, starting in French.

"I do. Do you wish to see it?" She seemed too old or too tired to smile.

"Please."

Madame deVine led the way slowly up what had once been a grand staircase. The wallpaper in the room she showed him was peeling, and the air was stale and spoke faintly of lavender and a dry decay, but the room was clean.

"If this does not suit you, I have others."

"No, this should be very satisfactory. How much is the fare?"

"How long will you be staying?"

"At least two or three days. I'm here on business and waiting for a decision to be made on a certain matter."

Madame deVine quoted a price. "Two days in advance, if you please," she added.

Abdul considered haggling, certain that she had few roomers, but then decided the price was really very reasonable. And he still needed Madame deVine's goodwill.

"That will be most satisfactory."

"Then come down to register."

Abdul filled out the registration card and placed two days' fare on the table.

"Your passport please, young man."

Abdul handed her his driver's license. "I'm afraid, madame, that my passport is missing. I was in a taxi that was caught in a fight at a roadblock two days ago and my luggage—except for what you see in my hand—was destroyed. I've reported it to the Jordanian consul and he assures me I'll receive a new one in a few days.

"He'd better be right," added al-Jabbar with a forced chuckle, "because I'm due in Athens next week and I won't be going anywhere until I get it."

Madame deVine squinted skeptically at him, then looked at the money. "Very well. Please bring it to me when you get it." Then, before he could thank her, she added "Lebanon is an impossible nation. I don't know how we all survive."

Once back in his room, Abdul moved its one chair over next to the window, pulled out his new PDA and hunted for a nonsecure WiFi circuit. He didn't really expect to find one in a neighborhood like this—he was certain he'd have to walk back toward the more affluent city center—but he surprised himself by finding one right away. Judging the name, it belonged to one of the neighboring families. Probably one with several children, for whom they'd managed to scrape up enough cash to get a couple computers and a router. They could, of course, detect him if they were out to do so, but he doubted they'd really understand what they'd come across before he was done. Within two minutes he'd opened his mailbox.

Nothing new except for another load of spam. With a quiet "shit," he signed off and started pacing. Then he looked in the mirror.

He'd seen Tareq ibn-Ali on the street near the electronics store. The bastard was closing in. At least it'd looked like the killer, and in his current situation a well-founded suspicion seemed more than enough. The disciplinarian was an animal, but he was a clever animal. He'd probably seen Abdul. Every Hamas agent and sympathizer in the city must have been shown his photo by now. There wasn't a great deal he could do about it, but there was something. He sorted through his meager collection and came up with his electric razor.

Ditching the mustache was easy. Shaving his entire head was going to be much trickier. He didn't have to worry about nicking himself and walking around with a half dozen telltale bright red slices on his head, but getting rid of all the hair and ending up with a shiny head was going to be harder. Even with a mirror he couldn't see it all. He'd have to use his hands to feel the hair. And he couldn't afford to leave odd-looking clumps. If he did, the whole world would notice him.

* * *

Faud el-Khodery sat next to Achmed in the front seat of the car and watched as the Mercedes carrying Nadine Mulki, its headlights cutting through the night, turned off the highway and onto the much narrower roads of the middle-class Christian neighborhood in which she lived. He still resented being there, but could do nothing about it. Except make sure the operation succeeded.

He continued to watch as two or three cars that had left the highway just before Nadine's passed through the intersection. "Now!" he said into his opened cell phone. Achmed jammed on the accelerator and the car jumped into the intersection just as the car driven by Ibrahim did the same from the other side. Behind the Mercedes another of Faud's cars moved into position to cut off any retreat.

Ibrahim jumped out of his car, pointing an assault rifle at the Mercedes's driver.

"There!" said Achmed. "The trap is closed."

With a thundering crash and a great burst of light, the Mercedes's driver fired a riot gun into Achmed's face and Faud realized he'd made a terrible error. Before that roar had even stopped echoing, he saw the flashes of gunfire behind the blocking car and heard the heavy thud of the weapons being emptied into it.

The bank had done more than provide its threatened servant with a bodyguard. It had sent a whole convoy of agents. And the bank was not interested in taking prisoners. Its objective was to make an example—to establish the principal that nobody tortures and kills its servents. Nobody! It was a necessary institutional strategy in a lawless land.

The car exploded around Faud as one of the vehicles that had preceded the Mercedes off the highway now turned and its passengers opened fire.

Unfortunately for Faud, and despite the best efforts of the bank's agents, he did not die right then and there. Instead, the Beirut and Byblos Bank made a gift of him to the Lebanese government, which was very interested in what he might have to say.

* * *

It wasn't yet dark in Virginia when Chaz Owens learned that Abdul al-Jabbar had used his Visa card to buy a PDA in the Hamra section of Beirut. The news electrified him. He called Pat McGrath and told him to get his ass in gear. McGrath promised to get everybody he had out in the streets just south of the university. Owens ordered that the Director of the CIA, the deputy director and a half dozen other interested parties, including Greta Sabbagh, be notified immediately. Greta started to call Alex, then decided it wasn't necessary at the moment. Alex and her friends were undoubtedly very busy where they were, twelve hundred miles from Beirut. And there *was* such a thing as data overload.

* * *

"Remember," said Mike as he and the Trident Force, dressed in black wet suits, stood in the shadow of a life raft on *Crepusculo*'s stern, "the rebreathers are to be used only as an absolute last resort. The more of you that's underwater the better target you are for any anti-intruder SONAR. Hopefully, whatever SONAR they do have will interpret the bottoms of our floats as the surface. And when you paddle or kick, do it smoothly, with no splashing. They may be using passive systems, too."

"Roger, Boss," replied the team, more or less in unison.

It was shortly before midnight and a heavy mist, impregnated with the smell of petroleum, lay on the dark, choppy surface of Tripoli Harbor. Forward, *Crepusculo*'s crew, their cargo of cement already unloaded, were cleaning up the ship and securing everything to be ready for their dawn departure.

The five Tridents made final adjustments to their gear. Jerry inspected each of them, then Mike inspected Jerry. They slipped over the side, one at a time, and climbed down a long, swaying Jacob's ladder into the water. Awaiting them were five half-inflated air mattresses.

While the rest of the team settled onto the barely buoyant floats, Mike lowered a beer can–sized array of SONAR transducers a foot or so into the water. The array was composed of a dozen small transducers, each sensitive to a different range of SONAR frequencies and connected to a small, waterproof monitor.

"You get anything, Boss?" asked Alex.

"No. Not even the units at the oil depot, but then we're still in *Crepusculo*'s shadow."

On Mike's signal they all started to paddle, their hands in special web-fingered hand fins. Once clear of the ship, they stopped, now catching the outgoing tide, which would, hopefully, carry them most of the way to their destination.

Barely afloat, the five drifted slowly through the almost invisible grayish haze. Mike forced his head up several times but couldn't see a damn thing except the glow of the floodlit docks ahead and all along the right. In his mind he could see the SONAR transducers and video cameras, heat and motion sensors, that undoubtedly riddled the harbor. He could only hope Manuel Sarmiento was right about the security system's spotty coverage, and his prediction that the team's presence would be so low-profile it would fail to achieve whatever thresholds the systems' designers had built into them.

Mike pushed down on the flaccid air mattress to keep his head as high as he could, and listened. The harbor was filled with muted sounds—the crashing and banging of *Crepusculo*'s crew at they secured, the muted throbbing of auxiliary engines aboard ships, the engine of a truck ashore, the tiny splashes of the tiny waves. All were distant and none seemed threatening.

It was a little ironic, he thought, that a country whose best known export was terrorists was so worried about them itself. They had, of course, had problems of their own with Islamic radicals, but that was many years ago. Now, it seemed it was the Americans that Colonel Khaddafi worried most about. Not his fellow Moslems.

A tiny, pale yellow orb flashed briefly ahead, then died out. It had to be one of the lights on the breakwater. He stopped kicking for a minute and could feel the slight water movement around him as his four companions hovered nearby. One of them grunted ever so softly.

He crossed his arms and rested his chin on them. The water was warm and so was the wet suit. The night was quiet and the waves' quiet *slap, slap, slap* was almost soporific. He felt himself beginning to relax, and stiffened.

None of that shit! Not now.

He raised his head again to look around. All seemed clear. He dipped the SONAR array again, and this time it detected the high-frequency active system at the oil depot. He crossed his fingers that the system wouldn't pick up the rafts; that they'd just blend in with the surface.

He looked ahead and couldn't see the target ship, but the pier lights were obvious enough. Then he heard a sudden cough followed by the roar of a big outboard being lit off. And not far away. Damn! Had they been detected?

* * *

Abdul realized he was facing yet another sleepless night. Every time he closed his eyes all he could see was visions of Robert, Juliette and Penny being shot or tortured, just as George clearly had been. All because of him.

He'd always liked to think of himself as a smart guy, and a lot of other people seemed to have agreed with that evaluation over the years, but it was now obvious he had to be the stupidest bastard in the history of mankind.

Initially he'd established the most careful of contacts with the PLO, through friends of his relatives. Friends whose sympathy for the movement might be known to the neighbors, but whose beliefs were never trumpeted and certainly never extended to violence or sedition. Friends who, like so many Irish-Americans who spoke fondly of the IRA and its most worthy cause, contributed quietly. Names had led to names, none of them as far as he could tell on anybody's list.

While he'd been in college, he'd been invited to attend a training camp in the Jordanian desert one summer. He'd firmly declined the honor, explaining that as he conceived his role he would use his technical competence to serve the cause. He'd be one of those who led Palestine into the twenty-first century. He had no desire to throw bombs or fire shoulder-held rockets. Neither did he want to appear on anybody's list.

The initial reaction to his response had been icy. Not among his friends but among the intermediaries. And several years had passed. But then somebody higher up in the system, somebody like Hussein Sherif—indeed, it turned out to be a friend of Hussein's—somebody who appreciated the full importance of mastering and utilizing technology, heard about and contacted him.

The plan was simple. He'd become a respected IT consultant. He'd have access to many of the most important computers in the world. When the time came, he'd deliver a crushing blow to key components of the Western infrastructure—the cyberworld that had replaced the infidels' minds and souls. He'd be a mole, a soldier with no uniform and no trail.

For several years it'd been an almost stress-free nobrainer. He'd traveled, lived well, played with computers and networked with those who controlled many of the most crucial Nets in the Mediterranean and Europe. Then the Chinese had appeared with their mines, and those who backed him had been seduced. They concluded he was one of the few who could deal with the devices. His role changed. His mission changed. Simultaneously, his view of the movement, and of the world, changed.

Maybe he'd just grown up. It wasn't the change of

mission that had placed him in his present, impossible position. It was the changes that had occurred in his head. And now, for the first time in many years, he felt totally lost. Except, maybe, for Penny.

* * *

Mike buried one side of his head in the half-inflated, water-covered mattress, waited and watched. If the patrol boat spotted them, there'd be little they could do. Blowing away a boatful of Libyan security officers was not an option—especially since the team would, undoubtedly, be apprehended and identified by other Libyan security officers. It would be just the sort of incident that, if any of them left Libya alive, would result in utter disgrace at home.

With one ear Mike could hear the roar of the approaching outboards. With the other, the one in the water, he could hear their high-pitched whine. Periodically, one of the little waves would break over the soggy raft and splash in his face. There was no need to try to signal his companions. They could hear as well as he could, and there was nothing he could tell them to do.

Had the Libyans been waiting for them specifically or was this just a random patrol? How alert were they?

He hadn't the faintest idea, but he was about to find out.

* * *

"Okay, Chaz," said the Director of the CIA, "you're still the point man on this thing. Where do we stand?"

Owens, ramrod straight as usual, with a severe frown on his face, looked around the table, then spoke, "Between Pat McGrath in Beirut and the Lebanese, we've got a great deal more than yesterday. The Sea Hawk's an American-educated computer jock who's in Beirut now and has visited Tripoli within the past month. And he just used a credit card to buy a PDA, so he obviously intends to communicate with somebody."

"Yes, we all know that. What are you doing about it?"

"We've got everybody of ours in the Med looking—especially Pat and his people. At the moment our coverage in Tripoli is a little sketchy. As soon as we have him in our sights, we'll neutralize him."

"And?"

"So far, we haven't managed to pin him down."

"What about his family and friends in New Jersey?"

"We've managed to round up the aunt and uncle and one other cousin. Only one of the cousins is a citizen. We've detained them all and charged them, for the time being, with terrorism, aiding and abetting terrorism, supporting terrorism and conspiracy."

"What have you gotten out of them?"

"Very little. A few names at al-Jabbar's university that haven't led to much. None of them are citizens, so we plan to send them abroad in the morning."

"Where?"

"You don't want to know, Director."

Greta felt as if she were going to be sick, but she didn't say a word. She understood the concept of survival as well as anybody. Of living to fight another day.

"So this guy's still lose with at least two more of those Chinese devices? He could zap another ship at any time. Probably will. And it could be one of ours. Greta, do you have anything Chaz hasn't mentioned?"

"Only that the special DOD naval group is attempting to find the devices themselves while we track down the operator."

"I dislike these private little groups that keep popping up outside the organizational chart," grumbled the Director. "Intelligence is supposed to be centralized, but it still isn't, and we really have no idea about their training. Or their real instructions, for that matter. Or their loyalty to The Homeland."

"They're on the chart, sir, and they've got a reputation for being very dependable. I'm working as closely as possible with them."

"What are they doing?"

"They're in Tripoli. The Spanish think al-Jabbar visited a ship that's moored there right now."

"Why wasn't I told of this?" snapped Owens.

"It's something the Trident people just stumbled across. I only learned about it a few minutes before leaving my office." Not the absolute truth, she thought, but close enough.

"They sound damn unprofessional to me," grumped the Director. "Why do the Spanish think so?" he continued, hoping to move the discussion forward.

"They have a source."

"What do we know about this source?"

"Nothing."

"Do they think the devices are still there?"

"They didn't say. All they said was that al-Jabbar was seen aboard this ship."

"Those damn people are so damn imprecise. Especially when they want to be. What about Mossad?"

"They've pulled all the stops out," reported Chaz. "The high technology of the thing really worries them. It's like the Arabs having a missile that could actually hit what it's aimed at. We're working with them. Pat especially."

"Ladies and gentlemen," intoned the Director, "I'm sure you understand the seriousness of this whole matter. We have the most advanced intelligence gathering systems in the world, and I expect you to get off your butts and use them. This al-Jabbar is holding the entire Mediterranean hostage. The public doesn't yet know about the other two devices, but eventually somebody's going to tell them. Then the screaming will start, with the fatheads on TV assuring everybody both devices are off Coney Island in New York. The president doesn't want to hear that kind of talk and neither do I. So get to it!"

* * *

Mike looked hard out into the opacity to his right, where the patrol boat had to be. He could see nothing. He closed his eyes for a second, then opened them again.

Was there a splotch of darkness over there? About where the sound was coming from? Instinctively he pressed himself down into the mattress. Then he could be sure—the splotchy darkness was moving. Without realizing it, he held his breath as, moving very slowly, he glanced around him, noting the four nondescript blacknesses awash in the lively black water around him.

The splotch seemed to be moving past—or was that just wishful thinking? The whine of the outboards continued, but its intensity began to drop. The boat was screaming past, he tried to reassure himself. They must not have seen them. Probably weren't even looking for them. He knew from personal experience that riding around in a patrol boat could deaden the senses. The engines were now definitely moving away. Fast.

After what seemed a prudent wait, he forced his head up again. He looked around and then ahead. The haze was still there, but the lights of the pier made it possible to see the outline of what must be the *Ameer Badaweyy* moored ahead and to his right, with several other coasters.

Too far to the right, he realized. He looked around at his companions. Based on the very faint reflections of their face masks, they were all looking at him. He started to kick and paddle just as furiously as he could without splashing.

Slowly the dimly lit ship grew in size until its dark hull seemed to tower over him. Reaching out, he touched the ship's badly fouled waterline with his hand fin. Then he felt one of the others brush against his leg.

Moving rapidly, and taking care not to drift under the pier, where there might be barbed wire or some other obstruction or sensor, the Tridents secured their mattresses, masks and fins to the ship's rudder post. Chambers then looked around at his team. Although it was dark under the ship's counter, the surrounding water was illuminated by the reflection of the floodlights. He signaled to them to wait. Then, every forty-something muscle in his body groaning, he dragged himself up on the ship's rudder—the top of which was just below the surface—shinnied up the nearest piling and pulled himself up onto the pier. Totally alert he scurried to the ship's brow and, crouched in its imperfect shadow, removed his Glock from its waterproof housing.

It was hard to see in the haze and the distance, but there appeared to be two guards on the pier, both now standing near the guardhouse at the pier head. His heart pounding from both exertion and tension, Mike scanned the *Ameer Badaweyy*'s deck, which was only a foot or two above the level of the pier. He saw no sign of life. He secured a line to the brow and dropped it down to his companions, signaling at the same time that they were to continue to wait. Three minutes later he was about to signal for the rest of the team to join him, when a moving shadow appeared outlined against a deck light. The figure walked slowly along the deck, past Mike, and then disappeared aft. Again Mike waited, until, finally, he saw a faint flash of light and heard a metallic clang as a door into the superstructure was opened and closed.

Satisfied that he knew as much as he was going to, he leaned over the edge of the pier and signaled for the team to join him. One by one they dragged themselves over the edge of the pier. He signaled Alex and Jerry to stay with him. He sent Ted forward to work his way out to the ship on its bow mooring line, past the rat guard. Ray was to repeat Ted's act on the stern line.

This was the part he hated most of operations like this, he thought, as he watched the others move into position. The final minute or two before they would charge into they-had-no-idea-what. And to make it worse, there was a very good chance that whoever they encountered would be totally innocent and, therefore, not even a legitimate target in terms of self-defense. If they ended up killing a crew of innocent Libyans, the whole situation might well spin out of control.

He turned and looked down the pier. The two guards were still standing near the guardhouse. A slight movement of his eyes allowed him to spot a shape slipping over the bulwark where the aft dock line came aboard. He looked forward and saw no sign of Ted. Since he hadn't heard a splash, the SEAL must also be aboard. Mike waited another minute, listening for any sign that Ray or Ted had been spotted and giving them time to secure their immediate vicinity. Then, moving as quickly and quietly as possible, he ran up the brow at a crouch, with Alex and Jerry right behind.

13

The deck amidships was well enough lit to enable Mike, now crouching beside the bulwark, to watch as Ted checked the hatch to the raised forecastle, which was almost without doubt where paint and other boatswain's stores were stowed.

As the SEAL worked his way aft, he spotted first Jerry, then Mike and Alex, and shook his head. There was nobody in the forecastle. Mike nodded back then crept aft—with Alex and Jerry following—to the starboard ladder leading up to the aft deck, where the superstructure was located. Ted moved rapidly toward the port ladder.

Continuing to move quietly and at a crouch, the four crept aft thirty feet until they came to the rust-pocked doors. Mike whistled, then threw open the door in front of him. On Chambers's whistle, Ted charged through the port-side door and, unseen by the others, Ray barged through another door that opened onto the fantail.

The first four Tridents found themselves in a lighted and far from clean mess room. Seated at the table, with his arms crossed on it and his head down, was an old man dressed in a torn, long-sleeved shirt, dirty trousers and ancient sneakers. The man lifted his head just as Ray charged into the mess room through the aft corridor, which was flanked on each side by berthing spaces of some sort. Strangely, the old Libyan showed no fear and only the mildest surprise.

The Tridents looked at the man's face and then looked at one another. It was obvious at first glance that he had double cataracts—one eye was totally, grotesquely white and the other was fast getting there. He was almost totally blind.

The man shook his head, as if to clear it, then mumbled something in what sounded to Mike like Arabic. Ray hustled over and asked him to repeat what he'd just said. The man mumbled again. As he did, Mike gestured to Alex to go below and search the engineering spaces, and to Ted to do the same to the bridge. "I want you on deck, Jerry," he added. "Keep out of sight and warn us if you see any threats."

"Captain," said Ray, "this man's Arabic's hard to understand, but I think he just asked if we're going to kill him."

"Ask him where the rest of the crew is."

Ray repeated the question and listened intently. The air in the mess was warm and close, further thickened by the sour smells of meals long past and infrequently bathed human bodies.

"He says he's the ship keeper hired by the owners to watch over the ship. The crew was paid off two weeks ago and he has no idea where they've gone."

Mike didn't have to ask who the owners were. Thanks to Gomez and Sarmiento, he already knew—a front corporation located in Piraeus, Greece. It was a factoid of no great use to him at the moment. He looked again at the old man. He was ancient, emaciated and dispirited, and he breathed with a rasping sound that suggested every breath, even when seated, was a monumental effort. Being blind, old and emaciated was no proof that he wasn't a terrorist, but the theory simply didn't wash in this case. As Chambers studied him, the ship keeper, his hands on his cheeks with his elbows on the table, mumbled again while staring straight ahead through his almost sightless eyes.

"He says please don't steal anything from the ship because if we do he'll be fired and not be able to get any other work."

Mike nodded, and Ray reassured the old ship keeper they had no intention of harming him or of stealing anything. Alex reappeared and shook her head. When Ted came down the ladder from the bridge, he had something under his arm. "I have a feeling this is the log, Captain," he reported. "We won't really know until Ray takes a look."

The SEAL handed Mike the battered book. Mike looked. Pretty damn ratty, he thought. "Alex, I want you and Ted to go down that little hatch amidships. I think it leads to the two holds. You know what we're looking for."

"Roger, Boss."

Mike then handed the log to Ray, who sat down at the far end of the table from the ship keeper and began to page through it. "The officers of this vessel—the former officers—have absolutely terrible handwriting."

"You sure it's not the language?"

"No, sir. But I can decrypt it."

Mike sat, his eyes and his Glock on the ship keeper, while he waited tensely for the sound of trouble in the holds.

"When did you say our man was in Tripoli, sir?"

"June 20 through the 27th."

There was a tapping on the side of the cabin. It must be Jerry, thought Mike, as he motioned for the others to be silent. Then somebody shouted something in Arabic from the pier. The old man's head suddenly jerked up.

"That must be the guard," whispered Ray into Mike's ear. "He's asking the old man if everything's okay."

Mike looked at the old man, who looked first at Ray and then at Mike.

"Remind him that we have no intention of hurting him or stealing anything. Tell him we'll be gone in less than fifteen minutes and nobody but he will ever know we were here. Then ask him if he will go to the door and tell the guard that everything's okay."

Ray repeated the offer. The ship keeper shrugged his shoulders and stood. Then, dragging his left leg behind him, he started to walk slowly around the table with Ray following closely. The old man stopped at the door and mumbled something—a loud mumble this time. Mike mentally crossed his fingers and found he was holding his breath. When the man finished, Ray gave Mike the one-up sign.

The guard on the pier shouted something then waved and walked off. The old man started to shuffle back toward the table. He stopped and asked Ray a question. Ray nodded "yes," and the old man sidled over to a sideboard, where he grabbed a used tea bag, placed it in a far-from-clean china cup and filled the cup with hot water from a rusty faucet. He then returned to the table, carrying his cup of tea, while Ray returned to studying the log.

"Captain, this log is damn sketchy—you'd never accept it aboard one of our ships—but I think it's going to be useful."

"Does it say anything specific about the device or al-Jabbar?"

"No, sir."

Just then, Ted and Alex walked in. "That guard almost spotted us," said Ted. "I was just coming up out of the hatch. Fortunately, he was looking at the superstructure."

"What did you find?"

"Nothing, Boss," reported Alex. "Both holds are totally empty except for some filthy, almost useless pallets and some lines and tarps."

"Ray?"

"As far as I can tell the ship got under way the 22nd and returned the 26th."

"Where'd they go?"

"They steamed west then turned around and came back."

"No record of entering any port?"

"No, sir, but they recorded their position every four hours, so we should be able to plot their route and get a rough idea where they turned around."

"No courses and speeds?"

"No, sir."

"Good work, Marine," contributed Ted.

Mike glanced at him, then back at Ray. And the log. He'd told the old man that they weren't going to take anything and that nobody would even know they'd been there, so he didn't feel comfortable taking the log. Anyway, he had no way of keeping it dry on the swim back to *Crepusculo*. "Ray, ask the man if he'll give us a piece of paper and let us use a pen or pencil."

Ray asked and the man nodded, then dragged himself to a small cupboard from which he withdrew a pen and dog-eared sheet of paper. Ray thanked him and set to work copying dates, times and positions. He then handed the log to Ted, who disappeared up to the bridge.

Mike folded the paper containing Ray's notes and stuffed it into a waterproof utility pack. He looked at his watch and groaned. "We've got another half hour at least before the tide starts flooding."

"We going to wait here or in the water, Captain?" asked Ted.

"Might as well wait here."

"What're we going to do with this old guy? The minute we leave, he'll probably start hollering."

Mike, who'd been asking himself the same question since they first found the ship keeper, looked at the old Libyan. He wanted to leave as little evidence of their presence behind as possible. The best way to do that would be to kill him and make it look like some sort of robbery. But if they got caught on their way back to *Crepusculo*, they'd hang for sure—or whatever the Libyans did to murderers. And the act would undoubtedly cause a crisis even more damaging than the revelation of the remaining devices would. It would provide stunning evidence of the utter callousness that much of the world already attributed to the American government.

He tried to look at it from the old Libyan's point of view. If he reported the visit after the fact, he'd undoubtedly lose his job. Everybody would agree it'd been his duty—no matter what the risk to himself—to report the invaders when he'd spoken with the guard on the pier. As it was, they were taking nothing, destroying nothing. And he didn't seem in any way patriotic. Or even anti-American. At most, he appeared totally lethargic and disinterested. Barely alive. If they managed to disappear into the night and he managed to remember to forget, he'd keep his job—pitiful though its rewards undoubtedly were.

"Ray's going to ask him to keep his mouth shut; remind him that we've done no harm to either him or the ship, and that he'll have a hard time explaining why he didn't alert the guards when he had the chance."

"Aye, aye, sir," said Ted, turning the matter over in his mind and, reluctantly, reaching the same conclusion.

* * *

While Chaz Owens's tone had been suitably modulated during the conference with the Director, it was considerably less so when he called Pat McGrath an hour later. "How much more do you need, for Christ's sake? You've got a photo of him and you know he's in the Hamra district. Hamra simply isn't that big."

"I've got everybody out looking, Chaz. What the hell more do you want?"

"Results! We've got people in the Lebanese Police and Army. Lean on them. Tell them to lean on the citizens if necessary. They're in a much better position to do that than we are. They can say it's related to the recent troubles. And you be sure to remember that if this guy manages to sink another ship—especially one of ours— it's really going to hit the fan. The director of national intelligence is beating on us. The president's determined not to be put in the position where the media can call him another Jimmy Carter. If that happens, we're all going to be in deep shit, especially now that we have something to go on."

"Don't worry, Chaz. You'll have your results."

"I damn well better, McGrath. I don't want to have to come over there and take personal charge. There's too much else going on in the world."

McGrath hung up. The call rankled because he was tired of hearing the masters of the universe at Langley tell him what he was doing wrong and what he should do to correct it. Those who'd once been in the field seemed to forget, the moment they settled into their new offices, how things really were outside Virginia. Those with no field experience, and there were hordes of them, hadn't the vaguest clue about the real world.

And Chaz Owens was the worst of the bunch. The son of a bitch's a control freak, McGrath thought. Command and control. And a fanatic. Pat McGrath believed everybody, and anybody, *might* be a terrorist. Owens believed everybody but Chaz Owens *was* a terrorist who just hadn't yet been caught. And he treated everybody accordingly.

Thinking about Owens made Pat edgy, almost twitchy. Dawn was arriving. He decided he needed exercise. He showered and dressed and—Beirut being Beirut, especially when it was having one of its endless crises—rounded up two armed thugs to accompany him. They climbed into a company car and drove to the Rue Sidani.

"Park," instructed McGrath. "We're going to walk a little. I want to get a feel for the area."

"Roger," said the driver.

McGrath got out of the car and started walking slowly along the still-dark street with the two toughs flanking him. Despite the early hour, pedestrian traffic was beginning to build. He turned north on the Rue Jeanne d'Arc, headed toward the university and stopped abruptly. There, directly in front of him and headed south, was Moshe Goren. Shit, he thought. He should have known that if he knew about the charge card so would Mossad.

"You're up awfully early, Moshe," he said.

"So are you, Pat."

"You know anything I don't know?"

"Probably not, but let's get a cup of coffee."

* * *

The float back to *Crepusculo* was just as nerve-wracking as had been the trip over—and even longer, due to the flooding tidal current's slower initial speed. Despite two near misses by the patrol boat, the Tridents made it back before dawn, only to discover a Libyan guard standing on the pier not far from the ship's stern.

"Damn!" mumbled Chambers as he backed slowly around to the side of the stern away from the pier and gestured the rest to follow him. He listened. All was quiet except for the harbor's background music of wind and wave. He couldn't even hear the welcoming party Manuel Sarmiento said would be waiting for them. He had to assume they were under cover.

After several long minutes the guard finished the cigarette from which he was clearly taking such pleasure and ambled off. A minute or two later there was a scraping sound overhead and the Jacob's ladder descended from on high. One after another the team pulled themselves out of the water and started climbing, dragging their gear with them.

"Welcome home," said Sarmiento as he helped each of them over the rail, a smile on his shadowy face. "Did you find anything of interest?"

"Indeed we did. Not what we were hoping for but something well worth having," said Mike as his middle-aged lungs struggled to do their job.

By 0800 they were all packed back in the void, shouting to be heard above the boomings and thunderings of the ship's main engine. While they squirmed, they all studied the plot Alex had created on a six-inch handheld GPS display. It was a record of *Ameer Badaweyy*'s travels between July 22 and 26. Five days of positions, noted every four hours.

"This appears to be their farthest west position," said Mike, pointing at a red circle. "Thirty-six degrees, one minute north, four degrees, fifty-five west. Just to the north of the Punta de Almina, near the northernmost point of North Africa and close to the middle of the Strait of Gibraltar. For us, the worst possible place."

Jerry squinted at the display and decided age was beginning to catch up with his eyes. The damn thing was simply too small!

"But they may not have dropped it exactly there," remarked Alex. "Their positions before and after look as if they were zigzagging or something."

"I wonder how accurate their navigation really was?" remarked Ray.

"They had a GPS unit on the bridge," said Ted. "But that doesn't mean they weren't still a little careless."

"Even if their navigation was perfect, we're still not sure precisely where, or if, they dropped the devices."

"They must have," grunted Jerry. "Why else would they go out there and steam around for a day or so?"

"The chief's right," commented Ray.

"Thank you all for agreeing with me," said Mike. "I want Alex to notify Greta and Mariano. If the devices are controlled from shore, his people stand a better chance of locating the operator than we do. It's his turf. I'm going to notify COMSIXTHFLT and suggest he discontinue *Lines*'s and *Abernathy*'s boarding operations, although they should continue to patrol for torpedoes. And to render assistance, just in case the worst happens. I'm also going to suggest he ask the Italians and Mariano's people to get their mine hunters out there ASAP. Unfortunately, it's still a huge area to try to locate a couple car-sized objects in."

"And there's nine hundred feet of water there, Captain. Up to a few years ago, before devices like these came along, it really wasn't very practical to mine this place."

"And there's nine hundred feet of water," agreed Mike glumly.

"It's a start," said Ray, trying to sound positive.

"And the mine warfare people will love the challenge," added Alex. "They don't get to chase real mines much these days."

"What about us, Boss?" asked Ted.

"We're headed back for Rota to see if we can rejoin *Abernathy*."

* * *

His eyes red from lack of sleep, Abdul gnawed on a cardboardlike mass of now-stale bread for breakfast. Much as he hated to do so, he was going to have to go out to get more food. And he was going to have to do it soon, while the sidewalks were still filled with the crowds of students headed for classes and others headed for work. Before going out, he decided to take one more look in his mailbox. He logged on and opened the box and there *was* mail. From Penny.

He stiffened, not believing it at first. Then he read:

Water Camel—

I don't know what to make of what you just told me. My first reaction was "screw you," you're part of all the killing and suffering I have to deal with every day. But then I remembered that I'm also part of it—I sometimes patch up people who then shoot somebody else a month later. It doesn't seem to be pure black-and-white and there always was something really good in you so tell me what you want me to do. And please don't betray me.

Abdul found himself shaking. He wasn't sure if it was from relief that there might yet be a way out for him or from fear that he might, in the end, disappoint Penny. Or get her killed. Quickly, before he lost his nerve, he replied that she must contact her friend in the CIA and see if the friend would try to get him out without letting Hamas, the Lebanese, the Syrians or Mossad get ahold of him. He then realized he simply had to eat, so he finished dressing and hurried out onto the crowded side-walk.

* * *

Everybody in Hamas knew of Tareq ibn-Ali's violent—some might say vicious—temper. That may explain why Faud el-Khodery's successor sent an attractive young man to report Faud's recent misfortunes. The messenger might equally well be viewed as either a gift or a sacrificial lamb.

When first told that Faud had managed to stumble into a trap, the disciplinarian had clenched his jaw and fists. With a sigh, he relaxed slightly as the seriousness of the situation sunk in and his survival skills shoved his emotions aside.

"Is he alive or dead?"

"We don't know yet," replied the messenger, hoping Tareq's evident relaxation was a good sign for him.

"Are you sure it was the bank's security people. Not Mossad?"

"I am told it was the bank's people."

It was most logical, thought Tareq. The Lebanese were like the Swiss—they took their banks and their officials very seriously. If Faud was still stupid enough to be alive, he would've been turned over to the army. How long before he talked, assuming he was still able to do so?

Tareq had to know more. He also had to move more quickly to find al-Jabbar. For all he knew the traitor might have already left Hamra. Maybe even Beirut. Or, he might be sitting having tea with Mossad.

* * *

"So what's your plan now?" demanded Alan Parker over the satphone.

"The trail in Tripoli seems dead, at least for now, so

we're going where we think the devices are. Back to the Strait."

"Fortunately the media knows nothing about you, because it seems to me you're just fucking around and they'd be the first to point it out. The Agency has made real progress tracking down the operators, and all you've done is paddle around in Tripoli. You still don't know for sure where the devices are."

"They're doing their job and we're trying to do ours."

"Your job is to kick ass."

"Thanks, Alan. We'll be on station in about twenty-four hours. Keep me posted."

* * *

It was midafternoon in Langley when Greta Sabbagh received Penny's e-mail about Abdul. To say it was a shock would be a serious understatement. She'd known the nurse was working in Gaza—in Hell, that is—but she'd had no way of knowing that while in nursing school Penny had known a young Jordanian Palestinian who was getting his master's in computer science.

God, what an opportunity! To help the Sea Hawk defect. And she'd find a way of doing it without certain other defenders of the American Way sticking their little fingers into the pie and ruining it. The guy wanted to defect to the United States and that he would. She even had a rough idea of how to do it. And, of greater importance, who would do it.

But she'd have to be careful. Need to know. Everybody at Langley would know everything they needed to know, more or less. And deniability. Her coworkers all loved deniability, and so did she in this case. That's why God had created Alex and her friends. The Tridents worked for SECDEF, not Langley. It was more than reasonable for her to provide them data, but nobody could expect her to be responsible for how they used that data or any little escapades they might indulge in. She'd get them started and then let them run with it. Virtually on their own initiative. The less they told her the better, but they'd have to run like hell so it was all done before anybody else could screw it up.

And once it was done, well . . .

She'd have to keep the Director informed about what she was sending the Tridents—and of what they might tell her about what they were doing—but that seemed manageable. Unfortunately, Chaz Owens would also have to be brought in. The situation required flexible thinking, and flexible was one way Chaz didn't think. He had an unhealthy and generally unconstructive attitude toward anybody he even suspected of terrorism. He liked blood and pain. He was more like a Saracen than even he ever imagined. He believed to the core of his soul that the only way to save The Homeland was by sword and fire. That Islam must be destroyed or reshaped into our image if we were to survive. His determination was unbending and his energy limitless.

Speed, she reminded herself, was of the essence.

But first, something had to be done about Penny. Greta realized how unprofessional of her it was to be thinking of the nurse's well-being at this point, but Penny had saved her life. Her physical life and also her emotional one. It was Penny who'd sat by her bed for days on end convincing her she should try to live when she really had no desire to do so.

Just being a nurse in Gaza meant Penny was up to her neck in shit already. Now that she'd become a conduit—the only conduit—to a man half the world wanted to slice slowly to pieces, she was in way over her head. Hamas would want her. Mossad would want her. Chaz Owens would want her.

She had to get the hell out of Gaza—right now—yet stay in the region.

With barely a pause Greta replied to Penny, telling her she'd find a way to do the deed and then begging her, ordering her, threatening her with an even worse hell than she already was in if she didn't get over the border and on the first plane to Cyprus.

Cyprus, Greta thought, was perfect. She'd be almost as safe there as anywhere, and it fit right into the plan forming in Greta's overheated mind.

As soon as she hit the send button, a small smile crossed her face. She was in the analysis business. It was her job to process huge amounts of data. That meant she got all sorts of strange traffic from all sorts of strange places. By the time counterintelligence spotted her exchange with the nurse, realized it didn't fit into her normal pattern and decided what to do about it, the deed would be done.

Greta had a well-deserved reputation for being impossible at times, so the Director would feel no shock. Everybody seemed to understand that, short of firing her, there wasn't much you could do—in terms of administrative penalties—to an angry, half-Lebanese girl with only one functioning eye. Push too hard and she might start throwing the china around the apartment.

14

Penny had been worried and confused when she'd received Abdul's first e-mail and grasped its full implications. When she received Greta's reply, her relief at being able to turn it all over to somebody who knew what she was doing was tempered by very real fear. Greta was right—while Penny had been doing her thing in the middle of continuous destruction and murder, she was now more part of the game than ever before. And it was entirely possible she'd now be a very specific target of those who were after Abdul.

Taking a deep breath, she walked across the dusty courtyard of the clinic and knocked on the door to Dr. Fayez's office.

"Come in."

"Doctor," Penny said, getting right to the point even before the door had closed behind her, "a very important personal matter has come up. I must ask for a week off to take care of it."

Fayez, who'd been dozing, looked at her with a frown. "Is it something serious? Of course it is, you wouldn't be here otherwise."

"I'm afraid so."

Fayez continued to smile. "How long have you been here?" he asked, knowing the answer perfectly well.

"Almost three years."

"When was your last vacation?"

"A week in Greece, a year ago."

Fayez shook his head slowly. "You've given so much and taken so little, Ms. Arnold. I assume you wish to leave as soon as possible."

"I know it's not a good time . . ."

"There's no such thing as a good time here. I have no desire to pry, but how can I help? One of the foundation's cars and driver along with your papers should get you through either the Egyptian or Israeli checkpoints."

"Israeli. I have to go to Cyprus, and there's a flight out of Lod later tonight."

"The car'll be ready in half an hour and I'll redo the duty schedule. You pack. I hope it all works out well. I know it will—even Moslems like me know an angel when we work with one."

"Dr. Fayez, we both know the Koran's filled with angels, and most of them are armed to the teeth."

"Few have served God as faithfully as you. Please don't repeat that. There are some around here who'd go out of their way to misinterpret my words."

* * *

Crepusculo Ardiente was about sixty miles north of Tripoli—well clear of any prying Libyan eyes—when the big SH 60 helo thundered into view. "There's your ride," observed Manuel Sarmiento.

"Can't tell you how much we've enjoyed the trip with

you," said Mike as he, Alex and the captain headed for the fantail. "Short but satisfying."

"And the accommodations?"

"Not as much as we enjoyed the activities."

As they were walking down a ladder, Alex's satphone buzzed. "Hello," said the Trident XO.

"Alex, this is Mariano. Progress, real progress at last!"

"Wait," shouted Alex. "There's a helo coming right at me, Mariano, wait a minute." She then stepped through a door into the superstructure, where the roar of the helo's engine and the sympathetic rattling of the gear on *Crepusculo*'s deck were somewhat muted.

"What's up?"

"No matter what some of your people say about our friends in Italy, they've come through this time. We now have a photograph of the girl and have already learned that she was in the Barcelona airport yesterday."

"How'd the Italians manage to come up with the picture?"

"Without going into details about why they wanted him, they put the man's photograph on all the TV stations around Naples. And the newspapers. An ancient aristocrat named Carlo Metello contacted them to say the man had rented the villa next to his for a week. Indeed, the man and his companion had dinner with Metello and his wife a couple nights ago. And both villas are directly on the Bay of Naples."

"What about the photograph?"

"It seems Don Carlo harbored certain wishful ambitions with respect to the girl. He took a number of photographs of her, some using a telephoto lens. Most show only the girl. A few also show al-Jabbar. They're much clearer than the passport photo."

"Did he learn anything about them?"

"Surprisingly little, although maybe it's not so surprising considering where his thoughts were. He found al-Jabbar to be a very intelligent and personable young man. As for the girl, he obviously found her fascinating. He said her Italian was of the highest quality, but he got the impression she might be Albanian. Other than that he seemed to learn very little about her."

"You think she's still in Barcelona?"

"We're looking from the Pyrenees to Gibraltar and beyond."

"Should we go to Barcelona?"

"I think it makes more sense for you to go to Rota. I still think the Strait is the place, not Barcelona. I may be terribly wrong, but I've learned that at times you simply have to make the best guess you can. Let Mike decide where he wants to go."

"He would anyway."

"Give me a call when you reach Sicily. I may have more."

"Roger. Do you want me to forward this to Greta?"

"No. I'll take care of it."

Alex stepped out of the superstructure, to find Mike and Captain Sarmiento waiting and the helo hovering impatiently. Shouting, she gave Chambers the news.

"Sounds to me like we're headed where the action is," said Mike, his face brightening.

As he waited to be winched up into the helo, Ted found himself staring at the Arab sailor who'd made him so uncomfortable before. The fellow was now grinning at him.

There are some very strange people in the world, thought the SEAL.

* * *

With the levanter having blown itself out, the morning air over the Strait of Gibraltar was cool and clear, perfect for watching the two American frigates as they slowly patrolled the narrow waterway, their haze gray hulls glinting in the early morning sun.

Magda stood on the balcony of the Tryp Ceuta, the only major hotel in Ceuta, and focused her binoculars out over the port and beyond, to the waters of the Strait. She watched as one of the ships—the more southerly, which was only a mile or two offshore—cruised from west to east, then turned almost directly in front of her and steamed back toward the west.

Today, she thought. I really should do it today, before they decide to change their operations.

* * *

The team was sitting in a lounge at Sigonella Air Base waiting for the mechanics to fix a defective pressure gauge in the jet that was supposed to take them to Rota. When the satphone buzzed, Alex reached for it because Alex always answered the phone if she could. That way she could be sure of knowing what was going on.

"Alex, this is Greta."

"Hey, what's up? Did you get our report about the course the *Ameer Badaweyy* followed a few weeks ago? When we think the Hawk was aboard?"

"Yeah. Good stuff. But I've got something even better. It's going to blow your mind."

"Okay, I'm sitting down."

"Do you think Captain Chambers will go for a little off-the-books work? It's not as bad as that, actually. It's utterly part of your current mission, in its broadest sense. It's just that a few people here may only be told what I think they need to know when I think they need to know it. You guys won't get in trouble."

"What about you?"

"If it works, a few people will be pissed and nobody will ever trust me again—not that they do now—but nothing substantive will happen. If it doesn't work, I can always find a new job. No matter what they might say, they won't really send me to Cuba."

"Why are you doing this?"

"You'll understand when I tell you about it."

"Okay. Give it to me."

"You remember my telling you about Penny Arnold, the nurse who talked me into wanting to live again after my head was almost blown off?"

"Yes."

"I just got an e-mail from her. She's still in Gaza and she just got an e-mail from a guy she knew in college. The guy's name is Abdul al-Jabbar."

"Oh my God!" said Alex, in a voice loud enough to cause the others to stop talking among themselves and turn in her direction.

"Oh my God is right. And he wants to defect. To us."

"How're you going to get him out of Gaza?"

"He's not in Gaza, he's still in Beirut, and you and your sailor pals are going to get him out."

"Really? Why aren't your people going to do it?"

"Because."

"Why not?"

"Alex, we both know that mixed in with all the good guys around here are a few creeps. Our man in Beirut, for example, dislikes both Arabs and Israelis almost equally but has managed to run up a big debt with Mossad. Whenever he can't get what he needs, they give it to him, so I doubt he can say no very often. And the deputy director for antiterrorism tends to be a little quick on the draw whenever he hears the word 'terrorist.' This may sound silly, but I really don't want Penny falling into the hands of any creeps. They may decide she knows something. I also don't like the idea of this guy being rewarded for defecting by going for a CIA swim. It discourages others from defecting. I'm positive if you can get him out—using whatever resources you normally use—we can keep control of him and get him into the right hands."

"So what's the starting point?"

"You guys get your tails to Cyprus and meet with Penny. Al-Jabbar wants everything done through her."

"I thought she was in Gaza."

"I told her to get the hell out for her own safety."

"Then what?"

"Then you and the navy get him out. And you don't even have to tell me what you're doing. In fact, it would be best if you tell me nothing from this instant on. Just listen. Otherwise I may have to tell Chaz—the terrorism czar—and then his people may try to horn in."

"Let me put Mike on, Greta, and you give all this to him. He's the one to decide."

"Roger."

Alex handed Mike the phone and Mike listened to Greta. "Give me a minute," he finally said after the CIA analyst had finished her pitch.

Chambers looked out the window at the airplane they'd soon—he hoped—be in.

"What did Mariano say about the Albanian woman?" he asked, covering the mouthpiece of the phone.

"That they've tracked her as far as Barcelona."

"You've informed COMSIXTHFLT about the *Ameer Badaweyy*'s track?"

"Yes, sir."

"How about Nichols aboard *Abernathy*?"

"I've informed both frigates about the track, and as soon as you give me the phone back, I'll tell both about the woman."

Where could he achieve the most? Mike asked himself. Mariano was much better equipped than he was to track down the Albanian. And with proper warning, *Abernathy* and *Lines* should be fully capable of defending themselves.

How would he explain it to Alan Parker and what would the deputy secretary say?

Alan didn't like sudden changes. He'd undoubtedly say Mike should keep his eye on the ball and find the devices. He'd also say Mike was intruding on Agency turf.

What else was new? And his mission wasn't to find the devices, it was to neutralize the Palestinian Naval Militia and prevent more ships being sunk.

He'd wait to inform Alan.

"Very well, Greta. We're in. We've got a plane, I hope. All I have to do is tell them to fly in the opposite direction. Where's the nurse going to be?"

"In a hotel near Larnaca, on the Greek end of the island. I thought that'll be safer."

"Anything more?"

"No, Captain. When I get more information, I'll forward it, but the details are up to you."

"Roger."

Mike turned the phone off and handed it to Alex. He then set out for the air base's operations office, where he informed the major who seemed to be running the place that the flight was going to have to be redirected.

"Do you care which airport? There are several civilian ones and two British military ones."

"Larnaca, if you can. Otherwise, any one that'll let us in."

* * *

Moshe Goren walked slowly along the Corniche, looking out at the royal blue Mediterranean and digesting the past twenty-four hours. Faud el-Khadery, a Palestinian well known to him, had attempted to kidnap an employee of the Beirut and Byblos Bank. That employee was the assistant to the IT manager, who'd been tortured and killed the day before. The IT manager was also the last person Goren knew of who'd seen Abdul al-Jabbar. Except for the desk clerk at the Phoenicia, whom he couldn't very well interrogate, because the Lebanese Police were already doing so.

Before he died—according to Goren's informant within the Lebanese Army—el-Khadery had blurted out that Tareq ibn-Ali had ordered the IT manager's kidnapping because he wanted to interrogate Hadeed about al-Jabbar. Considering the manner of the interrogation, Moshe had to assume ibn-Ali's intentions toward the Sea Hawk were not friendly. Why, he could only guess, but the reason didn't really matter at the moment. The Palestinians were always maiming or killing one another.

It might be very much worth his while to locate ibn-Ali and keep an eye on him.

Goren had no objection whatsoever to letting Hamas do some of his work for him. Just as long as *he* was the one who got the son of a bitch in the end.

* * *

Art Nichols sat in his chair on *Abernathy*'s bridge and worried. As he was paid to do.

According to Chambers's data, the device was probably located within an area of about fifteen miles by fifteen miles, and its range was estimated as at least five miles. The way he saw it, that meant the entire Mediterranean approach to the Strait was potentially lethal. And the business about the second terrorist—the woman—being in Spain suggested something was going to happen soon.

He looked around the bridge at the OD and the rest of the watch—the two sailors behind the conning console, the lookouts, the quartermaster and the messenger. They were all in battle dress. The ship was at Condition Two—half the crew on watch, all combat and damage control stations manned and the antitorpedo system streamed astern, making believe *it* was the ship and *Abernathy* herself was just a figment of somebody's imagination.

Over long periods of time Condition Two could wear down a crew, blunt their sharpness, but Nichols didn't anticipate more than a day or two of it. He'd maintain the condition until somebody gave him a reason to feel better about the situation.

He raised his glasses and looked off to the right, at Ceuta. He'd never visited the city and wondered if there was anything worth seeing there.

Nichols stood and stretched, then walked out onto the bridge wing. It was a beautiful day. The sun was high and the wind just right to drive away the heat. The ship looked good, too. Despite a long, busy deployment, the gray paint was smooth and bright and unblemished by rust. The deck department had been turning and burning. They'd all been turning and burning. He should be feeling good. Proud of his ship and pleased to be her commander. But he wasn't feeling good. He was worried sick.

* * *

Alfredo Sanchez couldn't help but feel a twinge of pride as he sat in the lobby of the Tryp Ceuta, his eyes fixed on the bank of elevators.

The light on his silenced cell phone blinked. "Alfredo, this is Gomez."

"Yes, Don Mariano?"

"You say she's at the Tryp Ceuta?"

"Yes, the desk clerk recognized her photograph."

"Is she there now?"

"Yes. I called her room, identified myself as the manager and asked if her accommodations were satisfactory. She said yes, so I thanked her and ended the conversation. I'm in the lobby now with an excellent view of the elevators."

"Excellent, Alfredo! I'm in Algeciras. I'm walking aboard the ferry as we speak and will be with you in an hour. In the meantime, remember that we want her alive. Also remember that she's extremely dangerous. Watch her. If she leaves, follow her carefully but take no other action unless it is absolutely essential."

"Yes, Don Mariano."

Alfredo waited, at one point walking over to get a copy of a newspaper. As he waited, he noticed the desk clerk seemed to spend most of his time in the office behind the desk.

An hour or so after Alfredo's conversation with Gomez, one of the elevator doors opened and out stepped Magda, dressed in jeans, sneakers and a white shirt and carrying a small purse. Without taking his eyes off her, Alfredo glanced at his watch. Damn! Gomez was probably already in Ceuta, probably only half a kilometer away. Why couldn't she have waited another five minutes?

* * *

Mariano Gomez was standing, furious, on the ferry dock in Ceuta when Alfredo called. "She left the hotel several minutes ago," reported the agent. "She pulled out on a white motor scooter and turned west on the Paseo. I'm following her in my car."

"Keep after her. The Guardia was supposed to have a car and driver waiting for us but they appear to have screwed it up. We'll join you as soon as possible. And keep me informed!"

"As you say."

"I think our car's here," said one of the two associates

Mariano had brought with him. Gomez snapped his cell phone shut, halfway through dialing the number of the local Guardia Civil office.

Gomez turned and saw the unmarked car. It was a tiny SEAT four-door micro-mini. The driver was looking at a photograph and comparing it to him. He strode over to the car, mumbling "idiot" under his breath and opened the rear door. "In!" he snapped to his two associates as he bent over double to fit into the front passenger's seat.

"Señor Gomez?" asked the driver.

"Yes, of course. As you can see."

"Where are we going, sir?"

"Our target is a young, dark-haired woman on a white motor scooter. She's right now headed west on the Paseo. I want you to also head west while I check with the man following her."

Alfredo reported that Magda had already gotten past the harbor and seemed headed out of the city on the Carretera de Benzu, which ran west along the edge of the Alboran Sea.

"How close are you?"

"Maybe five hundred meters. The traffic's unusually heavy, although she seems to have no trouble weaving in and out of it."

"Very well. Report any changes."

The driver slammed on the brakes and Mariano looked up and out the windshield. "Quickly, up on the sidewalk," he snapped when he saw that a minor accident of some sort was partially blocking the road. "Just don't hit anybody."

* * *

Alfredo, now roughly a hundred meters and four cars behind Magda, noted immediately when the target swerved off the road to the right, just where Punta Blanca jutted out into the sparkling sea. He immediately pulled off to the side and watched as she started to pick her way down the steep, rocky shore.

"The target's pulled off at Punta Blanca and is climbing down toward the water," he reported.

"*Mierda*!" snapped Gomez. What was she up to? Should he have Alfredo approach her or continue to watch? "How far are we from Punta Blanca?" he asked the driver.

"Perhaps five minutes, señor."

"Approach her slowly, Alfredo. Attempt to see what she's doing."

Alfredo continued to watch as Magda worked her way down over the rocks and then started to wade into the foot-high surf. Her stride was firm and confident as she seemed to kick the water aside. She stopped when the water was waist-deep, reached into her bag and pulled out what looked like a small radio. At first she seemed to listen to it, then she leaned over and stuck it in the water and held it there. Standing again, she looked out to sea. Only after Alfredo's eyes had followed Magda's—and seen the gray American frigate a couple miles offshore—did he fully appreciate what he'd just witnessed. He drew his pistol and started to run along the road toward her.

As Magda forced her way toward the rocky shore, carrying her bag in her right hand, she spotted Alfredo running toward her. She reached a large, low, flat rock and stepped up on it. Alfredo was stopped now, staring down at her, with his pistol pointed at her.

"Drop the bag," he ordered, believing incorrectly that she was holding it by the top. Magda fired the pistol she was holding in the bag right through the bag's side, opening a small but fatal hole in Sanchez's chest.

* * *

The hazard alarm sounded, breaking the near silence that existed on *Abernathy*'s bridge as the hazard display started flashing. Nichols, sitting in his chair, didn't even have to look to know his ship was in serious trouble. "Sound General Quarters. Set Condition Zebra.

"Right full rudder," he added as he studied the display, raising his voice to be heard above the General Quarters alarm. "Clear the engineering spaces. All hands prepare for possible torpedo strike."

Now, he thought, as he gritted his teeth, we'll find out if the engineering system can really operate on remote for ten minutes. "Steady on Two Six Five True."

The display said two minutes until impact. He continued to grit his teeth as he acknowledged the various manning reports that were coming in. He watched as the bridge filled with additional personnel. What the hell else could he do? The torpedo defense system was activated, he'd turned toward the torpedo, he'd prepared his ship as much as possible for disaster.

One minute to anticipated impact. "Pass the word for all hands to sit down or get a good grip on something and prepare for shock and concussion," he directed the boatswain's mate of the watch.

Sixty-five seconds later *Abernathy* shuddered, then rose almost straight up a few feet. Even before she had a chance to settle back into the deep waters, a hole opened in the deckhouse overhead and a great tower of flame and white hot gasses erupted just aft of the funnel. A massive cloud of overpressure air came with it and expanded in all directions, battering everything within its reach. Despite the warning, a hundred officers and sailors were thrown violently in all directions—some against bulkheads or down ladders, two all the way over the side. A cacophony of additional alarms sounded. Fire. Flooding. The ship groaned and coasted to a stop, her propulsion system already reduced to scrap.

Nichols turned to the phone talker to tell him to call Damage Control Central to demand a status report, then stopped himself. It was much too soon for them to know anything more than he did. He stood and walked aft, to the signal bridge. One of the signalmen was lying there, propped against the bulkhead. Clearly dead, a victim of the horrendous concussion of the explosion.

Somehow, the antitorpedo system hadn't fooled the device one bit. Was it possible the device's creators knew more than they should have about the system?

15

Mariano Gomez heard the crack of Magda's pistol as he pushed open the car door and headed for the railing along the *carretera*. He saw Alfredo collapse and cursed loudly. His eyes burning with controlled anger, he looked down at the rocks. Magda was standing there with the waves breaking around her and glinting in the sun. She looked up at him and his three companions, all of whom were advancing with pistols drawn. On her face was a fierce expression of defiance or perhaps contempt. By now, much to Mariano's irritation, traffic had come to a stop as the drivers attempted to guess what was going on.

"Don't shoot!" shouted Gomez, just as Magda fired and barely missed him. "Get down. We want her alive." His heart pounding but his hand steady, Mariano knelt and braced himself against the railing. Taking the most careful aim—he was considered by most who knew him to be an outstanding marksman—the Spanish agent fired and Magda fell, clutching her leg.

Mariano stood, taking a deep breath. Then, with their weapons aimed at her, the four Spanish officers approached the terrorist, who was now lying on her side on the large, flat rock. She was clearly in shock, stunned. Her pistol had fallen a few feet away. She looked at them a moment, her contempt clearly as strong as ever. Then, to Mariano's utter horror, her hand shot out and grabbed the pistol. With one continuing motion she pulled the weapon to her head and blew a hole in her right temple.

Gomez felt a wave of disgust sweep over him. With life, with himself. He was too old and had been in the business too long to slide into self-recrimination, but he did have to recognize that by carelessly allowing the woman to kill herself he'd done the civilized world no favor.

"Get this traffic moving," he snapped to one of his assistants. "There's nothing more for them to see."

Then he saw the yellow white flash at sea and heard the thunder. He looked out in time to see the volcano erupt aboard *Abernathy*.

* * *

Word of *Abernathy*'s crippling, and Magda's death, reached Langley, Virginia, shortly after seven P.M. By eight, a meeting had been convened in the Director's conference room.

"Up to now I've gone along with Greta's little game," enunciated Chaz Owens, "but it's time to take the gloves off. Four American heroes died a few hours ago, and there's still at least one device left. And one terrorist. This business of Greta's trying to get him in as a defector is bullshit. He doesn't plan to defect. He's jerking us around. If Greta can get him to show himself, my people will grab him by the balls and pull them off."

"A willing defector is generally much more—" started Greta.

"You still don't get it, after all these years! Our homeland is in the greatest danger it has ever been in. Al-Qaida and its allies are the most formidable enemies we've ever faced. We have to strike hard. No rules, no limits."

Greta had long known how Chaz felt, but she'd never seen him explode in this way. "I was pretty scared when the Brits burned the White House down a few years ago," she hissed, wondering if she could get a job with Alex and her friends.

"Don't be smart! Director?"

The Director looked at his assistant, then at the two combatants. This was just the sort of decision that had cost some of his predecessors not only their jobs but their reputations and public images. "The naval group will have to continue, especially since we really don't seem to have any control over them, but Chaz will move his people in and shadow them. If something goes wrong . . ."

Greta looked down at the table, feeling sick to her stomach. Chaz smiled. Before this was all over, he'd have this al-Jabbar prick. And he'd start by tailing the navy interlopers just as soon as they arrived in Cyprus. Once they reached Beirut, he'd use McGrath and his people. He'd be all over them. And if he thought Pat was fucking up, he'd fly out there himself.

* * *

"COMSIXTHFLT is calling you, sir," said the jet's co-pilot, standing in the isle next to Mike's seat.

"Very well," said Mike, who'd been studying a map of Beirut.

"This way, sir," said the copilot, leading him forward to the flight deck.

"Mike, this is Fred Townsend," said the voice of COMSIXTHFLT's intelligence officer. "I've got some very bad news. *Abernathy* was nailed about an hour ago by one of those devices. Right off Ceuta, more or less where you predicted."

"Hell!" mumbled Mike. "Hell! Hell! Hell! Casualties?"

"Four dead, twenty-seven wounded. As far as we know. It seems Captain Nichols was listening to your theory that the devices were aiming for the engine noises, because as soon as SONAR reported a torpedo, he cleared everybody out of the engineering spaces. Otherwise we'd have fifty dead."

"The ship?"

"She's still afloat and we hope to keep her that way. What's really disheartening is that the Spanish had located the woman in Ceuta and were closing in on her when she activated the damn thing. From what I hear, they're as upset as we are."

"I can believe it. At least we have the woman. She can tell us where the third is."

"The woman is dead. She killed herself before they could take her." Townsend paused a moment, then continued. "Mike, to be honest, there's a little confusion about what, exactly, you and your group are doing at the moment. First you head for Rota then you turn around and head for Cyprus. Admiral Simmons is hoping you'd clarify it for him."

"Al-Jabbar, the principal operator of the devices, is cornered in Beirut and has indicated he'd like to defect. In part, as far as I can tell, he's had a change of heart and in part he seems caught in the middle of a power struggle within the PLO. We're headed for Cyprus, then Beirut, to get him out before Hamas can get their hands on him.

If we can get him out alive, we're hoping he'll be willing to tell us everything we've ever wanted to know. Including the location of the third device."

There was a pause as Captain Townsend digested Mike's explanation. "So you're shifting your focus? Going after the terrorists?"

"He seems to be coming to us."

"It does seem like a good opportunity, especially since we're in no position to locate the remaining device—I assume they're only three in all—at the moment. I think the admiral will agree, so we'll just have to continue as we have been. If you need any backing and he can provide it, I'm sure he will."

"Thanks, Fred."

After signing off, Mike walked slowly aft and told the rest of the team about *Abernathy*'s near destruction.

* * *

Abdul's initial reaction to Penny's agreement to help had been near ecstasy. Now, he stood a chance. But the more he thought about it, the more his joy dissipated. Nothing was guaranteed. And then he thought of George Hadeed. If Hamas found out about Penny's involvement, she'd suffer the same fate George had. Worse, in fact, since Tareq had a reputation for especially disliking women who did anything to foil him.

The Hawk paced his room in the Pension Marrakech. His safest plan was to stay where he was until Penny got back to him. But he knew he couldn't. He felt trapped. In a cage. In a crypt. The air, the scent of lavender and decay, was choking him. At the very least he had to go out and get some food. And he had to assume Tareq still believed he was in Hamra. He also had to hope that shaving his mustache and head had changed his appearance enough so that nobody who didn't already know him could spot him at a glance. Taking a deep breath, he put on a pair of glasses and walked out into the corridor.

"Hello, Mr. al-Jabbar," said Madame deVine as he walked across the lobby.

"Hello, madame. How are you this evening?" From the expression on her tired old face, he suspected she might eventually develop into a problem. Showing up with no passport, then shaving his mustache and head. How could she not be suspicious? His only hope was that as an old woman with few boarders she needed every pound she could get her hands on. And that she'd seen so much of life in Beirut that she didn't really care who he was just as long as he wasn't going to rape and rob her. He didn't even know whose side she was on—she'd never said a word about politics. She was a Christian, so she probably sided with the government. But that was far from certain.

"Are you well? You've left your room so little."

"I'm fine, madame. As I may have mentioned, I'm a computer consultant and I spend way too many hours pounding on a keyboard. But even I have to take a break. Can you recommend a decent restaurant?" As he spoke, he had no intention of actually spending an hour or two in any public place, much rather a restaurant.

The elderly woman smiled. "I know nothing about computers. Maybe I would like to know more, maybe not. I will decide someday. Go to the Rum-Maan. The food is good and the prices are reasonable. Go out my front door and turn right. Then take the first right turn after that. After another few blocks you'll see it on the left."

"Thank you," he said. "Thank you very much."

As the Hawk stepped out onto the street, he decided to change his plan. Rather than buying food and bringing it back to his room, he would take Madame deVine's advice and look in on the Rum-Maan. He simply had to get out for a little while.

The Rum-Maan turned out to be a smallish, quiet neighborhood restaurant. After stepping through the door, he glanced quickly around, trying not to seem too interested in studying the diners. There were still enough customers so he wouldn't stand out like a sore thumb, but not enough to cause a problem getting a table. And he had trouble believing any of the other customers were Hamas thugs. Most appeared to be with their families. The place felt right.

"Sir?" said the young woman standing at the small counter near the door. Judging from the expression on her face, she'd already spotted him as an outsider.

"I'm famished," he said with his friendliest smile. "Can you give me a table?"

"Of course, and if you're truly famished you've come to the right place."

Abdul enjoyed that dinner, his first complete meal since leaving Robert and Juliette Saleh's apartment. When he first realized he was relaxing a little, he tensed. Relaxing was dangerous. But so was too much tension. It could lead to obsession-induced blindness and mental exhaustion.

Feeling confident now that Penny and her friend would, indeed, find a way to get him out, Abdul finished his meal of lamb and rice. Then, as he was enjoying his sweet, he noticed a change in the atmosphere. The young girl who'd been at the counter was now moving from table to table, speaking to the diners with an intense look on her face. As she spoke, her audience at each table started to look around the room, then seemed to start gobbling their food.

"I'm very sorry, sir," she said when she reached

Abdul, "but we'll be closing in a few minutes. It seems the agreement between the government and Hezbollah has fallen apart and there is trouble."

Abdul looked at her, then at his half-eaten pastry. "Of course you have time to finish that and your coffee. We'll be open again just as soon as things calm down."

The Hawk smiled back at her and said thank you. He watched for a moment as the other customers finished up. The initial shock seemed to have worn off and most left in a hurried but unpanicked manner, as if they'd been through all this before—which most of them had. Abdul then finished up himself, paid and walked out the door.

The night was cooling and almost silent, except for the rumble of diesel engines. Telling himself he really did have to know what was happening, he set out for the Place d'Etoile, about twelve blocks away. When he arrived, he found, parked between the elegant stone buildings, a half dozen army trucks and jeeps, with soldiers fanning out from them, taking positions around the area. He heard a clunk to his left and turned to find himself facing two soldiers, their rifles pointed at him.

"Excuse me," he said quickly, "I just finished dinner and was about to head back to my room when I heard noises out here."

The soldiers looked at him a moment, noting that he seemed to be both alone and unarmed. "Where is your room?" asked one.

"At the Pension Marrakech. I'm a computer consultant, here on business. My passport is at the pension, but I can show you my driver's license."

While one kept his rifle pointed straight at Abdul, the other accepted the driver's license and studied it a moment. "You look different here. You've shaved your mustache and head."

"Yes," said Abdul, his stomach cramping. "As you

can see, my hair wasn't much. It made me look old so I decided to try this to see if the girls like it any better. If it does no good then I'll let the hair grow back."

The soldier looked at him, a small smile flitting across his face. Then he looked at the other soldier and both shrugged.

"You'd better get back to your pension, Mr. al-Jabbar," said the first soldier as he handed back the driver's license. "You picked a very bad time to go for a walk."

"Thank you," said the Hawk, totally agreeing with the soldier. "I'm sorry."

It would seem, he thought, that the Lebanese government isn't as interested in me as they might be. If they were, they'd have told all their soldiers to look for me. Or maybe the two soldiers hadn't listened to their instructions. Or maybe they just didn't care. There was a lot of that in the world.

On his way back to the pension, Abdul came to a small store that was in the process of closing. The owner started to shoo him away but then relented and took five minutes to sell him two loafs of bread and a pound of cheese. "Perhaps you should take more," said the shopkeeper as the Hawk headed for the door. "There's no way of knowing how long this *merde* is going to last." Abdul turned and asked for another loaf of bread and a bottle of middling French wine.

* * *

Penny's flight to Cyprus was a short one. While the Lebanese went back to practicing street politics, she landed at Larnaca Airport and, within an hour, was settled into a room at a hotel on the shore, not far from the airport. A room reserved for her by Greta Sabbagh.

Under any other circumstances, she would have immediately taken a walk along the beach to celebrate her release from the terrors of Gaza. She would have danced into the blue green water in joy. Cyprus might have its problems, but they paled in comparison to those she'd suffered with in the Strip. But tonight wasn't any other circumstances. Greta, by pointing out the obvious, had scared her more than she'd ever been scared before. In Gaza she'd known she might well get killed, but it wouldn't be because somebody wanted to kill Penny Arnold. She'd just be collateral damage. Now it seemed all too possible that somebody might show up for the express purpose of killing her and nobody else. She'd been released from Gaza, but she was far from free. If Abdul was being chased, then she was, too. She locked and bolted the door then turned off the lights and plunked herself down on the couch. There she waited, staring at the lights along the dark shore, for the arrival of somebody named Alex Mahan. Greta's friend.

* * *

Art Nichols shuddered inwardly as he leaned over the temporary railing and looked down at the greasy, glob-filled water rising and falling with deceptive gentleness around the scrap that had once been *Abernathy*'s engine room. It stank, he thought. The whole damn ship stank— of oil, and burned oil and burned plastic and other burned things. It was overpowering.

He felt somebody bump into him from behind. "Sorry, sir." He turned to find an engineman struggling across the shattered mess deck, carrying a role of fire hose. Hanks. Hanks was his name, thought Nichols. Hanks's dungarees were soaked with a filthy mix of oil and water and covered with soot. As was Nichols's uniform. And the man looked as exhausted as Nichols felt.

"Don't worry about it, Hanks. Keep up the good work."

The torpedo had blown a big, elevator shaft–like hole in his ship. Four dead and twenty-seven wounded. Ten percent of his crew. It could have been five times more if he hadn't known to clear the engineering spaces and those immediately around them. For the most part the blast had been directed straight up—from the engine room through the mess decks, through an electronics repair shop and then out the top of the superstructure. Fortunately, the ship had been buttoned up, so the flooding was limited and controllable, and the damage control parties had been on station and ready to fight the fires.

Unfortunately, according to the Spanish naval divers who'd already examined the bottom, the ship's back appeared to be broken. Even from where he was, he could see that the deck aft was no longer on the same plane as the foredeck. The ship was twisted. His ship.

Abernathy was now lying just inside the breakwater at Ceuta, surrounded by an almost solid mass of oil and water, with a yellow pollution containment boom rigged all around the foul mess. While he wished otherwise, Nichols felt certain she was most likely headed for the scrap heap. They might be able to repair her, but it would cost almost as much as it would to build a new ship.

He looked up through the hole and could see the gray dawn sky and the drizzle drifting down from it. What more could he have done? he asked himself bitterly. Avoided the danger zone? How could he? The danger zone was the entire Strait of Gibraltar and it was their job to patrol that space. What about the Spanish? Why hadn't they caught that fucking woman!

They'd done their best, and in his heart of hearts, he suspected they'd probably done the best anybody could've done under the circumstances. He'd never much liked after-the-fact recriminations. No excuses, he reminded himself. No regrets. No passing the buck.

Enough of that maudlin shit! Both he and his ship were out of it now. For a while, anyway. He hoped Chambers—or somebody—got that other terrorist and located the final device before it got somebody else. In the meantime, he had work to do.

* * *

Penny sat on the couch in her hotel suite, looking out over the sparkling, wind-kissed, blue and white Mediterranean, and saw none of its beauty or romance. She'd sat there all night, not leaving the couch except to go to the bathroom. She'd sat there, fists clenched, waiting for death to break in on her. She'd sat there, wondering if she was doing the right thing. Or if Abdul should just be thrown to the sharks.

Greta was right that she'd have been in great danger if she'd stayed in Gaza. But Greta knew as well as anybody that there was no safety anywhere—the entire Eastern Mediterranean was always at a half boil—a cauldron filled with radicals and messiahs of all sorts moving freely around—and had been since the fall of Rome. If she had enemies in Gaza, then those enemies would have no trouble finding her here. It was only a matter of time.

There was motion outside her window and her eyes focused on it. On the beach. Two small children were there, running and splashing each other, and the sun had barely made it above the horizon.

She'd loved beaches once. All water sports, in fact. Beaches were a place for fun. To swim, to sun, to drink illicit beer, to talk to your friends and hope that some of the boys talked to you.

Gaza had beaches. One whole side of the Strip was one long beach. But that beach was different. The sand was the same hard, pitiless sand that covered the whole place. Sand in which little to nothing grew. Sand that got everywhere—in your clothes and eyes and mouth and soul—when the wind blew the wrong way. And the Mediterranean, blue and cheerful in the distance, was, in reality, just one more wall around the prison. It was a body of water that was able to provide only the most limited reward to the fishermen who continued to hope and try.

Now that she'd lived on one for three years, Penny hated beaches. All beaches.

She should have stayed in Kansas, she reproached herself. Except it was Oregon, not Kansas. But she should have stayed there anyway.

There was a knock at the door. Her back stiffened. Was this the Alex who Greta said was coming, or was it somebody she didn't know? And didn't want to know.

The temptation to stay right were she was—seated, clutching her hands and staring out the window, the temptation to make believe there was nobody outside the door—was almost overpowering, but she forced herself to overcome it. She walked to the door and opened it, holding her breath slightly as she did.

"Hi, I'm Alex," said a tall, attractive young woman with dark hair. "Greta Sabbagh told me to look you up." Her accent was clearly American.

A wave of relief swept over Penny. She was close to breaking into laughter at the triteness—even inanity—of Alex's greeting. Then the fear and doubt swept over her again, but she forced herself to control it. "I'm Penny and I've been waiting for you. Come on in."

"Great," said Alex. "Can my boss and one of my associates also come?"

"Yes," said Penny, her voice still a little tight. Was she making an awful mistake? Should she be calling hotel security?

"Mike Chambers," said Mike as he walked in. "Ray Fuentes," he added, pointing to the captain of marines who was following him.

"Before we go any further," said Penny, "are the three

of you with the CIA? Abdul's a little nervous about them."

"We're the navy, Penny," said Mike, "as odd as that may seem."

"Mike's a navy captain," added Alex, "and this handsome fellow is a marine officer."

"And you, too?"

"Not originally. I used to work with Greta, but then I met some sailors in a bar and they fed me drinks and talked me into changing sides. By the way, just so you won't be surprised, there're two more of us. One's in the hall and one's in the lobby. They're keeping an eye on the place."

"Why'd they send the navy?"

"Because we're the ones trying to find the devices your friend has been using. And, I'm going to be honest with you, Greta's a little worried that some of the people at her place might be tempted to grab your friend and make him disappear. Some of them also work closely with Mossad, and there's a certain amount of information that gets exchanged."

"There's nothing in the Middle East that's straightforward," sighed Penny.

"There's nothing anywhere that's straightforward," grumbled Ray as he opened the sliding door and walked out onto the balcony. To savor the view. And to carefully examine the surrounding roofs and balconies while he was at it.

"Can I get you anything?" asked Penny, the bad habits resulting from paying attention to her mother coming to the fore. "Coffee?"

"I think we all could use a cup," said Mike. "Ray's fully qualified to make it, so why don't you, Alex and I sit down with this map of Beirut and get started?"

"Okay."

"Before we get started, though, you're going to have to tell us more about you and your friend Abdul."

Penny sighed. "There's really not much to tell. I was raised near Seattle. My father's dead now, but he was an executive at a trucking company. My mother's a fifth grade teacher. I have a sister. She's a teacher, too. When I graduated from high school, I wasn't sure what I was going to do. Then a friend had a car accident and I went to the hospital with her. While I was at the emergency room, I realized that maybe nurses and doctors were the only people I'd ever seen who were doing something constructive. I went to college in Florida and got my BSN. While I was there I met Abdul. At a convenience store."

"And Abdul?"

"He was born in Jordan. When he was about ten or twelve his parents were killed in a car accident and he was sent to live with some cousins in Pennsylvania."

"Do you know what sort of things he did in high school?"

"He studied, tried to have fun and swam. He was a hot high school swimmer. He also swam in college."

"Did he enjoy life in Pennsylvania?"

"I think he did."

"Why didn't he become a United States citizen?"

"Because, I think, he never lost the Palestinian thing. His cousins were Palestinians, of course, and I gather they were happy staying in America, but he wanted to come back here and try to do something positive. I'm beginning to wonder just how positive his activities have been."

"Did you date him?"

"For a while."

"Do you mind describing him? Not what he looks like, what he was."

Penny stared out the window a moment then turned back to Mike.

"He was quiet and nice and very smart. And often he was funny."

"Did he talk a lot about politics?"

"Not politics, but occasionally he did talk about Palestine and how he thought the Palestinians were being screwed by the entire world. But he never screamed or shouted or hung out with weird people."

"What was your reaction?"

"He convinced me. After I'd graduated and spent two years in a nice, clean, orderly, suburban hospital, I decided maybe I should go out and help someplace that was really desperate. I considered Africa and South America and even some inner cities in the United States, but I guess I'd listened too carefully to Abdul, because I ended up in Gaza City."

"Does that mean you don't consider yourself politically active?"

"I never did until the doctor I work with pointed out that by patching up the combatants, we're really making ourselves part of the whole mess. Since I've patched up all sides, though, I'm really not sure which side I'm on."

"Did you love Abdul in college?"

"I think so. Maybe."

"And now?"

"A lot's happened. I really don't know. No, not the way you do in college. I wish him the best. He's still an honored friend—at least until I learn even more bad stuff about him."

"Did he take a lot of grief about being an Arab?"

"Not that I saw. The other guys on the swim team seemed to love him. But I'm sure somebody said something sometime. Somebody always does."

"Thank you, Penny, for not biting my head off."

"I figure you have to know who you're going to be working with."

"I do. And if you'll excuse me a moment, I have to call Greta about you again. She was going to do one final background check."

"Coffee," said Ray, placing a cup on the table in front of Penny, while Mike walked out on the balcony and called Greta.

"Sabbagh."

"Good morning, Greta. This is Mike Chambers. You're up early."

"Good morning, Captain. You know about that worm business."

"Yes."

"What's up?"

"We're with Penny right now. I've spoken with her, but before going on I wanted to check to see if you've come up with any surprises about her."

"I've dug and dug, Captain, and I can't find a single bad thing. What you see is what you're getting. Just remember, the clock's ticking."

"The deal's going to be done before you know it."

"Outstanding! You wouldn't believe some of the rumblings going on around here."

"Yes, I would."

"Now," said Mike, walking back into the room and spreading the map on the coffee table, "do you know where al-Jabbar is in the city?"

"I have no idea. He contacts me by e-mail."

"He believes that Hamas is after him?"

"That's what he says."

"And he has no passport, so it's dangerous to move around?"

"I assume so."

"Once upon a time we might've just flown a helo in

at night and picked him up on some field, but both the Syrians and Israelis are keeping tight control over the airspace. And we can't take him out by commercial airliner or car without a passport."

"We could easily get him a new one," offered Ray from the kitchenette.

"That would probably involve some of my old friends," said Alex.

"You don't trust the CIA? Greta works there and so did you," said Penny, a slightly confused expression on her face.

"I trust Greta and I trust ninety-five percent of the people she works with, but there's another five percent who sometimes go overboard." Then, turning back to Mike, Alex continued, "How about through the mountains and into Jordan on some back road?"

"Take too long. We've got to move quickly. Anyway, everybody's patrolling that area, and Jordan isn't particularly fond of terrorists. Even homegrown ones. Ray, I want you and Ted to fly to Beirut this afternoon and check a couple things. We'll follow in a day or two. In the meantime, Penny, do you mind having Alex as your roommate?"

"No, I'd feel better. Is Abdul going to be able to hold out that long?"

"We'll work as fast as we can. I'm going to take a quick walk around the place with Jerry. Alex, will you please get Ray and Ted on the next flight to Beirut?"

"Roger, Boss."

"And get them into a good hotel. Beirut's the sort of town where image can be very important."

"First class! Deluxe. They're worth it, especially the way Ray makes coffee."

16

Abdul's initial reaction to Penny's e-mail that help— help not directly related to the CIA—was on its way was another burst of elation. And then fear—nervousness— returned. When the time came, he'd have to come out and expose himself—either tell them where he was or arrange to meet them somewhere. There was no avoiding it. And they had to move fast—he only had enough cash for two more days. He replied, saying he could only last two more days and that whether he met them somewhere or they came to him, they had to bring Penny. How else would he know them?

As he sent the demand, his disgust with himself started to overflow again. He was putting Penny in ever-increasing danger just to save his own neck. He only hoped he could give them enough valuable information to justify—in his own mind—his vile actions. Both present and past.

* * *

Ollie Mathews sipped his third cup of coffee at a snack
bar in the main concourse of the Larnaca Airport and
watched as Ray and Ted walked across the hall and
into the corridor that led to the flight to Beirut. Once
they'd disappeared through Security, he opened his cell
phone and called Pat McGrath in Beirut. "Pat? Okay,
two of them just walked by. They should be boarding
right now."

"Which ones?"

"The marine and the black SEAL."

"None of the others?"

"Not so far, but I'll be here to see when they do
come."

"Okay."

Pat digested the report, then told Beth to forward it to
Chaz Owens.

* * *

Tareq ibn Ali was standing on a street corner on the Rue
Mahatma Gandhi, a block or two south of the American
University, when he saw him.

Moshe Goren, the son of a whore!

But Tareq was enough of a professional to admit to
himself that Mossad frequently had good intel. He had
no idea where the Jewish creep had gotten his, but if they
both thought al-Jabbar was still in Hamra, then there
was a damn good chance that he was. He walked over to
the car in which Zeid—Faud's successor as Hamas chief
in Beirut—was sitting, talking on his cell phone.

"You see our friend over there?" he asked, pointing at
the Mossad agent.

"Goren?" said Zeid, following Tareq's pointing
finger.

"Yes, if he thinks the Hawk is here and we do, too, then he must be here. I want you to get every man you have throughout the city and start going from door to door. I want to find him before the Jew does."

Then he spotted two Lebanese soldiers walking down the street. "We'd better move on before those two pigs start asking stupid questions. Perhaps they'll continue on and nab Moshe for jaywalking for something."

* * *

Ray and Ted landed in Beirut shortly after noon. Much to their surprise, the airport, if not jammed, was crowded, with as many people headed in as out. Curious, Ray stopped a uniformed cabin attendant—towing her wheeled luggage behind her—and asked about the seeming calm.

"I haven't been downtown this trip," she replied after first turning up her nose and trying to turn away, "but I understand nothing really happened yesterday or today, and it's tourist season." Without further elaboration she then strutted off, her heals clicking and her butt swinging in a restrained manner.

"I guess you're not as irresistible as you thought you were, Captain," observed Ted.

"I was counting on you, Ted. You're the one with the phenomenal physique and lightning moves. Anyway, no more 'captain' while we're here. We're just Ray and Ted."

Getting a rental car turned out to be no problem at all, and they walked right by Janet Dove on their way out to the parking lot. Janet followed them just closely enough to read the license plate of the light blue Honda they climbed into. She immediately forwarded the information to Pat McGrath.

"Okay," said Ted about twenty-five minutes later, as Ray drove north along the western tip of Beirut, "you see those two big rock spires sticking out of the ocean? That's Pigeon Rocks. The street names keep changing, but this seems to be what they call the Corniche. We're supposed to start familiarizing ourselves with the turf and checking out these beaches and marinas the Boss has marked for us." As he talked, the SEAL's eyes hopped between the GPS unit in his lap and the tourist's guidebook in his hand. "How'd he know which places to mark?"

"I think he once visited here."

"I hope you're able to see more than I can," said Ted a few minutes later.

"I'm not. The road's too damn wide. We're going to have to go on down to the port area then turn inland and check out the downtown area then circle back and head west along the shore."

"Okay," said Ted, looking out his window. "This part of the place reminds me of Fort Lauderdale or some place like that. All these new, glitzy buildings along the shore."

"And Alex has us booked into two of them."

Ted's face glowed. "It'll be nice to be in a decent hotel for a change, though two does seem like overkill. Does the Boss know?"

"He insisted on it."

"I liked his line about the importance of having the right address."

"I'm hungry, Ted," said Ray as they approached the American University campus.

"Whatever you say."

Ray found a place where he could turn off the Corniche into a side street just east of the campus. A street that seemed to be continuous restaurants and cafés on both sides. Whether it was because of the delicate political situation or despite it, both sides of the street were jammed with cars, making it difficult to advance and even more difficult to park. Patience and fortitude, those two great lions of character, finally triumphed, and they found a place no more than three blocks from the café they'd decided to try.

* * *

It can't be said that Tareq ibn-Ali never missed anything, but in fact, he missed very little. When he walked past the café, he noted Ray and Ted sitting at an outdoor table, experimenting with various forms of *mezze*—little dishes of various concoctions—eggplant, chicken, lamb, fish. Arab tapas, to Ray's way of thinking.

Clearly they were Americans. But then, the city was often filled with Americans. All the same, there was something about them. Perhaps it was the expressions on their faces. Or just the way they sat. They didn't look like they were on vacation. Tareq filed the information away and continued on, returning to the immediate problem—locating Abdul al-Jabbar.

* * *

"Good stuff," said Ray as they walked back to the car. "I could do with a siesta now, but I guess we don't have time."

"No," agreed Ted. "I don't think so either."

After wandering around several narrow, student-jammed back roads, they managed to find their way back on the Corniche and continued east to the port. There they turned inland, stopping to check into the Phoenicia Hotel. After surrendering their passports at the hotel, they drove through the center of the Place d'Etoile, only to spend at least twenty minutes stuck in traffic. Once they'd worked their way out of the mess, they cruised the surrounding streets, then returned to the Corniche and started west. In the course of familiarizing themselves with the less-traveled streets, they passed the Pension Marrakech. At the time they had no idea of its significance.

"Okay," said Ted almost immediately after they'd found their way back to the Corniche. "Turn right here. This is the St. George Yacht Club. One of the places the Boss wants checked out."

Ray turned off and they soon found themselves at a gate. "We were told at our hotel it's possible to arrange for temporary memberships here," said Ray in his fault-less French.

"Yes, sir," said the armed security guard after eyeing them and concluding they probably could pay the fare. "May I see your tourist cards?"

Ray handed the cards to the guard. He noted their numbers in some sort of register. "Please go to the club-house and ask for Ms. Masri," said the guard, pointing at the clubhouse.

They had no trouble locating Ms. Masri, who was filling in at the desk while the normal clerk went to the bathroom. Ray explained that they were in Beirut for a week on business and were staying at the Phoenicia and would like to arrange to use the facilities. After calling the Phoenicia to confirm at least part of their story, Ms. Masri explained the procedures and offered to give them a tour as soon as the clerk returned. Ray proposed that he and Ted take a quick look around on their own since they had to appear at a meeting in a little while. At first skeptical, Ms. Masri finally agreed.

"I like this place," said Ted twenty minutes later after they'd walked all around the pool and the marina and along the L-shaped breakwater that protected it from the open Mediterranean. "And the chick liked you."

"It'll work fine," agreed Ray. "Don't tell my wife."

They returned to the clubhouse and used their credit cards to pay the impressively large fees for two-week guest memberships.

"I think we're under surveillance," remarked Ted as they drove back out onto the Corniche and returned to checking out the rocky shore and the beaches that lay in between the rocks.

"It's probably the Agency," said Ray as he pulled into a parking place. "Alex said her friend in Langley thought they might keep an eye on us."

"I suppose that's good. In case we need close-in support."

"I suppose so."

* * *

The second time Tareq saw Ray and Ted—he was driving along the Corniche and passed them while they were standing, leaning on the rail and studying the shore and the surf pounding on it—a bell rang. A minute later, when a white Saab with a blond male driver also passed him, going in the opposite direction, his interest was definitely aroused. The same Saab with the same driver had been parked within viewing distance of the café where the two Americans had eaten. Why would one American be shadowing two other Americans?

"Pull over, Zeid. After I get out, turn around and park on the other side of those Americans." Tareq stepped onto the sidewalk and walked back toward the two Tridents. He walked casually, neither too fast nor too slow, admiring the Mediterranean as he went and not bullying the other strollers.

The two Americans were definitely not tourists!

Was it possible, he wondered, that they might be connected with al-Jabbar? That instead of dealing with Mossad, as he had assumed, the traitor was dealing with the Americans? The idea was ridiculously unlikely—there were thousands of reasons why American agents might be wandering around Beirut—but al-Jabbar was

on his mind and he had nothing to lose at this point by
keeping an eye on the two men. Alert for any calls from
his search parties concerning the traitor, Tareq continued
to follow the two Tridents as they made one more stop
to examine the shore and then disappeared into the Riviera Beirut Hotel.

* * *

After hearing Ray's report, Mike paced back and forth
and looked out the window at the darkening Mediterranean. He knew the Agency was shadowing the operation
and wasn't sure what they had in mind. Greta had told
him to steer clear of them as much as possible, so he'd
made no effort to establish contact. He also had to assume that both Hamas and Mossad were out there somewhere. Both had a very big interest in getting their hands
on al-Jabbar. He had no idea where they were or what
they were doing, but he did know that every extra minute and every unnecessary act increased the risk that
one of the potential interlopers might foul the operation.
It had to be totally quick and clean. And the risk to Penny
had to be minimalized to the maximum extent possible.
He and his people were, in the end, expendable, but she
was not. Yet she was totally necessary for the operation
to proceed.

"Ladies," he finally said, "Let's gather around this
map."

Alex and Penny gathered while Jerry remained outside, prowling through the hotel and its grounds.

"We've identified two good pickup points. Both on
the north shore. One's in West Beirut, the other's in the
center. Which one we use will depend on where we pick
up Abdul—the less time he's riding around, the better.
Penny, will you please e-mail him and tell him we'll be
picking him up tomorrow, late morning or early after-

noon? If he won't tell you where he is now, tell him he's
going to have to tell you when you e-mail him tomorrow, when we arrive at the Beirut airport."

"Okay."

"Alex. Call Ray and tell him we're going to move
tomorrow and he's to arrange for the boat now. Also tell
him it'll be one of the two places he and Ted recom-
mended but we may not know which until tomorrow.
We'll call him from the airport."

"Roger."

Mike then called Admiral Wolf's intelligence officer,
and gave him as much of an update as he could.

An hour after Penny e-mailed him, Abdul replied that
he was ready but didn't want to reveal his location until
the last possible minute.

* * *

It was a little after five in the morning in Langley when
Chaz Owens finally jumped out of bed after a long,
sleepless night. It was time to act, he told himself. No
more fucking around. There was a very dangerous terrorist running around, and the way things were going,
the son of a bitch was going to escape.

Defector my ass, he thought. The animal was just
playing them for fools. He should never have agreed to
let Greta and her naval pals take the lead. This was
Agency business, antiterrorist business. Not only did he
doubt they had the slightest idea what they were doing,
but Greta claimed she didn't know much either. He'd
even called SECDEF's office, and they'd had the balls to
claim all they knew was that the group was on Cyprus.

Shit, he knew that. And that deputy secretary he
ended up talking to, Parker, was an utter ass. And so was
Pat McGrath, he thought as he grabbed the secure
phone.

"I'm disappointed in you, Pat," he said the instant McGrath had assured him the connection was secure at both ends.

"What?" demanded Pat. "The al-Jabbar business? I've been shadowing Greta's little operation, just like I was told to do."

"But from what you've reported, it doesn't look like you're really on top of it."

"I reported that two of them have left Cyprus and come to Beirut and spent the day driving around."

"None of that's actionable. Anyway, half of it came from my guy in Cyprus. Do you know where al-Jabbar is? That's the only thing that's worth knowing."

"No."

"I'm coming over to give you a hand. I'll be arriving a little before noon tomorrow, your time. Have a car at the airport for me."

"You've got it, buddy."

Before leaving for the airport, Owens called Duke on the West Coast to find out what he'd managed to learn from Penny's mother and sister.

"They talked their heads off from the very get-go but didn't tell us anything that's actionable."

"What do you suggest?"

"I think there's more there. There always is. Considering this nurse's role in the whole thing, their behavior appears to me to be not inconsistent with conspiracy to aid and abet."

"Okay, I'll let you know. In the meantime, keep the pressure on them."

* * *

"Yes, Mr. ibn-Ali, it is as I said to Zeid. One of the Americans is down on the dock in the marina talking to one of the men who rents speedboats."

"Very good," said Tareq. "Does it look like he's going out right away?"

"I have no way of knowing, sir."

"Of course. Keep your eyes open and your phone in your hand. I must know immediately if he goes out. And tell me if he returns to the hotel also."

"Yes, Mr. ibn-Ali."

* * *

Pat McGrath had felt like spitting when Owens told him he was coming to visit. Screw him, he thought. He didn't like him, didn't trust him and didn't want him messing around in his station.

He also suspected that Chaz's enthusiasm was going to prove detrimental to the cause.

Pat didn't really like Arabs, or Jews or most other Americans for that matter. He was a cause man, not a people person. Whatever his dislikes, however, he lacked Owens's burning hatred of terrorists. He could see the value of making a deal every now and then. He could also see the value of voluntary defectors. Especially high-profile ones. Helping al-Jabbar get out of Beirut made sense to him, and he was willing to let Greta—no matter how irritating she was at times—and her illicit little group of sailors do the job. He was willing to screen the operation and only participate in an emergency.

But Chaz was such an inflexible bastard! The minute he arrived, he was going to insist they step in and take the operation over, even though it was far from clear exactly what the naval group was planning to do.

There was no choice—he was just going to have to play it by ear.

* * *

"That was a damn good meal," remarked Ted as he and Ray walked out of the hotel's most expensive restaurant, toward a bank of elevators. "I'm going to have to learn more about Arab food. Maybe I'll give Hannah an Arab cookbook for Christmas."

"That's always the best kind of present to give to your girlfriend. That way you never have to worry they'll ask you to marry them."

A tall, blond guy stepped up in front of them and blocked their path to the elevators. "Sorry, mate, you'll have to wait a minute where you are."

The thug was smiling but his eyes were cold. Security guy, thought Ray. Somebody's bodyguard, maybe. Australian or South African. He couldn't always tell the accents apart.

The two Tridents did as they were directed while the thug turned and stopped several other guests from approaching the elevator.

As they watched in silence, an elevator door opened and a small man in a Western business suit walked out, accompanied by two other men and several women much younger than he was.

"Who's the dude?" asked Ted after the small entourage had passed.

"The emir of Qataban, mate," replied the thug.

"Where the hell's Qataban?"

"Doesn't matter to somebody like you. All you need to know is that he's got enough cash to buy this whole country."

17

The sun was making its first efforts to struggle up from behind Lebanon when Mike, Alex, Penny and Jerry packed themselves into a taxi at the door of the hotel. Forty minutes later they were boarding the first flight to Beirut, a fact which Ollie Mitchell noted and reported to Pat McGrath. One hour later they were working their way through Lebanese Customs.

"Arrived Beirut. Where are you?" sent Penny to Abdul while the four of them sipped paper cups of coffee.

"Pension Marrakech," replied Abdul five minutes later. "143 Rue du Sannine."

Alex glanced at the address and punched it into her PDA, which was already logged onto MapQuest. "I've got it, Boss. It's south of the center of town, maybe a kilometer from the Place d'Etoile."

Mike studied the display a moment then called Ray. "The St. George Yacht Club. Be off the end of the breakwater in an hour and a half."

"Roger."

The four then walked out to their rented Honda and drove out of the airport, toward the city. Pat was again notified, this time by Janet Dove.

* * *

To the casual passerby the neighborhood around the Riviera Beirut Hotel was no more crowded than usual. Only the truly discerning and well informed would have spotted the luminaries present, mixed in among the increasing numbers of Lebanese out for·a breath of fresh air. Tareq ibn-Ali and six of his thugs were there. Sitting in cars, leaning on the railing along the Corniche, hunched over café tables making each cup of coffee last as long as possible. So was Moshe Goren and three of his people. And Pat McGrath. Hell, he belonged there. He was practically part of the operation.

* * *

"We've got to move," urged Ray as he and Ted darted across the Corniche from the hotel to the Riviera Marina. "We're running a few minutes late."

"Roger."

The two Tridents checked into the marina office, where they picked up the keys for the boat they'd rented and ensured that its gas tanks had been topped off. "Do I have time to hit the head?" asked Ted.

"Barely," said Ray. "Snap it up." Then he walked around the building and headed down the finger pier.

"Shit," mumbled Ray a minute or two later. Standing in the middle of the pier, between him and their boat, was the Australian bodyguard. "Sorry, mate," he said without the faintest hint of sorrow on his face, "you can't go any farther."

"For how long?" snapped Ray.

"Not until the emir and his party finish loading their

boat and leave." As he spoke he nodded at a good-sized cruiser moored to the next finger pier over. "I'd say a good half hour. Probably more like forty-five minutes."

"We can't wait that long."

"Whether you want to or not, mate, you're going to." As he spoke, the guard tensed slightly, clearly expecting an attack.

Ray had to assume the Australian—or whatever he was—was as well trained as he was. The bastard was also considerably taller. He thought he might still be able to take him, but it would take time and he didn't have time.

"I'm not going to put up with this," he grumbled. "I'm going to see the dockmaster." With that he turned and trotted down the pier.

"You just do that, mate," said the thug to the marine's back, a small smile of supremacy on his face.

Ray hurried around to the far side of the building and caught Ted just as he was coming out of the bathroom. "We've got a problem. That Australian stud won't let us go to the boat until the emir finishes loading his boat at the next pier over."

"You have a plan? Something we can do without creating too much of a ruckus?"

"Of course. That's what they pay me for. You still remember how to hold your breath?"

"That's the first thing they teach you at SEAL school, along with keeping your mouth shut. Am I going to like this? More important, is Captain Chambers going to like this?"

"You're both going to love it," Ray assured him as he led the way to the edge of the building. "Can you see the thug?" he asked, pointing down the pier.

"Yes."

"Good. While I walk back, still making a scene, you're going to work your way out there, in the water from boat to boat, until you're in position to pop up and grab the fucker's leg. Then yank! If possible, pull him into the water."

Ted studied the situation a moment. "Good plan. This water's a little murkier than along the beaches. I'll blend right in."

"You said it, not me."

"Let's do it!" With that, Ted disappeared between some cars and managed to slide into the water at the pier head without Ray even seeing him do it. The marine captain waited a few minutes then headed back out to the pier, grumbling as he went.

"You can't do this," he griped to the Australian. "The dockmaster says I can go out to that boat."

"I don't give a rat's ass what the dockmaster says. You aren't going any farther than this until I damn well say you can."

Out of the side of his eye Ray caught a slight motion in the water right next to the pier and breathed a quick sigh of relief. He couldn't keep the act up forever. He then moved as if to lunge at the Australian, although his weight was positioned for him to retreat. The thug, underestimating Ray, took the bait and went after him with almost blinding speed.

Like a pilot whale breaching, Ted suddenly rose up out of the water and grabbed the thug's leg. He then yanked. All in one smooth motion.

The Australian's legs spread like a ballet dancer's— one in the water and one across the dock—and he crashed down, face-first, onto the planking. Before he could even begin to recover, Ray lashed his wrists with his own restraints. The marine then grabbed the thug's pistol from his jacket pocket and dropped it in the water. "Keep your mouth shut," he snarled as he tore off part of the Australian's shirt and stuffed it in his mouth.

As far as Ray could tell, most of the action had been

out of sight of the guards nearer the emir's yacht, although they could undoubtedly see that the Australian
had disappeared from sight. Ray leaned over and helped
Ted out of the water. "Well done. Now let's get the hell
out of here."

The two Tridents scurried down the pier to the center
console fish killer they'd rented and lit off the engines,
which exploded to life with a bang and a cloud of
smoke.

"Cast off," directed Ray. Ted had already done so.
Then, hoping Jerry never heard of his unseamanlike behavior, the marine jammed the throttles forward and the
boat leapt out of its slip into the basin. Ray turned
sharply left and headed for the opening in the seawall.

By now the emir's guards on the other pier *had* realized that something was happening, even if they didn't
know exactly what. Trained as they were to shoot first
and ask questions later, they opened fire on the boat as
Ray twisted and turned past them into open water.

Twang! Twang! Two shots tore through the fiberglass,
then they were out in open water and headed east.

* * *

"Look for me at 10:45. In the street."

Shaking, Abdul stared at the text message for several
seconds. 10:45. An hour from now. It would all be over
in another hour or two after that. Either he'd be dead or
he'd be free.

But he still had no idea how they planned to do it, so
maybe it would take longer. And would he really be
free? The news was full of the sinking of the American
ship off Ceuta. Four dead. Four Americans dead. It must
have been Magda. They said the terrorist was killed, but
they didn't say if it was a man or a woman.

Would they really accept him as a defector or would

they treat him as they'd treated so many others? He thought what he could give them would be of great value, but they might not even believe what he said. Or they might insist he knew more than he really did.

He tried to lie down and couldn't. Instead, he forced himself to sit in a chair and look at TV. Two soccer games, an ancient American cowboy movie and some politician saying nothing.

10:15. He walked over to the window and looked out over the courtyard and onto the street. As he'd hoped, there were a few empty parking spaces, so they wouldn't have to double-park.

What if Tareq and Mossad were following the Americans? What if the Americans had lied and were working with the Israelis? What if they already knew he was here and were just waiting for him to come out on the street?

He stared at the wall and the ceiling and the tattered Oriental rug. He tried to look inside himself but found the view much too confused to understand. He had not known that he'd come to hate the smell of lavender and decay.

At 10:40 he could no longer stand it. He walked over to the window and stared nervously down into the street as a couple of elderly women walked by. He waited.

At 10:46 by his watch a Honda pulled up and stopped in front of the courtyard to the Pension Marrakech. The right front door opened and a blond woman stepped out.

Was it Penny? It was Penny! It was really happening!

He placed the room key on the table, along with all the cash that remained to him. For Madame deVine. Then he dashed out the door, almost running into that very same Madame deVine in the hall.

"Good morning, Mr. al-Jabbar."

"Good morning, madame."

"Is there something wrong?"

"No, but I'm on my way to meet an old friend who I haven't seen for many years."

"Ah!" Madame deVine's eyes followed Abdul's back as he ran down the stairs and out into the courtyard.

"Penny!" shouted the Hawk as he dashed through the gate and out onto the sidewalk.

The nurse looked at him a second, as if not recognizing him. He's different, she thought. He's shaved his head and grown older. And inside, how much has he changed there? Then she made the connection and stepped toward him, a look of lingering doubt on her face. Was this really him? Was he a monster? A reformed monster? A fool? Was she doing this for him or because she thought it might do some good? Was it the right thing to do?

"Quickly, Abdul, in this car," she said, pointing to the Honda, which was now parked about six cars down the street.

So far, none of the dozen or so passersby had given any indication of even being aware of the encounter.

When Abdul reached the car, a solid-looking middle-aged American was holding the back door open for him. He dove in and found himself next to a tall, dark-haired woman while Penny got back into the front seat. Then the middle-aged guy got in beside him and closed the door. His breath caught. He was surrounded. Imprisoned. Did the wrong people have him after all?

"I'm Alex," said the dark-haired woman as the car pulled away from the curb. "On your other side is Jerry and Mike is driving."

Unsmiling, his face showing the strain, Abdul nodded all around. Except for an occasional direction from Alex, who was holding the GPS unit, nothing was said until after they'd driven sedately around the rotary in the Place d'Etoile.

"Damnit!" grumbled Mike as they approached the port. Everybody looked up and around. There was a roadblock about three blocks ahead.

"Take this left, Boss. This one you're coming up on now," directed Alex.

* * *

From the Corniche, Tareq ibn-Ali watched the struggle on the finger pier and was unsure precisely what to make of it. He was, however, probably the first of the three watchers to appreciate that Ray and Ted had left the Riviera Marina without waiting for a passenger. They're going to pick up the traitor someplace else, he said to himself calmly. Someplace along the shore. Actually, there were countless places they might turn in and meet a man who'd stepped out of a car and scampered down to the rocks.

He jumped into his waiting car and headed east, struggling to keep the speeding boat in view and finding it more difficult than he'd anticipated.

* * *

"One more block, then turn right. We can get back on the Corniche here."

"Roger," replied Mike, hoping the Lebanese Army—who else could it be?—wasn't using multiple road-blocks.

A few minutes later Mike turned off the Corniche and down the driveway to the St. George Yacht Club. He stopped at the gate. "My name is Chambers," he said to the somewhat bored-looking security guard. "My friend, Mr. Fuentes—I understand he arranged for a temporary membership here—asked us to meet him. He's getting a boat from some place and is going to give us a tour of the coast. He said he was going to call you."

The guard looked at Mike then leaned over and

looked inside the car. "Do you have your tourist card with you, sir?"

Mike handed him the card he'd received at the airport. "Will you need all of ours?" he asked, mentally crossing his fingers. If the guard said yes, they'd have to neutralize him, and he didn't want to have to do that.

"No, sir. Yours is fine. Mr. Fuentes did call." Then, after making a notation in his records, the guard directed them toward the harbor.

Mike stopped at the shoreward end of the large, L-shaped breakwater that enclosed the marina. He paused for a moment, looking at the waves breaking along the outside of the breakwater. He then looked out at the white speedboat approaching from the west, bouncing in the chop as it came.

"Now," said Mike without turning, "we're going to walk fast—don't run—and join Ray and Ted for a little cruise."

The car's four doors flew open and the five of them stepped onto the long, stone structure. They walked rapidly out toward the end, where Ray and Ted had turned into the entrance and were waiting, idling a few feet off the protected inside of the breakwater.

* * *

If the outline of the plan to take the terrorist was clear to Moshe Goren almost as quickly as it had been to Tareq, the Mossad agent's response was greatly more vigorous. Not only did he follow the boat, but he radioed for an Israeli Defense Force helo gunship to be sent to intercept the boat in case he was unable to stop it. He had no intention whatsoever of letting the terrorist escape.

* * *

"Pull over," shouted Tareq to Zeid when he saw the boat slow off the St. George breakwater. Even before the car had come to a complete halt, he jumped out, rifle in hand, and ran across the Corniche. He hadn't been fast enough, he thought, but all was not lost. As he ran, he looked up and down the wide road. There were a few idlers and sightseers visible but not a cop, or a soldier, in sight. He paused when he reached the rail along the sea-ward sidewalk and tried to catch his breath. He watched as the blond woman stumbled on the breakwater and the faithless whoreson of a traitor slowed to steady her.

The boat now had its bow up against the end of the breakwater. Mike and Jerry were up to their knees in the blue water, holding it in place. Abdul had just started to work his way down the loose riprap of the seawall to-ward the boat when Tareq, after bracing the rifle against the rail, fired a rapid volley. The traitor was slammed forward and down, falling face-first on the very hard rocks.

Ignoring the shocked pedestrians around him, Tareq paused to remove the now-empty clip and replace it. He wanted to make sure the traitor was dead, but he never got the chance. Before he could finish reloading, four slugs slammed into the right side of his chest, under his raised right arm, knocking him to the concrete side-walk.

* * *

Fifty feet down the rail, Pat McGrath shoved his pistol back into the pocket of his blazer and turned to his com-panion. "Son of a bitch was shooting at our people," he said, half to himself. "We've got to get the hell out of here now before the Lebanese decide we've had some-thing to do with all this."

"What about the defector? He's down," asked his companion as they hurried to their car.

"That's the navy's problem." Then he noticed Chaz Owens getting out of a car and walking toward them. It wasn't possible for the prick to know what had just happened, but he still looked pissed. He always looked pissed.

"Chaz," he said, walking toward him. "Welcome to Beirut. Let's go to my office—we don't really want to be here right now."

* * *

"Oh, no!" cried Penny as Abdul pitched forward beside her, blood pouring from his now misshapen right shoulder.

"Get him in the boat," snapped Mike.

Between them they got the defector into the boat, then crawled over the gunnel themselves. With his passengers aboard, Ray backed carefully away from the rocks then turned and shoved both throttles forward, so they screamed directly out into the whitecaps.

As the boat pounded over the chop, Penny bent over Abdul and studied his wound. Then she shook her head in despair.

"How is he?" shouted Alex, fearing it was one of the stupidest questions she'd ever asked in her life.

"There's nothing I can do for him here except maybe try to cushion the shock."

"Okay. Let me help."

Between them they managed to get a layer of cushions and life vests between Abdul and the pounding deck, while Penny tinkered ineffectively at slowing the blood flow. All the while, Mike scanned the horizon for pursuit.

"Can we slow down," shouted Penny a few minutes later, struggling to be heard over the outboards, "so we don't bounce so much?"

Mike and Jerry—who was at the wheel—exchanged glances. The chief boatswain's mate then turned the bow to the right so that instead of slamming into and pounding over the waves the boat started to slide and roll across them.

"That's the best we can do, Penny," said Mike. "We're in a very exposed position at the moment."

Penny nodded.

When they were about three miles offshore, Abdul opened his eyes and tried to say something to Penny. She tugged at Jerry's trousers to attract his attention and signaled for him to slow down.

Jerry and Mike exchanged glances again. Then Mike nodded "okay." Jerry throttled way back and the boat slowed, settling back on her stern and beginning to roll slightly less violently.

"I wanted to give you so much to help pay for my redemption," whispered Abdul, "but now . . . Thirty-five degrees, fifty-nine minutes north; five degrees, sixteen minutes east. Remember that." His eyes then closed and he lapsed into unconsciousness.

"Thirty-five, fifty-nine north; five, sixteen east," repeated Mike. "Everybody keep repeating that. Jerry, is there anything to write with in that console?"

Jerry looked frantically and finally found a pencil. Along with an owner's manual for the engine.

Twenty minutes later, as they were approaching the twelve-mile limit of Lebanon's sovereignty, a helo appeared on the horizon. Their initial joy was quickly tempered when they realized it was an Israeli gunship.

"Boss?" said Alex.

"There's nothing we can do. Let's hope they're just keeping an eye on us."

"Let's hope," echoed Ted. "They've been known to misidentify targets, though. I really don't want to die from friendly fire."

The gunship approached rapidly, its turbine whining.

Then, to clarify its desires and establish the seriousness of its intentions, it fired a burst of cannon shells ahead of the boat. Yet again, Jerry and Mike exchanged glances and the chief throttled back.

"They must be after our passenger," observed Ray, "but I'm not sure what they can do with him at this point."

"They'll probably just be pissed," sighed Ted.

"Phantom, this is Seahorse," squawked the handheld radio on the console. "We have you in sight. Our ETA four minutes."

"There!" said Alex. "Look to the west. The cavalry is coming."

All eyes turned to the west, where three dots on the horizon soon morphed into three helos, a big SH 60 and two smaller AH 1 gunships. The Israeli gunship, which presumably had been tracking the approaching American aircraft by radar, decided it didn't like the odds and drifted off to the north.

Within seconds the SH 60, roaring and snorting, was hovering overhead, its prop wash pounding the choppy waves almost flat. Its crew seemed especially on the ball to Mike, because the first thing to come down, instead of a lifting yoke, was a Stokes stretcher. Holding their breath, the Tridents and Penny rolled Abdul into the wire carrier and, after strapping him in, signaled to the helo to hoist him.

"Okay, Penny, you're next," said Mike as the wire returned with a yoke on it.

Ray, Alex, then Jerry followed her up.

"The Riviera's not going to be happy, Captain," shouted Ted just before he slipped the yoke over his head.

"That's one of the many reasons we've got Alex. She'll arrange for a nice big check to be sent to them and everybody will be perfectly satisfied."

"How about Mr. Parker?"

"He'll cope with it.

"Instruct the gunships to sink that boat as quickly as possible," shouted Mike to the helo crew when he was dragged through the door.

It had been some time since the gunship crews had been allowed to actually sink something, so both immediately fired a rocket. The boat promptly exploded and was gone within two minutes, and the three helos turned west toward *Bastogne*.

18

Thirty-five degrees, 59 minutes north; 5 degrees, 16 minutes east. Without further details, an area two miles by two miles. A position roughly five miles from *Abernathy*'s location when she was torpedoed. An area filled with the remains of twenty-five hundred years' worth of wrecked ships. Even knowing the position, it had taken the USNS *Vector*, an American survey ship, and a Spanish mine hunter a week to locate the third device.

"Alex," said Mike, looking out the side of his eye, "please stop playing with that. I know it's been deactivated, but it still makes me nervous."

Alex stopped playing with the little SONAR transmitter Mariano Gomez had found in Magda's purse. It made her nervous, too.

At the time, Mike, Alex and Jerry were standing with an explosive ordnance disposal officer and his assistant, a chief, in *Vector*'s underwater operations control room.

"Al-Jabbar was clever," remarked Mike as they

watched a civilian operator use a joystick to guide an ROV nine hundred feet below them. "If he hadn't given us the position, we'd be looking all over the Med for this thing when it was right next to its brother."

"I think he wanted to tell us a lot more," said Alex. "It's too bad he didn't make it."

"What does Greta say about Penny?"

"She thinks she's convinced her to avoid the Middle East for a few years—I doubt it was really hard to get her to agree. She thinks she may go back to college and get her master's."

"If she were my daughter, that's what I'd want her to do."

"Looking at Kenny, you must be a great dad, Boss. It's too bad you didn't have a daughter, too."

"Knock it off, Alex. There's no way I can get Alan to give you a raise. Has the Agency cleared her?"

"Hell, no! You know they never will. Not her, not her mother, not her sister. They claim they all knew, or should have known, what al-Jabbar was doing. Greta doesn't think they have enough to indict, but it's going to be hanging over their heads for the rest of their lives."

"And they ended up deporting the al-Jabbars?"

"Yep. All of them, even the one who was a citizen. They're all back in Jordan now."

"Okay," said the EOD officer. "I think we've got enough photos of this gem. Now let's see if we can get it up."

Mike looked at the display. The device looked pretty much as he'd assumed it would. A torpedo set on a metal carriage. It was the software within that made it so utterly dangerous. And so very interesting. What would the programming indicate about Chinese knowledge of American antitorpedo technology?

A few minutes later a second ROV came into view of

the first's cameras. As they watched, the second vehicle swam over to the device, dragging a lifting wire behind it. After three tries it managed to attach a snap-hook to a small lifting ring set into the torpedo's top.

"I'd get that second ROV out of there before we try anything," remarked Jerry.

"Couldn't agree with you more," said the EOD officer.

Five minutes later the ROV had been recovered and hoisted aboard. The EOD officer glanced at Mike, who nodded.

"Heave around slowly," directed the EOD officer over a phone.

At first the scene on the monitor didn't change. Then it became possible to see the lift wire more clearly as the slack was taken out of it. When the wire appeared almost up and down, they all held their breath. Suddenly, the picture disappeared and a row of lights started blinking on the control console.

"God damn it!" shouted the EOD officer. Within a few seconds *Vector* shuddered as if somebody had hit her in the belly with an immense tree trunk. A moment later a seething bubble of gas and heat exploded in the water twenty yards away.

"That was the warhead," remarked the EOD officer. "They must've booby-trapped it."

"At least it didn't sink us," said Mike.

"Or anybody else," added Alex.

"But we lost a two-hundred-thousand–dollar ROV," griped the EOD officer.

"Going to be damn hard to recover enough to pin anything on the Chinese," said Jerry.

"Much as we'd all like to try," said Mike, "we're going to have to leave it to somebody else. We have to get back to Tampa. Then I have to present myself in Washington to explain it all to Alan."

Tom Clancy's
SPLINTER CELL®

CREATED BY #1 *NEW YORK TIMES*
BESTSELLING AUTHOR TOM CLANCY,
WRITTEN BY DAVID MICHAELS

penguin.com

M223AS0709

More from #1 *New York Times* Bestselling Author

Tom Clancy

THE TEETH OF THE TIGER

RED RABBIT

THE BEAR AND THE DRAGON

RAINBOW SIX

EXECUTIVE ORDERS

DEBT OF HONOR

WITHOUT REMORSE

THE SUM OF ALL FEARS

CLEAR AND PRESENT DANGER

THE CARDINAL OF THE KREMLIN

PATRIOT GAMES

RED STORM RISING

THE HUNT FOR RED OCTOBER

penguin.com